The KINDRED GATHERING

J. R. Hatmaker
David E. Bader

BV Wespat
PMB 197
1641 North Memorial Drive
Lancaster, Ohio 43130

The authors have made every attempt to trace ownership and, when necessary, obtain permission for quotations used in this book. From time to time they have been unable to determine or locate the author of a quote. In such instances, if an author of a quotation wishes to contact the authors of this book, he or she should contact them through the publisher. Portions of the "Walking Man" are based upon Mary Louisa Duncan's recollections of her father, John Buchanan Hatmaker, a one-time Tennessee lawman and politician. Photo of "Hootmocker" Hospital is courtesy of Gerri Lyn Hatmaker. War of the Regulation quotes are from the actual correspondence between Regulators and Royal Governor William Tryon.

All rights reserved. No part of this book may be reproduced or transmitted in any form or by means, electronic or mechanical, including photocopying, recording, or by any information storage and retrieval system, without the written permission of the publisher, except where permitted by law. For information address: BV Wespat, Lancaster, Ohio

Copyright © 2002 Jerry R. Hatmaker, David E. Bader
TXu 1-053-780 Certificate of Registration

Library of Congress Control Number: 2002095876

ISBN 0-9713342-1-8
Printed in the United States of America.

Times Square Printing
296 Royal Palms Drive, Atlantic Beach, FL 32233

About the Kindred

J. R. Hatmaker, in addition to *The Kindred Gathering*, is the author of *The Coalwood Misfits* and *Shoddy and Ox*. All are loosely connected and part of *The Clear Fork Series*. Also, he has written or co-authored several historical and genealogical titles, including *Biographical Sketches of Some Early German-American Pioneers* and *Dillweissenstein to Carolina and the Mohawk Valley*.

While researching another book, he heard of a strange group of people called Melungeons. Supposedly, there were still clans inhabiting the upland regions of Appalachia. His curiosity remained with him and a year or so later he visited southwest Virginia and Upper East Tennessee just to see the lay of the land and the isolation of some of its inhabitants. It struck him that the high mountains and narrow valleys were much the same as those that cradled his place of birth, Coalwood, McDowell County, West Virginia.

After months of research, it became obvious that many physical characteristics attributed to Melungeons, also, could be found in some families he had known in McDowell County; and during his career of extensive travel, he had met many people who fit their physical profile, chiefly in the general region where West Virginia, Kentucky and Virginia meet, an area which lies in close proximity to Upper East Tennessee

With ancestral links to Campbell and Anderson counties in Tennessee, old Orange County, North Carolina and Montgomery County, New York, he began to piece together a possible migration route for an historical novel.

After teaming up with **David E. Bader**, a former Navy journalist and college professor, the two began the developmental and final research stages for a book. Utilizing and weaving together known historical fact, Mr. Hatmaker, along with David, decided to write a story that would bring to light in an entertaining way the mystery of the Melungeons, their weaknesses, strengths, and their accomplishments. Thus was born *The Kindred Gathering*.

Sally Skunza painted portions of the front cover. She's a well-known artist in Central Ohio, focusing on wall and furniture art. Sally attended Ohio University and Columbus College of Art and Design.

John Lott is an associate of Time Square Printing and an expert in the field of Graphic Design. He lent his know-how and creativity to the project. Mr. Lott has a long history in the instruction of Graphic Design.

To the memory of

Jack Klotz

"She waited for him to open her door, and momentarily she stood in awe between the beauty of the gleaming white community church with its towering steeple and the grandeur of the massive Clubhouse. She took a deep breath, released it slowly, and then walked briskly up the stone steps and into the great room of the Clubhouse."

White structures, left to right: Dantzlers' House, Coalwood Community Church, Clubhouse, Post Office building—housed the dentist's office, doctor's office, library, barber shop, and Women's Club meeting room (later, a Scout Room).

CONTENTS

Acknowledgments................................8
A Word..9

1. The Plan.................................. 16
2. Expedition to the Fork of the Tug.... 29
3. War of the Regulation................... 45
4. The Spigoting...............................65
5. Micager................................. 71
6. The Decision............................. 78
7. The Cabin............................... 91
8. Vardy's Valley 101
9. The Finding 108
10. The Walking Man 112
11. Whitaker Werd....................... 119

12. The Posting 128
13. The Talking 139
14. Hootmocker Hospital 146
15. Duty Calls 154
16. The Professor 162
17. Marianne's Trip 176
18. Waiting and Watching 181
19. Bought and Sold 191
20. The Discovery 197

21. Judge Ballard's Court 201

22. The Reckoning 214

   Afterword.................................218

Acknowledgements

We owe a deep debt of gratitude to Ronald Farris, Rhonda Hatmaker, Ronald Pearman, Rhonda Cox Wilson, Elizabeth Ann Lanier Berry, Eloise Quarles Hatmaker and Rita Looney Parsons for their contributions. An even greater debt is owed to Vernon Eugene Dagley, who first told us about the Melungeons, and to Mary Louisa Duncan for her wonderful recollections of her father, John Buchanan Hatmaker. Without their generous assistance and thoughtfulness, this book would have been much harder to write. Their help has been important and greatly appreciated.

Also, we would be remiss if we didn't extend a word of thanks to the people at Times Square Printing, Atlantic Beach, Florida. Jeff Klotz and his superb crew worked closely with us and steered the manufacturing of *The Kindred Gathering* to fruition.

But, as always, the foundation for the characters is of utmost importance, so much of our gratitude and respect must go to the extraordinary Melungeons and other kindred spirits who explored and settled Appalachia, and to this day remain in the shadows of its beautiful mountains. After all, it is to a great degree their story. Without them, *The Kindred Gathering* could not have been written.

A Word...

For centuries a strange and mysterious people have inhabited the upland regions of Appalachia. They are said to have already been in America when the first European settlers arrived. Supposedly, they lived in hewn log cabins, spoke broken Elizabethan English and claimed to be "Porty-gee." Legend has it that French explorers first discovered them and tagged them *Melange*, meaning *mixture*. Eventually, the word evolved to the more English spelling, "Melungeon."

They are thought to have removed from the coastal lowlands in front of the westward migrations of European settlers. No one knows exactly where they came from and no one knows how they came to be on the isolated ridges of Appalachia, but once the white settlers reached them, they became oddities, even outcasts in a land they had inhabited for generations.

What is known is they are neither Caucasian nor Negroid, nor are they Indian. Although today, they are most commonly associated with Hancock County, Tennessee, there are descendants all over the region. They can be found in East Tennessee, western Virginia and North Carolina, eastern Kentucky and southern West Virginia.

Their men are sometimes unusually tall and have an oily reddish-brown skin, almost coppery in color. Their women present a strong suggestion of an Old World background; they are generally very pretty, have thin lips, high cheekbones, small graceful hands and feet, and "dreamy" eyes. It is said that those with pure bloodlines have slightly curved shovel-shaped upper front teeth. Many consider them to be of Mediterranean origin.

Suspicious whites mistook them for blacks, and discriminated against them. They were prohibited from attending white schools, but they refused to send their children to school with blacks, maintaining they were not Negro. Many were deprived of a formal education, and predictably they sank farther into the ignorance and isolation that once permeated the high mountains and long narrow hollows of Appalachia.

As a result of their isolation, over time some intermarried with the only groups that would associate with them, probably runaway black and mulato slaves, indentured servants and white bond slaves, Indians, and mixtures of convicts set loose in the Virginia low country. In many families their "look" today is not as apparent as it once was. In fact, when there have been relatively recent admixtures with other groups, many cousins, brothers, sisters and close relatives have significant differences in eye color, facial structure and even skin color.

Recognizing those differences, as early as in the late 1800s, many Appalachian cousins were identified as black or white. For example, two first cousins named Elijah, one showing characteristics of the mysterious group, and the other German, might commonly be identified as "Black Lige" and "White Lige."

They were never slaves, and until 1834 they enjoyed all the rights of citizenship. At that time, the Tennessee Constitutional Convention reclassified them from "free persons" to "free persons of color." In effect, they were legally considered non-persons, and prohibited from owning land, voting or testifying against white people. They had no legal standing. Therefore, they could bring no suits against whites in a court of law. Many lost land, homesteads and personal possessions, and physically suffered at the hands of land-hungry whites.

Some had soldiered heroically in the French and Indian War, the American Revolution and the War of 1812, and they took their ill treatment hard, nursing their hatred of whites.

And once the Civil War began, many refused to join either the South or North. Instead, they moved farther into the mountains, where they huddled together, a culture distinct from the common society. They made their own laws and contracts and became a separate entity within the larger one. They became marauders; bands of them roamed the highlands of Appalachia swooping out of the shadows to raid, bushwhack, loot and burn.

As a result of their unfortunate circumstance, their descendants refused to speak of their heritage, hiding their blood links to the odd group. Trying to distance themselves and their offspring, many claimed to be descendants of Cherokee or other Indian tribes.

In 1887 the State of Tennessee, trying to redress their grievances, gave them a separate legal existence. The state officially recognized them as "Croatian Indians," lending official weight to the theory that they are descendants of the Lost Colony, which disappeared in 1587 from Roanoke Island, North Carolina.

But there is something else about them, something that greatly confounds historians—it is not only the question of their race and origin. It is far more unusual than that. It's the rumors, the legends that they had once worked gold and silver mines and that they and their kindred had been wealthy clans, minting their own coins and secretly maintaining a network to deal with conflicts that might threaten the clan as a whole.

They were rumors that endorsed the legends of the Kentucky, Cumberland, Clinch and Big Sandy river basins—that for centuries kindred clans had concealed their discoveries of caves with large deposits of ore. One in particular, "the great cavern of the Shawnees," a huge cave with an entrance on opposites sides of a steep mountain, was claimed to be the richest of them all. Supposedly, trains of pack mules trudged over a series of high ridges to carry much of the great cave's wealth to the land between the Clinch and Powell rivers, and that some ore was taken into the Catawba country of North Carolina, and to a settlement along the Great Alamance.

With their great wealth, they could have enjoyed a lavish existence, but instead they chose to live humbly and modestly, frugally and discreetly using their wealth only to maintain and defend their bloodlines whenever it became absolutely necessary.

Nobody ever found their mines, although many tried. Prospectors wandered the mountains from Guest Station to Big Glades, Castle's Camp, Pound Gap and Jeffersonville to Cumberland Ford, Poor Fork, and Paint Lick Station. They waded creeks and followed deer trails looking for the great cave, sure the next bend in the creek or the next rise of cliff or the next ridge would give up the secret. But in their headlong rush for fortune, nobody heard the quiet voices of Cherokee elders—nobody heard the tale of a lone Frenchman and a great Shawnee war party that trailed northward from the Cumberlands and waded the Sandy and disappeared into the narrow valley of the Tug.

So, are they a secretive clan of several wealthy close-knit families, a mysterious race that uses wealth and strength only when it is a matter of survival, or are they simply a deprived and misunderstood loose association with no real cultural history?

We may never know, but whoever they are—descendants of Phoenicians, lost colonists, deserters of Hernando de Soto's expedition, shipwrecked sailors, Welsh explorers or even a lost tribe of Israel—they are still among us.

Look closely and you'll find them. When you do, make sure you treat them with great deference. And take them at their word. If you don't, they will fiercely and proudly defend their possessions, themselves and their blood—and you might be the one to suffer at the hands of the kindred known as the *Melungeons*.

Fonda, NY •
• Penn Yan, NY
Hootmocker Hospital

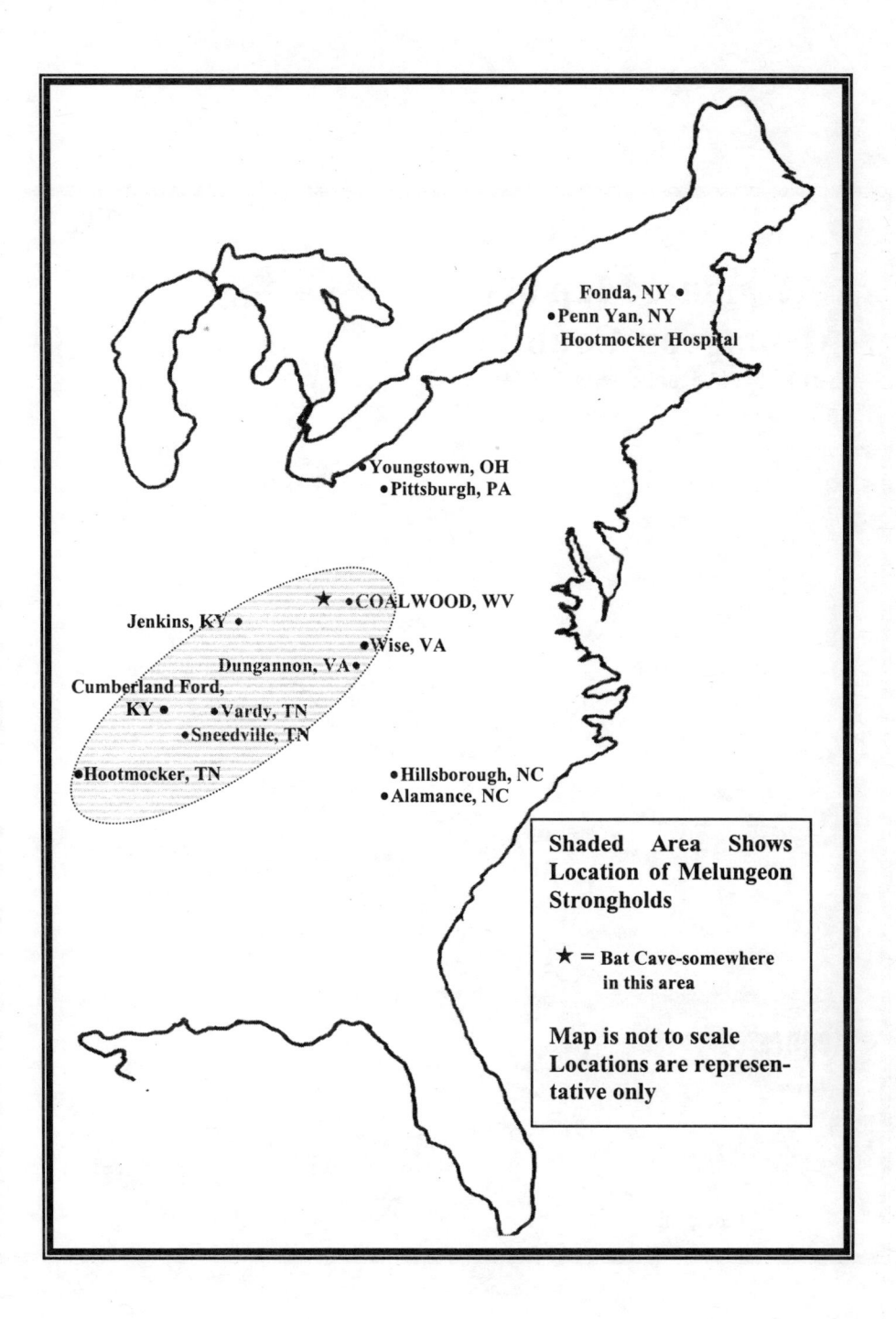

• Youngstown, OH
• Pittsburgh, PA

Jenkins, KY •   ★ • COALWOOD, WV
              • Wise, VA
       Dungannon, VA •
Cumberland Ford,
     KY •   • Vardy, TN
         • Sneedville, TN
• Hootmocker, TN
                    • Hillsborough, NC
                    • Alamance, NC

Shaded Area Shows Location of Melungeon Strongholds

★ = Bat Cave-somewhere in this area

Map is not to scale Locations are representative only

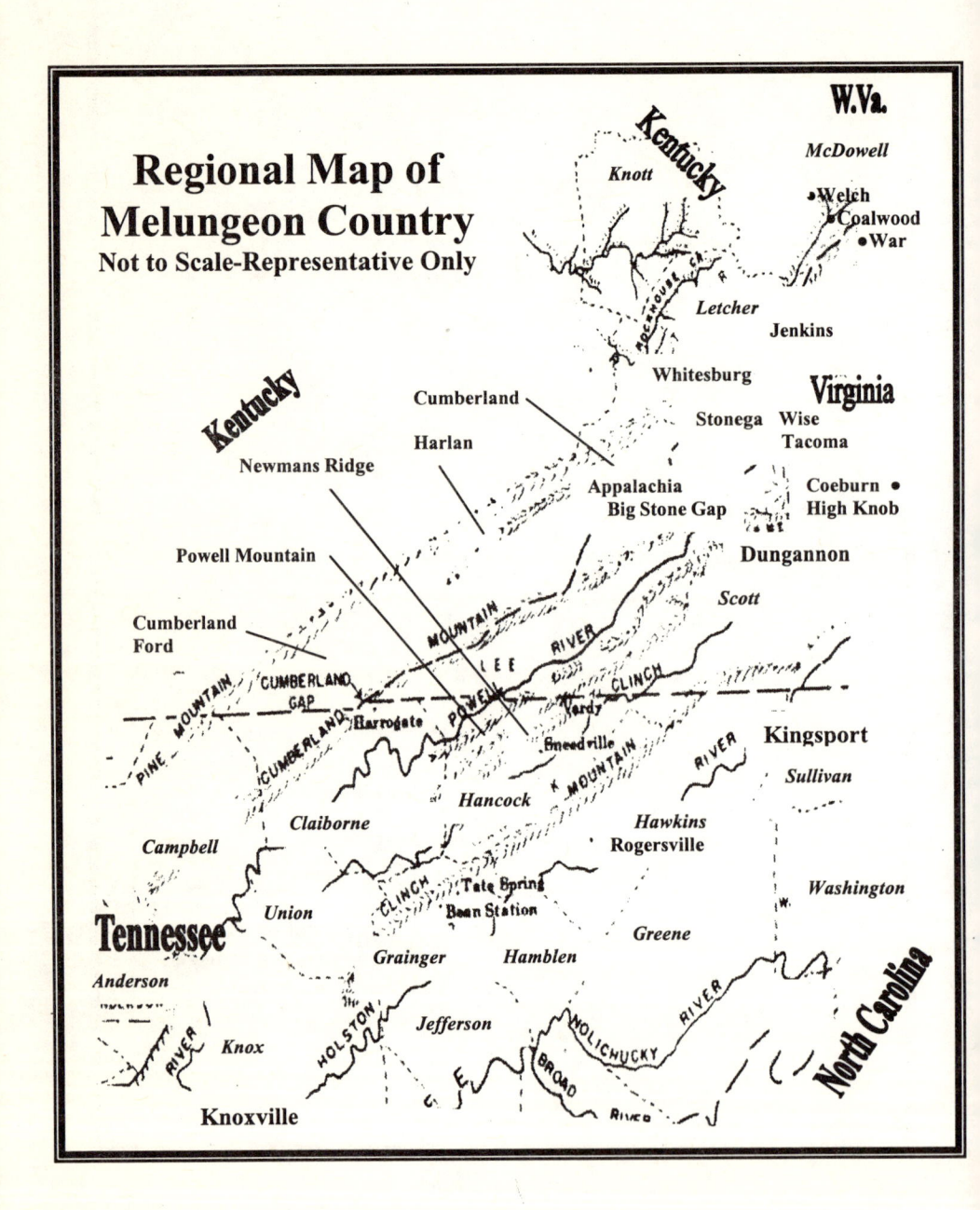

Regional Map of Melungeon Country
Not to Scale-Representative Only

The Kindred Gathering

J. R. Hatmaker
David E. Bader

1

The Plan

Youngstown, Ohio—1963

J. **Frank Hutson, Chief Executive Officer** of Champion Sheet and Tube, prepared to address his board of directors. He signaled to one of his cronies to close the lone mahogany raised-paneled door and dim the lights in the windowless room. He flipped a switch to a backlit map that abruptly illuminated the entire forward wall of the room. He could hear huffs and gasps of surprise from the eight men and one woman who comprised the board.

"It *is* quite unusual," he thought, "an eight-foot high map that spans almost the entire wall, every detail crisp and clear against the backlight." Hutson grinned openly in the darkness of the room's corner. "Just wait until they hear what I've got to say," he mumbled to himself. He drew the metal pointer from his shirt pocket, extended it to its full six-foot length, and walked smartly to the edge of the map. He began smoothly and confidently, rolling every word in a sharp northern accent:

"Good morning, gentlemen." He chuckled to himself, knowing there were many ways to ignore the one female board member—to make her irrelevant. "We have no time to waste so I will get right to the point. The land in question lies along this narrow ridgeline," he tapped the pointer twice against one end of the ridge, and moved it slowly along the run of the mountain. "Starting on the northwest bank of Wolfpen Branch...here...it passes by

Snakeroot and Mudhole hollows, Jim Branch—the locals call it Vint Carroll—and Mankins hollows, and continues on to Daycamp, Meathouse, Abbcamp branches and Copperhead Junction; then it follows this ridgeline in the same general direction all the way...to here...right here to the junction of Clear Fork Creek and Tug River. I'll go over it once again," Hutson snarled, glaring mockingly at his audience, and thoroughly enjoying the attention he was getting, while moving his pointer slowly over a long run of the map, "The land lies on both sides of this ridgeline, from here to here.

"Now, the angle and horizontal borings you were told about took place all along that line, some eighty tests in all. Once the borings were analyzed, we were astonished and pleased to find that we have discovered what appears to be one of the richest seams of bituminous coal ever found in North America. It's on the edge of the Pocahontas Field, but it's not part of it.

"It runs from here...to here...to here, and stretches more than eight miles" Hutson tapped the pointer solidly on the length and breath of the coal field, and all along the lengthy ridgeline, repeatedly striking it loudly just for emphasis.

"Gentlemen, at its minimum the seam is thirty feet high and four hundred yards wide," he paused to let those facts soak in, "and...and...listen to me now...at its average it is some forty-five feet high and six hundred yards wide."

It was difficult to plainly see their faces from the corner of his eye as he faced the crisp light emanating from behind the map, but he could hear their sighs and breathless chatter, and he could sense their disbelief.

"But, that's not all there is...no sir, gentlemen...at this point...at the head of Mankins Hollow is an old log collection point, where the wall of the hollow meets the main run of the mountain...here! Right here...right here...under that collection point the coal seam increases to a width...are you ready for this...a width of more than a thousand yards and it carries a height of over sixty feet. Now, that's high coal for you!" He laughed as the room lit up. He continued, looking directly at

Marianne Bretz, the only female member of the board. *"Boys, now that's Montana and Wyoming strip coal for you, right there in McDowell County, West Virginia.*

"If that's the case then why haven't we found it before?" Howard Mills, his old nemesis, asked sarcastically.

"Well, Howard, I didn't see you out there. Had I known you were in the room I would have spoken much more slowly and in simpler terms."

"Okay, Hutson, we know that we don't like each other—now, answer my question."

"Sure, Howard. The reason we didn't know the coal was there is that we dropped our original shaft about three miles away. The first workable coal seam we hit was at the seven-hundred-foot level, way below this newfound seam."

"It isn't on the same level?"

"No, it isn't! That's what I've been trying to tell you. The crown of the seam is only down thirty to forty feet. Just like seams of western coal and lignite. It's the strangest seam we've ever found in Appalachia, or for that matter ever heard of.

"The seam was hidden all these years because it lays across the hump of the mountain. A cross section would look much like the back and rib bones of a skinned fish; the seam is in the form of an arch. And if a horizontal line were drawn about two-thirds of the way up the imaginary arch, the main part of the seam would be found from the middle of that line to the apex of the arch.

"What! There's never been a coal seam like that, and that close to the surface!" Mills interrupted, not wanting to believe what he was hearing.

Hutson ignored his outburst and continued, "The formation is quite unusual. Our best geologists speculate—and that's all it is—that millions of years ago there was a slippage of the earth's layers caused by some sort of catastrophic event...say, an earthquake of a magnitude of unthinkable proportions. Or...and they say this is quite feasible...that somehow the movements of glaciers had something to do with its unique formation, and the lateral moraine actually caused it. There is some indication of this already widely known in West Virginia. One has only to look at the area between Green Bank, Cass and Seneca Rock to see vegetation and minerals indigenous to Canada.

"The second theory seems to be the better of the two, since our drillers found a small river, actually a creek, that appears then disappears on both sides of the mountain, finally flowing free for a short distance on the Roderfield side...right here," Hutson tapped the spot on the map to make his point.

"What's even more of interest is the creek flows uphill at times, leading them to believe there is a large glacial lake under the mountain, somehow pressurized, maybe from a lava upheaval that's coming from a still cooking volcano, one that is active far below the earth's surface.

"There is a series of parallel intrusive dikes of andesite-cut quartz, unremarkable by their estimation; but along with it is a layer of dark gray clay as unique and as fine as China Clay. Evidently the layer of clay helps to keep the stream contained and guides it along a circuitous and undulating course. Under the clay is the finest limestone to be found anywhere in the world. The stream winds through the limestone, and its waters are highly filtered.

"We had the water tested and it is one hundred percent uncontaminated. Nothing, I'm telling you, there is nothing in that water. Never have our testers seen anything that wholesome, that pure. The water in itself is worth a fortune. Beer companies, whiskey companies, medical companies, or any company making any sort of liquid would pay dearly for unadulterated water."

"What a find!" "Unbelievable!" "Undoubtedly important!" Gasps of excitement filled the room, music to Hutson's ears. He smiled proudly.

"Gypsum Drilling, pretending to be a local gas company, did the testing. It was my idea to test without the knowledge of Brownlow Bean, our General Superintendent at Coalwood. That's where this seam is...at our Olga Coal property. We wanted the test analysis to be objective, so we didn't want his people involved. You know, we've spread the word that Olga's seams are quickly working out, and to involve any of them might have created problems. They would have been biased, for sure. Besides, there's something about Bean that bothers me. He's a strange bird, I think.

"So, as a consequence, the results of the test bores will be kept secret from Coalwood residents and mine officials, and for that matter everybody except only one or two handpicked men outside this room."

"But, Hutson, if the seam is that big and rich, already confirmed, and easy to get to...you'll just strip it, right?" Mills asked rhetorically, "Then why haven't operations begun?"

"And there lies the rub, my friend. You see, we don't own the property!"

"What do you mean, 'we don't own the property'? Of course, we own it. We bought off every politician and judge in McDowell County. I know that for a fact. I paid a couple off myself!" A member in the second row blurted, then sheepishly turned away from the surprised eyes of his fellow board members.

"Yes, we did gather all the support we could. And gentlemen, everybody cooperated, except for one. Remember, when Sheet and Tube bought the properties from old man Carter? Remember, there was an entry in his journal about a stretch of land that he had never been able to purchase. We tried to contact the man who supposedly owned it; but, if you recall, he would not sell, and for that matter, he refused even to talk to us.

"We never found him, remember? We never pursued it, because we never thought to look for coal on a mountaintop. After all, unlike the Pocahontas Fields, there were no outcroppings to be seen. No way for us to know of these huge deposits.

"Well, gentlemen, that same man owns the whole darn mountain range from Wolfpen Hollow all the way down to the Tug." In clear frustration, Hutson banged the pointer several times on the map. *"He owns it all!"*

"That's right! Now, I remember. It was that Whitaker fellow. They called him *Pappy*. His real name is Ezekiel," someone yelled.

"Yes, that's right, Ezekiel Whitaker. He's one of those backwoods inbred hillbillies who'll be hard to deal with. I doubt that without a little help he'll ever sell to us."

"Yeah, I'll bet if you did an ancestral line on him it would be a straight line all the way back for hundreds of years—probably nothing but Whitakers, Collinses and Mullenses on the chart. Consanguineous half-breeds."

"Now, now, my friend, don't take your frustrations out on the man's poor ancestors."

"Okay, you've got a point! Now, just how secure is his claim?"

"Well, he maintains, and it has always been accepted, that his land was a grant from General Washington to his ancestor, Micager Whitaker, a bounty for his service during the Revolution. Apparently, he helped to rid the Carolinas of the British, which led to the surrender of Cornwallis at little York Towne. Legend has it that he single-handedly turned Nathaneal Green's retreating army, and led a ferocious onslaught against the Red Coats at Eutaw Springs, South Carolina.

"Washington made sure that Micager got as much and whatever land he wanted. In fact, they claim the signature that actually appears on the warrant is that of President Thomas Jefferson. And that makes sense because it was about the time military districts were authorized, and the land began to be warranted.

"Washington kept very detailed records of those who helped the cause and win the freedom. I'm sure that's how Jefferson came to be the one who signed the warrant. The only real question is: Why did Micager pick that particular ridge out of all the others he could have had? Maybe, just maybe, he knew what he was doing. Maybe, he knew all along."

"Maybe, maybe, maybe gets us nowhere! Now, where's the warrant?" Mills asked crustily. "Has anyone ever seen it?"

"No one that we know of has ever seen the paper."

"No one has seen it for sure? Can't we find a file copy somewhere?"

"No, can't find it. We checked the courthouses in McDowell County, West Virginia, and the one in Tazwell County, Virginia—nothing in either. We also sent people to the Virginia and West Virginia State Archives, and to the National Archives in Washington, D.C. Again, there was nothing on file. The curator in D.C. told us the land grant certainly was made, but the British probably burned the record during their attack on Washington City in 1814. That's why there's no record of the bounty land grant to be found."

"I'll bet ten to one he doesn't have papers. This'll be an easy one!" Someone chuckled.

"Maybe so," Marianne Bretz replied thoughtfully, "But we still have a dilemma: How do we get ownership of the land Ezekiel Whitaker claims as his own? And if he cannot produce proof of ownership, the original grant to Micager, then what do we do? We can't just take it. We'd have to lie about it and put the poor man and his family through an awful time. I couldn't live with myself."

"I agree with Marianne. Wouldn't be right. If he's got papers that's one thing, but if he doesn't we just can't take it through hook and crook. We'll just have to deal with him. After all, that family has lived there for generations without interruption or challenge. So, there must be legitimacy to his claim." Mills offered.

Hutson was ready for that one. Ignoring Mills, he roared, "Marianne, are you living in some imaginary land—in your own Cockaigne, where the streets are paved with pastries, the houses made of sugar cakes, and the people supplied and fed for nothing?"

"I resent that—"

"—So, what?" He growled, and turned away from her, ending the one-way conversation. "She's weak, just like a woman," he thought. "No place for women in a corporation." He chose to ignore Marianne's begging look, and turned toward Mills, answering her through him. "We have to do what's best for our stockholders. Sometimes you have to take a manly stance; men are tough and from time to time men have to do what needs to be done, no matter what the means. The results will justify our actions."

"But J. Frank, you can't—"

"—Oh, yes, I can, Marianne. Champion has a big stake here. This is no time for touchy female reactions," Hutson scoffed. "Besides, we've already paid...uh...contacted one of our judges in the county. He has issued an order to the Sheriff. His name is...uh...let's see...yes...yes...Greenwalt Christian. He's a long-time county sheriff. He has been commanded by the court to serve a Non Payment of Taxes Notice upon one Ezekiel "Pappy" Whitaker, posthaste. I have a copy of it right here. I'll read it to you, and then maybe you'll understand how big business gets things done. The summons reads in part:

The Free Sate of McDowell

To Greenwalt Christian, Sheriff of all districts of the Free State of McDowell,
GREETINGS:
You are hereby commanded to summon Ezekiel "Pappy" Whitaker
If to be found in your districts, personally to be and appear before the Justice of our Court of Pleas and Quarter Sessions, to be held for the county of McDowell in the Court House at Welch on the 4th Monday of September next, then and there to testify and present proof in a certain matter of controversy in our said court, depending, concerning said non payment of Real Estate taxes. And this you shall in no wise omit, under the penalty prescribed by law.

"You mean you're setting this poor man up? You're a disgusting person, J. Frank—"

"—Oh, shut up, before I have you voted off the board! We don't need your kind anyway. We've got enough female tokens in the lower ranks—where they belong!"

Marianne stormed from the room fuming and promising herself that if she got the chance she would get her payback. He had belittled her for the last time.

"We've got him for sure...!" Someone giggled as Marianne slammed through the door.

"Good riddance to her," J. Frank said under his breath. "Yes, we've got him for sure. Taxes are the key, no record of any paid."

"Whaaat! You mean to say the Whitakers have never paid taxes on their land holdings?"

"No, sir, we can find no payment at all, and no real documentation. There is an anonymous notation, though, in the tax books at Welch that states..." He fumbled through some papers, "Of course, without being witnessed it means nothing, but... yes... here it is. I'll read it to you:"

'President George Washington waived all taxes for Micager Whitaker and his heirs forever, including but not limited to, taxes on land, whiskey, gunpowder, furs, timber, animals and all else the Whitaker family might ever own, produce, make, barter, buy or sell in the United States of America and its territories, if any.'

"So, it all depends on the court. Even if he has a paper, the original could not have survived after all these years. Our lawyers will call it a forgery, and he'll not be able to prove otherwise. The judge will refuse to enter his paper as evidence, if he produces it. In the meantime, let's watch to see what the Sheriff does with our...uh...the court's order. If he does not serve notice on Whitaker promptly, then we'll offer him—" Hutson stopped in mid-sentence and winked at a frowning Howard Mills, and then, "Well, let us say...we will make Greenwalt Christian a very, very rich man—in his mind. Every man has a price, and I don't suppose a man of his poor circumstance will covet much more than a few hundred dollars. Cheap purchase by any measure."

"Well, J. Frank, maybe your lack of faith in the good in people will be borne out. Maybe you're right, maybe everybody is just like you," Mills spit out sarcastically.

"Like I said, 'everybody has a price.'"

THE CLEAR FORK

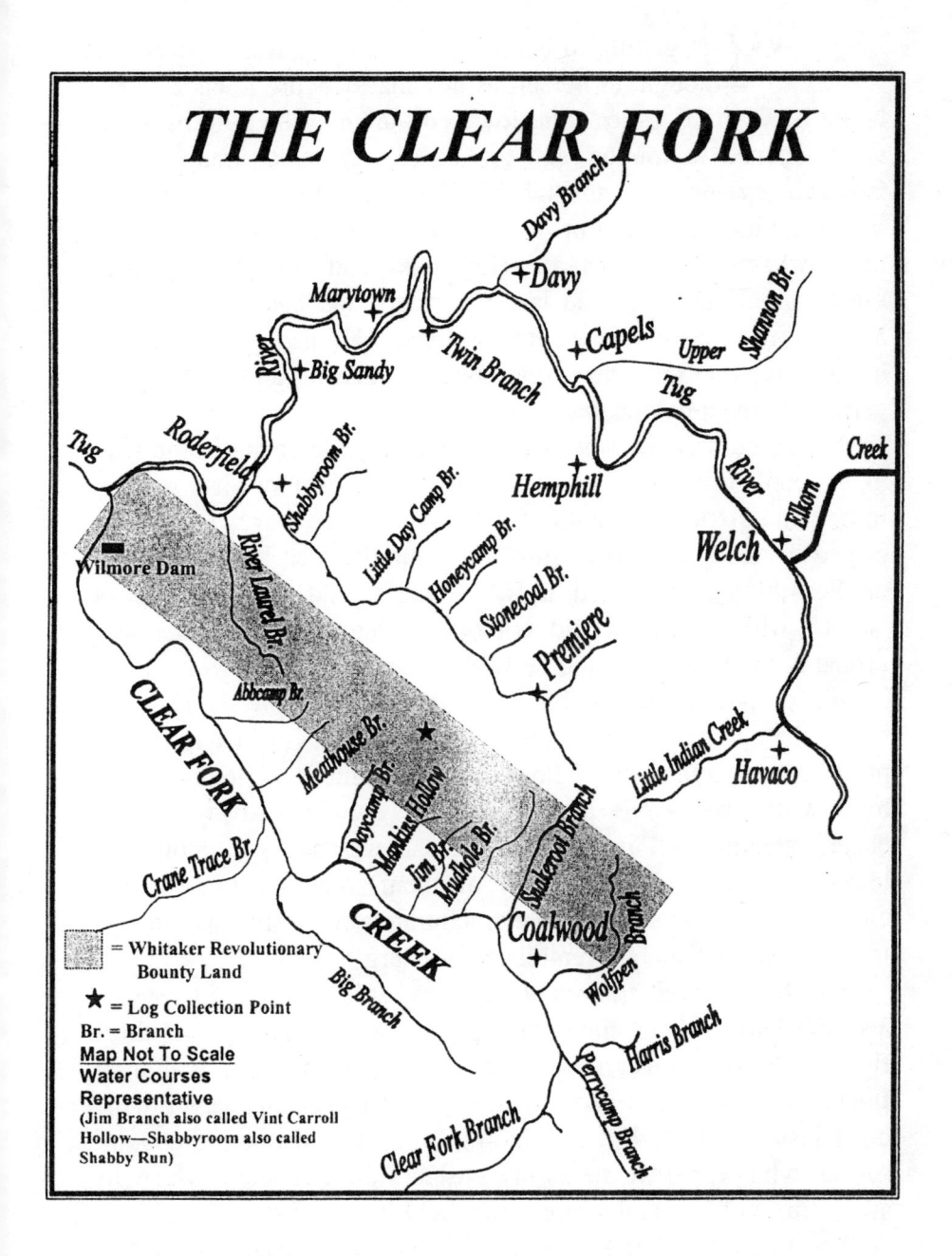

"I'm getting to be an old woman, I guess," Marianne thought to herself as her chauffer drove back to her home in Warren, Ohio. She lowered the small built-in make-up table, opened its mirror, and looked closely at her image. She frowned, eyeing the unmistakable lines of crow's feet, thin taut lips and a dark gathered brow that seemed to protrude from a noticeably wrinkled forehead. Her looks had definitely deteriorated, albeit slowly. The last few years had been difficult for her, trying to cope without her husband. He had gone fast, unexpectedly; one day they were jogging, kissing and playing together, the next day he was dead.

Marianne was not a beautiful woman. At least not in the way most people think of beauty. She was fairly healthy for a woman in her mid sixties. Still, the telltale signs were there. Excess fat ringed her body and tiny lumps of tissue drooped here and there on her thighs, arms and hips. Some would describe her as 'stout,' while others would not be so kind. Unremarkable was probably the best that could be said.

But despite her advancing years, and obvious physical limitations, she had managed to retain a distinct facial attractiveness, a pleasant appearance that held a certain magnetism, helped along by a wide, easy smile and bright blue eyes that always had a cheery gleam. All in all, though, she was realistic about her looks, and she made the best of them, wearing loose-fitting clothes and a neck scarf, and maintaining good posture while trying her best to display a semblance of energy.

She had learned to accept the inevitable, aging with grace, and she harbored no apparent regrets about losing her youthful figure. "I was never very pretty, anyway. I never had men flocking around me," she thought, "and I probably never will, but I just wonder if I'm ever going to meet someone. Someone special who will treat me as my husband did; someone who will accept me as I am, and appreciate what I have to offer."

She had taken her husband's place on Champion's board of directors. Although a minority holder, the family owned a great number of shares. She had accepted the position reluctantly, giving in to the urgings of J. Frank Hutson. He had been nice at first, showing great deference to her, but the more she disagreed with him the nastier he had become. Evidently, his motive for insisting that she replace her husband was based on his assumption that he could control her. "I might be getting old," she whispered to the mirror, "but that arrogant, pompous man will never tell me what to do."

She was not a vengeful woman but she believed that Hutson deserved his comeuppance. He deserved to be taken down a few notches. He ran roughshod over the Board, his management team, and even lowly employees who were unfortunate enough to catch his attention. He was a snot of a man, not worthy of his position. And today he had once again proven his worth. "I never thought I'd say it, but if the truth were known, I guess I hate J. Frank," she mouthed to herself, "and I just can't stand by and let him take that poor man's land."

Today's meeting had only confirmed once again what she already knew, and she had finally made up her mind. She would do what she could to fight Hutson, to change the atmosphere at Champion, even if it meant financial loss for herself. She reached for the radio's control and turned up the volume, and Paul Anka's *Puppy Love* filled the back of the limousine.

2

Expedition to the Fork of the Tug

The Appalachians—1763

They gathered at the farm of Captain "Big" Aaron Sharp, high in the rolling hills of the south bank of the Great Alamance, near its junction with Stinking Quarter Creek, and a few miles southwest of Haw River.

Big Aaron stood near the back of his house looking down at the throng of militiamen milling about, waiting for their orders. "I wonder how cocky they'll be after a few months in the high mountains," he thought to himself as he watched the mustering of contemptuous young men, many not more than sixteen or seventeen. He had seen their likes before, swaggering, boastful, overconfident, disrespectful, immature farm boys itching for a fight with the Indians, the French, or both. Yes, he had seen them before, and the changes a few months in the field would bring to them. Soon, they'd be just like all the others, innocent youth marked by the terror of war.

Once they knew firsthand of lonely and gruesome deaths at the hands of tomahawk-wielding red men, the Indians' thirst for blood, the killing and the highs of war, they would change.

An atmosphere of dread would descend upon his little army, and the once clean-shaven, loud-mouthed, foul-tongued volunteers, smartly dressed in linen hunting shirts, three-cornered hats and fringed buckskin, and carrying their prized powder horns and gleaming muskets, would become just what he wanted: determined soldiers, full of hate and loathing of the red man. Men who had seen their own, their brothers and their comrades, die in remote all but forgotten places in the high mountains of Virginia.

A lifetime of screams awaited each of them, images of pain and terror of dying men penetrating the lonely forests. Wrapped and hidden in their minds for as long as God granted them time to live on this earth, apparitions of blood-crazed Indians slaughtering their friends and relatives, tomahawked and scalped; men, red and white, who lay in pools of blood that only grew larger with each beat of a dying heart. Sharp knew those facts for certain. That would be their future because it was his future, too.

Big Aaron scanned the crowd, looking for the few familiar faces that he knew would be there; finally his eyes found those of Cager Whitaker and Vardimen Collins. Cager had served faithfully with him from the first days of the war. He was always there; whenever there was a mustering, Cager would come, and if Cager came so would Vardimen. And they came quietly, dutifully, fully aware of the dangers and the horrors that awaited.

It was said that Cager was from Virginia and that he and some of his close family and friends had removed to Orange County in hopes of buying land from Henry McCulloh, who owned over a million acres of the best land in North Carolina. He was selling it off cheaply and quickly, and hundreds of settlers came from all directions to take advantage of his offerings. The Whitakers, Collinses, Joneses and Gibsons had settled along the Alamance.

But the Germans and Scots-Irish in the area did not accept the new families, believing their copper-color skin was due to Negro blood. Most left the Piedmont, returning quickly to their Virginia hills. But not Vardimen and Cager. They stayed on, despite the bigotry.

Sharp had always believed they detested living in the Piedmont's low rolling hills; that they preferred the high mountains and narrow hollows of western Virginia and North Carolina; and that they continued to stay only because their neighbors didn't want them to. Many times he had heard Cager say that his ancestors were on the Alamance long before the British and Germans found it, and even before the French named it. He would leave he said when he felt like it—not because someone didn't like him.

They were both tough souls, men he desperately needed. Their expertise in mountain warfare and survival was critical. And their knowledge of the high mountains was invaluable to his command and mission. He trusted them, and depended upon them. They would be loyal to him long after all the others had deserted him. He made up his mind that after this expedition, his last, he would let his superiors know of their great contributions; he would be certain to inform Colonel Washington.

Cager acknowledged Sharp's stare with a knowing nod and a slight grin. He also had been looking over the green troops, gauging their commitment and battle readiness. He, too, was unimpressed by what he saw.

"He's a pitiful figure," Big Aaron thought.

Cager had only recently returned from scouting the backcountry; he had entered the New River Valley and made his way up through the Big Walker, Brushy and East River mountains, finally ending his exploration at the upper reaches of a strangely named river, Tug Fork. According to tradition, an old prospector bored holes in some crude silver castings called pigs and strung them together with a leather strap called a tug. One day while crossing Sandy River under Indian fire at a fork of the river, he dropped a tug with its load, and thus the name "Tug Fork" came about.

It was a small river that wound around the rough contours of steep mountains and through treacherous narrows and chutes lined with rugged boulders and edged by jagged cliffs. It was an unforgiving river and it had taken its toll on Cager.

His appearance revealed the sacrifices he had endured. His body was leathery and gaunt. Two braids of dirty, lice-laden, coal black hair framed a thin face, half-hidden by a scraggly beard and spindly mustache, and reached to his waist. Two distant yet intensely determined and knowing eyes broke a field of dark, reddish-brown skin. A round-top slouchy black hat with a wide brim canopied above his eyes, shading them, lending more mystery to his already odd appearance.

But his demeanor and appearance didn't fool Big Aaron. "He's one man I can depend on, a man that will protect his own and his friends," he thought as he turned away from Cager, clearing his throat and spitting out a small stream of brown tobacco juice.

He began his speech loudly, immediately drawing the attention of his men:

"Volunteers! Men of the Crown! Brave men who will protect our families and our country! We are called! King George calls us all! His Highest Eminence commands us to eradicate the French scourge from our beautiful countryside, and drive the red plague away from our homes and farms.

"Men of conscience! Men of high principles, landed men, and all free men of North Carolina and Virginia! King George wishes us to make 1763 the year of the defeat of French oppression and exploitation against all his peoples. Join me! Join me in this calling, in this important mission; a mission to protect, defend and honor our King, our brave fathers, our defenseless women and our innocent children; a mission that finds us with a clear mind of resoluteness and steadfastness. Join us now, march to the fife and the roll of the drums!"

On cue, a ragtag marching band appeared; fifes trilled and bagpipes pierced the air. The excited young men, smiling and waving, began to fall in behind the small band, marching briskly to the cadence of the accompanying drums. They paraded through the old Trading Ford where the Alamance flows over the ancient trading path that once ran from Petersburg, Virginia to the lands of the Catawba and Waxhaw Indians.

The formation trained to the northwest, toward Manakosy Creek, where the Moravians had in recent years completed the small settlements of Bethabara and Bethania. In the mid 1750s contingents of the Moravian Unity of Brethren had trekked down the Great Wagon Road from Bethlehem, Pennsylvania and picked those sites on which to build.

Bethabara was called the *House of Passage,* illustrating the Moravians desire to build an even larger congregational town to be called Salem. It would be Bethlehem's southern counterpart. Bethabara and Bethania were communes that stood in a valley the Moravians described as *Wachovia,* or *Pleasant Valley.* It lay relatively close to the German settlement of Heidelberg on Dutchman's Creek.

Sharp's small army skirted the Moravian lands, and continued on to the south fork of the Muddy, a tributary of the Yadkin River. They forded the upper reaches of the Yadkin, and at Fancy Gap traversed the Blue Ridge mountain range that frames the south side of the Shenandoah Valley. Once firmly inside the great valley, their scouts led them across New River, and northwest into the shadowy Big Walker, Brushy and East River mountains of southwestern Virginia, and through the Clinch Fields; eventually they turned into the narrow confines of the Tug Fork Valley.

Cager and Navarrh Vardimen Collins were the two scouts who roamed several miles ahead of the small column, observing the accessibility of the mountains, their direction of lay, steepness and width. From time to time, they backtracked to the column, giving details of the topography and directions for the easiest passages.

They had left the column early that morning, and were well ahead when they noticed an Indian trail. They followed it to a fork, a mile or so along the mountain wall. Vardimen took the right trail, which appeared to be the lesser-used path. Cager turned onto the other trail; it looped and snaked high above a small clear stream.

They had specific instructions from Captain Sharp not to engage under any circumstances, except those that might be personally life threatening. If either of them encountered an Indian force that appeared to be of significant size, or a scouting expedition that might precede one, they were to determine its numbers and its direction of march. He had reiterated that neither man was to engage even one Indian, in any way, certainly not in combat, except to preserve his own life or that of his fellow scout. It was absolutely necessary that any information learned regarding heathens, hostile or otherwise, be returned as quickly as possible to Captain Sharp; thus the secrecy of the expedition would be maintained.

After he and Vardimen split up at the fork, Cager continued down the west side of the mountain, maintaining a distance from the trail of over one hundred yards, while Collins traced the less-used path from its east side, also from a distance of nearly three hundred feet.

Cager moved silently through the thick undergrowth, stopping every few feet to listen for any human-caused sounds: the high-pitched and hurried chirps of birds, their sudden launch into the air, the soft sound of a moccasin striking the ground, the crunch of a leaf, the pop of a broken tree limb, and muffled conversation. He heard none; nothing, nobody was there, unless obscured by his pounding heart and heavy breath.

He was alone and frightened. His eyes moved from side to side, squinting at the shadows that sneaked through the forest, waltzing with them as their dark presence skulked from tree to tree, bush to bush; prowling farther and lingering longer with the size and shape of the clouds that floated and rolled from the southwest.

Every tree could hide an Indian, every limb an arrow, every shrub a headdress, every rock a dropped tomahawk, and every sound a precursor to tragedy. Sweat oozed from his brow, coating his eyes, rolling over his cheeks and nose and into his mouth—and he could taste his body's salty reaction to his stress. "I gotta settle down," he thought. "I won't be able to hyeh 'em 'fore they see me 'less I settle down." He stopped, resting against a huge black walnut, and took several long, deep breaths; he closed his eyes, holding the fresh mountain air inside, letting his lungs and heart harvest its oxygen. His composure returned slowly, but it came all the same, as it always did; he continued, slowly moving up the trail.

Suddenly, he heard it! The shrill gobble of a turkey, and then the rustle of leaves as the rangy bird dashed toward him, some one hundred feet to his west and south. It stopped, hiding in the shadows; and then he heard its powerful wings launching it into a low soar directly toward him. He saw its blur! He froze, as it landed not more than thirty feet away. "Now, whut do I do," he thought, suddenly feeling exposed. Fearing that it had been flushed out, and knowing that he could do nothing, not even move a limb without compromising his position and thus alerting whatever or whoever had caused its abrupt flight, he remained motionless, grateful only that a laurel protected his position, giving him small comfort and some camouflage.

He watched as the skinny bearded turkey stretched its neck from side to side, aware of every movement, every sound. It shifted its body to face the trail; its keen eyes gazed intently through the jungle of laurel, tree trunks and thick undergrowth. Warily, it cocked its head, listening.

Yes, there *was* a rustle of leaves! Cager had heard it, and so had the tom. Instantly, its body tensed, and long, powerful legs catapulted it aloft into a frenzied smear of feathers and flapping wings. It glided just above the undergrowth past Cager and out of sight.

No more than sixty feet away, the surprised Shawnee warrior jerked the reins and dug his heels into the flanks of the spooked pony. It whinnied, reared, and twisted head-to-flank, throwing its rider into the waters of a clear stream, a stream that Cager had not noticed. The pony, as if in slow motion, reared on its hind legs, and at the highest point it teetered, losing its balance. It fell thunderously backward, splashing onto the already dazed and frightened Indian, pinning him beneath its full weight. Then it rolled quickly away, regained its footing, and splashed out of the stream and bounded down the trail.

The Indian, yelping and moaning in pain, escaped the clear mountain waters and clawed his way up the gray clay covered bank nearest Cager. He leaned against a large oak tree, his chest heaving, expanding and contracting rapidly. Slowly, though, his breathing slowed and he regained his self-control. Taking a deep breath, he picked up his musket and began a slow trot toward the trail, away from Cager.

Seeing the Indian running away, Cager decided to move toward a huge hickory; fat with age, its enormous body soared above the canopy of pin oaks and short-needle pines. Just as he moved, the Indian stopped and turned! Cager froze.

Both men stared; their eyes locked onto each other's. The Indian's forehead was awash with blood that poured from an open wound. The rest of his face was so horribly scarred and twisted that Cager could hardly hold his gaze. In sudden realization of danger, each man's eyes widened in recognition of the enemy before him.

They dove for cover! Quietly, each listened for sounds of the other's advance or retreat. It was two hours before one of them moved; it was the Indian—and he was the first to shoot. Cager quickly returned fire, the first time of many.

Counting between shots, he could calculate almost exactly when the Indian could shoot next, taking nearly a minute to reload and ram the powder. Cager had the advantage in that respect; he could reload and fire in less than thirty seconds. The army had taught him that, and years of practice had honed the skill.

A weary silence crept over their small personal battlefield; a pause in the fighting that seemed to be an eternity. Cager knew that to stay there would mean certain death. If this Indian were what he believed him to be, a sentinel, then surely more would be coming; a large war party probably trailed him.

He weighed his situation, soon realizing that it was untenable. If he tried to run he would be shot in the back. If he gave himself as a target, and if the Indian missed, he would have only one shot, a shot that would have to be made at more than a hundred feet through a dense fence of limbs, leaves and shadows. And if his bullet missed its mark, there would be a fierce hand-to-hand struggle, and the Indian would surely be the winner of such a fight. If he stayed and did nothing, the face-off would continue and he would be overrun by the war party. "No," he thought, "Iffin I am to survive, somehow, I gotta git 'im to come closer an' he's gotta fahr first. Din and only din will I git me chance."

Cager made his musket ready to fire. Then, with his back hugging the fat hickory, he weaseled out of his hunting shirt, hung it over the barrel of his musket and stuck his slouchy black hat on top. Holding the musket by its stock, he stretched one shirtsleeve with his left hand. He inched his back up the trunk of the tree until he was in a slight crouch. He slowly brought the contraption around the tree and in sight of the Indian. Nothing! He held it there for just a second, and repeated the maneuver several times—still no response. "Maybe," he thought, "he ain't a-lookin'."

He coughed, not loudly, just enough to make the Indian think he was trying to hold in the sound. Making sure it was close to the ground, he once again exposed his contraption. A shot rang out! A lead slug burst through the center of his shirt, leaving a gaping hole. He dropped the lure, and immediately screamed in fake pain, groaning loudly. At the same time, he slipped his musket from the shirt, pulling it along the ground toward him, leaving his hunting shirt and hat where he had dropped them.

He heard the piercing war cry as the Indian jumped to his feet and charged for the final kill—and a scalp to brag about at the council fire. Shaking, forcing himself, Cager slowly counted under his breath, "One... two... five... ten... fifteen... now!"

He turned to his left, quickly peeling away the protection of the fat hickory, and faced the Indian. Thirty feet away, holding a huge tomahawk high above his head, the warrior charged the empty hat and hunting shirt. Suddenly as he neared the rumpled clothing, he skidded to a halt; his dark, brilliant eyes screamed with understanding. It was too late!

He yelled at the top of his lungs, lunging forward, just as the shot cleared Cager's musket barrel. The bullet ripped into the Indian's chest, throwing him backward. As if reaching for the heavens, he raised his arms in praise of the gods of the sky, or maybe in defiance. He crumpled slowly onto the soft loam of the forest floor, dying quickly.

Cager, stunned by his success, reloaded, retrieved his hat and hunting shirt, and walked toward the Indian. Stepping closer to him, he poked the body with his rifle, making sure he was dead. Satisfied, he walked to the stream where the Indian had fallen from his horse.

It was a strange sight. A beautiful, clear stream protected by gray clay banks appeared from the mountain wall, and then disappeared after flowing a few yards around the contour of the mountain. It was unusually high up on the mountain, too; and it seemed to flow uphill to the spot of its disappearance from the surface of the ridge. Cager looked about, quickly checking the lay of the mountains around him, looking for landmarks. To his right, farther up the hill, jutted a primordial cliff. A fortress of thick laurel almost completely hid it.

The craggy overhang laid horizontally, roughly perpendicular to the rise of the mountain. Even though he knew he should leave quickly, he walked toward it, lured by some unknown force. Once he parted the thick laurels, he saw its face. There before him was a mysterious black opening in the wall of the cliff—an ancient cave!

He knew he had found something unusual and mysterious, a discovery that he had to know more about—he would return later. Pausing momentarily, he let his eyes take in the mountain ranges that humped far into the distance; he stored the location of this particular ridge in his mind. He turned to leave the ridge.

Just as he passed the carcass of the Indian, he heard the war party. The dull sounds of moccasins falling against the hard mountain path came from a few hundred feet away. He listened intently, hoping that it was the sound of a grouse pounding its wings against the hollow of a log; but he was not mistaken. The party was coming, and coming quickly. "Ain't no use in a-runnin' back to the trail, they'll see me, fer shore," he thought. "I gotta find a place to hide out." He didn't panic. He still had some time. Looking around, his eyes were drawn to the laurels that hid the entrance to the cave. Crouching, running low and quietly, he made for the dark green thicket of laurels. Pushing them aside, he once again stood before the cave opening. He took a deep breath, and quickly entered the cave.

Only a few feet beyond its gaping mouth the cave floor turned dry and crusty, and a dim glare bounced from its white brittle skin. Light flowed through from the outside, allowing him to see the floor fairly well. There appeared to be no tracks, no traces of humans. It pleased him to know that no one had been in the cave recently; that he might be the first man ever to walk its dark tunnels. "I'll be safe hyeh," he thought. He hunched against the side of the tunnel, listening for the war party, waiting to see if they would discover the opening. Hour after hour, he waited and listened, but they didn't come.

Darkness began to choke off the thin spray of light that filtered through the opening. Outside the sun quickly set behind the mountains, and the tunnel became an abyss of blackness. The cave's stark coldness and desolation inundated him, and frightened him. He reached for the wall, hoping to find something of mass, something left of reality to grasp. He hugged the cold dry wall, and then...and then...at his moment of greatest fear, there came a steady whooshing sound against the backdrop of a great hum, a vibration of enormous power coming from deep inside the cave.

Waves of absolute dread rolled through his body as the roar grew louder, and the piercing, high-pitched and hell-like noises began. Blind in the darkness of the cave, above his head he could hear ghostly wings piercing the air, flapping, pounding the heavy cave air. "Hit's gotta be bats," he thought.

He slumped to the floor just as the invisible river of bats rushed past him. Their frenzied flow churned the air, creating currents of wind around him, frightening whirlwinds moving against his body, searching for his soul. And then just as suddenly as it began, the roar of the river was gone. The bats had broken into the outer world. They would search the forests for flying things, insects that could present no defense to the speed and viciousness of hungry bats. And Cager knew they would return, but next time he would be mentally prepared; next time he would know them as friends.

He was weary now, worn-out, almost exhausted. His wit, strength and courage had been tested to its fullest, and he had survived. Recognizing that his danger had retreated and that he was safe, his heart rate and breathing turned slow and steady; giving in, he relaxed against the coolness of the cave wall. He pulled his hunting shirt tightly around his body, closed his eyes and dozed off; sleep had finally overtaken him.

The bats jolted him awake. He chuckled as they flew past him, talking to them, letting them know that he was their friend, too. Their home had saved him, provided him with protection and shelter; he would remember them. When the last stragglers had flown by, he stood and walked in the opposite direction, toward the cave entrance.

As he staggered from the cave's darkness, the light rushed about his body, blinding him yet warming his soul. It was good to feel the warmth and pleasure of a renewed day. He stepped into the morning's brightness, into the rays that dropped through the canopy of green leaves that filtered a bright Appalachian sun.

Standing, bending backwards, stretching, ousting his stiffness and the coldness of the cave wall, he sucked in a huge dose of fresh mountain air, and released it in a steady drawn-out sigh. That's when he heard the shout. It seemed to come from above him.

"C-a-g-e-r! Cager W-h-i-t-a-k-e-r! Ye hear me?"

"Hyeh, down hyeh, Vardimen! Hyeh!"

Vardimen crashed over the ridge, stumbled on a log and promptly fell through the fortress of thick laurels growing above the cave's entrance. He tumbled, kicking and grabbing at roots and limbs growing over the low-lying cliff, finally landing directly behind Cager.

Surprised by the suddenness and violence of the fall, Cager turned, knowing that he would find Vardimen injured and unconscious, head and body smashed against the rock outcroppings. But, there he was, giggling, lifting himself up, and beating his floppy black hat against his knee.

"Whoooa, that wuz shore 'nough a s'prise, huh, Cager?"

"Ye okay?"

"Shore am, I got the best of that dang cliff—hit got right in me way. Yes, sirree, I got the best of hit though! Dunno whut got in me, a-runnin' like I did."

"I heared the shots. Crawled over 'em mountains almost right in the lap of a big Shawnee war party, jest 'bout a whoop an' a holler away from 'em—prob'ly be some of Chief Cornstalk's. Had to hold up all night till they skedaddled. Whar ye hide out?"

"In the cave!"

"Cave? Whut cave?"

"Well, stare yor eyes 'hind ye!"

"My, my, oh my, shore gives me 'em jimjams, Cager!"

Cager and Vardimen walked to the cave, pausing only to pull some corn shucks from the small leather sacks attached to the belts at their waists. They braided them around and over one end of the branches they had cut and stripped from the laurel. Lighting a shuck, they moved deep into the cave, their torches casting eerie shadows against the black shiny walls; they inspected every nook and cranny, every turn and every fork of the tunnel. Eventually, they came to an underground room, huge in all proportions and fresh with air and current.

Overhead and to the rear of the room, they could see the bats; thousands of bats hanging upside-down, their droppings falling continuously like a blizzard of sleet on a windless day. The men dug their shoes into the predictably crusty floor of the cave, scraping up large piles of the cave dirt with ease. They looked for their footprints—there were none. The niter had sprung back almost as soon as they had taken their next steps. They marveled at their trackless path, knowing they had found something of great importance, something the army needed desperately.

The cave was an armory of niter—the most and best niter they had ever seen in one place. The floor was covered with a layer of almost pure saltpeter, a layer the thickness of which probably could never be determined. It had piled there for thousands of years, maybe million of years, each day becoming thicker and more compressed. The bats had been there forever, it seemed. Thousands of generations of bats had made this place their home.

"Lookie, Vardimen, look at all dis bat manure; dis hyeh cave must've bin hundreds of feet high 'fore 'em bats come."

"Ye right 'bout that. I aint never seed dis much in all me life."

"Hit's a great cavern fer shore; 'em bats shore used hit a lot. But now luts quit air exploring' 'cause 'em Injuns might come back. Gotta git back to Big Aron and 'em other boys."

Their torches low with shucks, they headed to the back of the great room, back to the tunnel that would lead to the cave entrance. Suddenly, Vardimen stopped and screeched. "Ca...Cager...look, lookie over hyeh! Light some more shucks, fast!"

Cager pulled more shucks from his bag, quickly tied them around the end of his stick, lit them and held the torch high, exposing a narrow side-tunnel and lighting up the glittering outcropping that Vardimen was excitedly pointing to.

"Oh, my, my, my, Vardimen! Is that whut I thank hit is?"

"That's zackly whut hit is, Cager. Hit's zackly that. Look at hit! Ain't hit beeyuteeful?"

"We gotta test hit." He dug out a piece of ore with his hunting knife. "Take a bite of this hyeh, Vardimen."

"Cager, ye have to do hit. Ye know I ain't got no dadblame teeth." He handed it to Cager.

"Hit's soft, Vardimen, soft! Look at me teeth prints. Lookie thar, boy! Thar, and right thar, too. See, that's solid quartz hits in! We boys are rich. Hit's solid! Hee! Hee! Hee! Look at hit Vardimen! Feel hit's weight!"

"I see hit, I see hit! Hit's dadgum pure all right!"

Cager and Vardimen locked their elbows; dancing in small circles they shuffled their feet and kicked their heels, and loudly sang:

> Hit's a-hyeh fer us!
> Hit's a-hyeh waitin' fer us
> We goina see hit agin
> As soon as this hyeh war is done
> We goina git hit one by one
> We goina come back to pop a cork
> We goina come back to this hyeh clher fork!

Kicking up small dust storms of loose white niter, they danced until they were out of breath. Finally, bodies exhausted, faces glowing red, they sank against opposite walls of the passageway.

"Phyuuweee! That wuz sum dance thar ol' Vardimen! Luts ketch air breaths, din we'll load up air packs!"

"Yes sirree, This is excitin'; we goina take hit back to North Carolina, down to Cleghorn Crick, right? Them boys'll shore know 'bout hit thar? They got ther secret stash, right?" Vardimen asked as he scooped his pack full.

"Yep, they'll tell us fer shore."

"Okay, now whut?"

"Now, we gotta hide air findin.' Hyeh, hep me roll this hyeh big rock in front of that little tunnel openin' over yonder. Hit'll hide hit good!"

"Okay! Ahhhh, hit ain't so heavy to roll. Hep me now! Thar now, we got hit!"

"Now, lut's get outta hyeh!" They left the cave quickly, racing against the withering flame.

Once outside, Vardimen expelled a low whistle, saying, "Cager, whilst I wuz in that cave, after we cel'brated, I figgerated that we might well supply the whole army wit that powder and *that thar*. Colonel Warshington needs to know 'bout hit. He needs to know 'bout this hyeh cave. Ye wit me?"

"Hold on now, Vardimen, me friend. I might be a-thankin' 'bout settlin' jest right hyeh. I say we keep this hyeh place a secret. We'll work together, mine this hyeh stuff, and sell hit out right, maybe we'll pack hit south over them big mountains This'll give ye the start ye need to enter that land that's near the Clinch ye bin talkin' 'bout. Close to Blackworter Valley, I thank ye sed.

Ye can marry that purty little Gibson filly and settle in that valley y'all liked. Ya'll's youngin,' little baby Vardy, ye namesake, would like that place, fer shore.

"No, sirree, Vardimen, we gotta explore hyeh some more. Who knows, b'cuz of whuts in this hyeh cave, summers out yonder might be air youngins' futures. Ye little Vardy might do great thangs 'cuz of this hyeh niter, *and ye know whut else!*" Cager chuckled devilishly, referring to the find. "What'll ye thank, mister rich man Vardimen Collins?"

"Ye right 'bout little Vardy. He'd like that valley. If we cud sail 'nough saltpeter—we'd all be rich to buy a lot of this good earth. Won't tell 'bout air other find, though. Mums the werd wit hit. No sirree, nobidy will know nothin' 'bout hit! I'm in wit ye, Cager. Hit's air secret cave, this hyeh big ol' cave wit 'em bats."

"All we do is send werd to Warshington that we can maybe mine a little saltpeter fer 'im, and make 'im a bit of powder. He can send werd. That's all. Right?"

"Right!"

"Okay, Vardiman, cut ye fanger. I done cut mine. We can mix air bloods soins the secret of...this hyeh...ba...*bat cave* will be hid fer all time! We goina meet right hyeh at Bat Cave on this hyeh chler fork after the war is over, agreedment?"

"Agreedment! But, Cager, don't ye thank ye oughtta be callin' this hyeh cave, *Shawnee Cave*, seeing as how you done kilt one right hyeh? Kinda be like a soovinear thang."

"You call hit whut ye wont, Vardimen. Hit's goina be *Bat Cave* to me—'em bats near skeered me outta my skin."

3

War of the Regulation

Orange County, North Carolina—1760s and Early 1770s

After the 1763 Peace of Paris, which ended the Seven Years War of which the French and Indian War was only a small part, Cager and Vardimen returned to the Piedmont and once again settled-in along the Great Alamance at its junction with Rock Creek, and began raising their families. Each had a boy first. Little Vardy was Vardimen's special joy, and Cager took great pride in Micager. When Cager first saw the copper-skinned, black-haired fledgling Whitaker, he exclaimed, "My little...my... my...myyyy Cager," so Micager became his name.

There was a brief interlude of normalcy throughout the Colonies for a few years after the war. The farmers of the Piedmont took to their chores with renewed determination to better their everyday lives and their prospects of even better ones.

Vardimen and Cager were no different. They worked hard to make their farms more production and their families more comfortable. Activities on their farms were directed toward everyday survival, and passing along their skills to their sons.

The boys were learning how to use frontier ingenuity and tradition to meet the family's daily needs. And there were many. Almost ever single thing in and around the farm was the result of their individual and combined efforts. The family made all the meals, the few snacks, the chairs, the clothing, their medicines and paints; and even their eating bowls were made from small blocks of wood hollowed out by hand. Being busy every day making and doing things that would ensure their survival gave them an extraordinary awareness and appreciation of life.

The first day of August was the day people gathered to give thanks and celebrate their harvests. They used long "harvests tables," the tops almost always were made of one wide solid board. During the festival, loaves made from the first ripe grain were consecrated. Huge gatherings of Piedmont farmers and their families could be seen throughout the countryside.

The Collinses and Whitakers, though, were never invited to their Irish and German neighbors' farms to celebrate their harvests. They were avoided because of their odd-colored skins. It seemed that no one claimed to be their kin, not whites, Negroes nor Indians. They were outcasts, men without ties, men without history and tradition. But Vardimen and Cager didn't let the obvious bias bother them. They still had a fine time with a few of their old Virginia neighbors who also had settled in Orange County.

With the first hot days of August came the dog days of summer and the blistering hot weather that seemed to breed cicadas, and since they appeared in every manner to be gigantic houseflies the settlers called them Great Harvest Flies.

The family's wide-ranging guide for everyday life was the almanac. It was a periodical that contained astronomical and meteorological data arranged according to the days, weeks and months of a given year; it often included an assortment of other information. The moon and weather lore directed their every activity. A waxing moon meant they could begin above ground planting, harvesting, transplanting, grafting or firewooding. During a waning moon, underground crops could be planted or harvested, structures could be shingled, timber could be cut and fruit picked. Between a half-waning and half-waxing moon, the period of most light, cross-country travel or night farm work was recommended. Working at night was a frequent activity of the Collins and Whitaker families.

Young Vardy and Micager busied themselves gathering black walnuts and butternuts under the tall trees along the banks of the Alamance. After a night of high wind, their fathers always sent them to collect as many as possible—not only for baking purposes but also for snacking. Dried goods of all types were an important part of their daily diet, and especially necessary for long hunting or visiting trips.

They each made their own burden carriers by folding a three-foot square of canvas called "summer cloth." It was easy: fold over into a triangle, fold again from each side, lower the forward flap, use a thorn or pin to secure the folds, and use the back flap for a shoulder handle.

They filled their homemade bags and grudgingly carried their loads along the bank to Vardimen's forge house, which sat a short distance from the main house. Its roof was low and shallow, sloping over the lean-to. They placed the hulled walnuts side by side on the roof for drying. They gathered up the hulls and smashed them with large heavy blunt cuts of wood, and then placed them in a sturdy cooking pot for boiling.

After their mother boiled down the hulls, vinegar and salt were added. This *set* the mixture. The solution remaining was brown ink, to be used with their quill pens—either slit or curved. For black ink they could add indigo or lamp black (soot). Blue ink required a mixture of two parts powdered indigo, one part madder and one part bran with water. After letting it stand, it had to be strained well. Their ink well was a soft river stone with a hollowed-out center in which to hold the ink. After writing, a small amount of clean creek sand could be sprinkled over the wet ink to absorb the moisture. Then the sand could be blown away.

Because of the stains inflicted upon them by the lowly walnuts, Vardy and Micager didn't care much for nutting. No amount of scrubbing with creek mud and sand could remove the stains. They were destined to wear the marks for several weeks afterward or until they had grown completely new skin on their wrists and hands.

There was one job the boys really liked, though. They loved to soot the fruit trees. From time to time, their little orchard was infested with insects, so the corrective procedure was to fill two shovels with soot from the forge house, mix it with one shovel of Quick Lime, and place the mixture on the ground windward of the trees. When sprinkled with water, a generous quantity of gas developed, rising into the trees. The insects would be destroyed with no harm to the trees, and with big smiles and popping eyes the boys would amaze at the huge clouds of sizzling gas.

The tanning of hides was common labor for backcountry families. They used chestnut bark they called "acid-wood" or "tan-bark" for removing the last fine hairs from the hides. The family made moccasins, coats, strops, hinges, shirts, gloves, harnesses, and countless other products to ensure their survival.

Apple drying was another practice they had to learn. By slicing the apples and hanging them on long woven grass drying trays, supported from hooks embedded in the ceiling beams over the fireplace, the heat from the fire would soon dry them. Drying trays were almost continuously in use during colonial days, except when a Saturday-night bath was necessary. Then, blankets were hung on fireplace hooks for the bather's privacy. This manner of drying ensured that a good supply of raw or sugared fruit would be available to the family during the winter and early spring. Apple trees were so essential to the survival of the pioneers that in some places it was against the law to cut down a tree, since one tree could provide raw fruit, applesauce and butter, dried fruit, cider and vinegar.

The boys loved to pick apples. After all, they could eat all the juicy, snappy fruit they could stand. They picked eating apples by the stem for storing and packed them without touching in straw; then they placed them on stone shelves in the cellar. The best of the remaining apples, those not fit for storage, were used for drying. The rest were used for making applesauce, butter and vinegar. To reach apples hanging high in the trees, they made apple sticks, long poles cut from straight tree limbs, forked at one end. A pot was fastened just under the fork, so when the fork pushed the stem, the apple dropped into the pot, keeping bruises to a minimum.

There was much to do on the farm. The everyday reality of life was that the family had to be constantly busy maintaining, improving and building new structures in order to store and preserve staples for themselves and their livestock. For example, the boys learned to stack hay around a center pole. They stacked it so tightly in forming a hayrick that a hay knife had to be used to cut the hay from it. The knife was made much like a big sickle, with the sharp side out. On top of the rick, which looked like an inverted bell, the boys always placed their favorite homemade rick ornaments. Sometimes they made rick vanes, or various animal or bird forms fashioned from strands of hay, tied together by twine, all connected by a straw-covered stick attached to the top center pole of the rick.

They built corn cratches, later *cribs*, by making two crosses and placing them on their sides at a desired distance from each other. Then the upper part of the structure could be framed and covered with a shingle roof. The V-shaped sides of the cratch were made of slats, spaced apart for ventilation. The ends were covered, but a door on one end and a vent on the other were necessary.

Every July and early August, the families looked for blackberries, especially the shade berries that grew under the trees on the banks of the Alamance. It wouldn't take long for the boys to breach the oath of "no eating the berries." Normally, their transgressions were exposed early in the gathering. Dark tongues, stained lips and teeth, wide sheepish grins and empty containers were evidence enough.

After gathering enough for a couple of pies, the remaining berries were turned over to their fathers. They called it medicine, so the boys watched the procedure very closely, thinking that it might save their lives at some future time. Vardimen and Cager mashed about two gallons of blackberries, added two quarts of boiling water and let the mixture stand a full day. Then they strained it through a coarse cloth, added six quarts of water and four pounds of brown sugar, mixed it well, and poured it into two large jugs, leaving the corks loose. They'd always leave the jugs in Vardimen's cool cellar. Along about October they'd invariably catch some sickness and have to drink, sometimes a lot, of that smelly, ugly medicine.

In spring the work schedule began again. The entire family moved to the fields, planting seeds they had stored over the last winter, and the few they had managed to buy at market. Planting time was a hopeful, cheerful labor and they one and all worked to the tunes of several songs. One of their favorites was:

> *One for the blackbird*
> *One for the crow*
> *One for the cutworm*
> *And one to grow.*

Piedmont tobacco was in great demand throughout the Colonies, and as an export to Europe. Almost every farmer in Orange County cultivated at least one field. The tobacco economy was big then, and many plantations raised hundreds of acres of the plant, but many like Cager and Vardimen were small growers. They were called "men of one hogshead," because about all they could harvest was a hogshead or two, so they strove for quality, hoping that superior leaves would make up what they lacked in quantity.

But raising tobacco required great skill and year-around work. Seed plants were grown in protected areas, and when they reached the size of a shilling they were transplanted into long rows of hills that the family had formed before planting.

The families hunched in the fields for several months, weeding, topping, suckering, cutting and worming. During worming—the removal of cutworms, flea beetles and hornworms—inspections were made for leaf rot and hollow stalk.

When the leaves began to spot and discolor they cut off the six- and seven-foot plants from their bases. They left them in the fields until they had wilted, then they were brought to the curing sheds and hung upside down, far enough apart to promote sweating with good air circulation. If the air became foggy and heavily laden with moisture, they made smothers, smoke fires, to ensure a steady drying process.

Six weeks after cutting, the curing and drying were finished and they stemmed and stripped the leaves, binding them together in small bundles called "hands." Finally, they "prized" them, packing them in layers in wooden barrels called hogsheads. They were roughly four feet high and two feet in diameter, and the "hands" were packed loosely so as not to *squeeze them to death*. Then they secured the "head," placed the hoops that encircled the barrels and marked each one. After loading the hogsheads on their two-wheeled cart, Cager and Vardimen drank a toast of applejack to a rich and timely market. Their "good as gold" product was ready for market.

Flax and corn were also staples on all farms. Flax grain was used widely in Europe and in the colonies in the manufacture of oil; its fiber was used in making paper and linen. By using a flax brake, comb and dresser the woody parts could be prepared for spinning.

Corn was always planted as soon as possible after a place for settling was found. Once a family harvested its first corn crop, they made a spiritual and practical transition from pioneers to farmers. On every farm in every region of America corn was the foremost crop. The Indians called it *maize, that which sustains life,* but most settlers and newcomers referred to it as *Indian corn*.

Corn was easy to grow, easy to store for long periods; it had high resistance to insects and drought. It required minimal preparation, and could thrive in new ground. It would germinate after years of storage and would mature in a few weeks, and it yielded three times more than wheat and required one-fourth the seeds. Its food value was retained for years, and its harvest time was not critical, since it could be harvested at different times during the growing season and used for different purposes. Although corn brought little at market, it found its way there in livestock, poultry, their by-products and whiskey.

Corn was roasted, boiled, pickled, stewed with meat, dried, ground and powdered; it was popped for delicious treats, and when mixed with grains of high gluten content, it could be made into bread. Depending on the region, families called their creations mush, swamp, hoecake, johnnycake, dodgers, corn pone and a whole host of other pet names. Many settlers called it the *plant of gods*, but some considered any end product besides whiskey to be unnatural and a sacrilegious waste of a heavenly gift to all men. Whiskey was the therapeutic product of the heavens, and one could feel heaven's warmth with every sip.

Corn cobs, leaves, husks and stalks were used for fodder, garden fences, snow breaks, caulking, banking material, stuffing mattresses and chairs, insoles of shoes, seats, chair backs, horse collars, kindling, plugs for holes, corks for fishing, stoppers for jugs and bottles, tool handles and sanitary supplies for the outhouse. Torches were also made from corn shucks. In fact, at many get-togethers, the signal for returning home was, "It's time to light the shuck."

Vardimen and Cager had recognized the uniqueness of the Piedmont, even when they first laid eyes upon the two adjoining parcels of 265 acres they each had purchased from Henry Eustace McCulloh.

Their land was isolated from the diseases brought by ships into Charleston and other eastern seaports. Due to the lack of swamps and lowlands with their mosquitoes and waterborne diseases, typhoid, malaria and yellow fever were virtually absent. Cholera and smallpox outbreaks were rare, because there were few contacts with overseas foreigners. Hygiene and sanitation were generally good and as a result eight to ten children per family normally survived into adulthood.

The Piedmont also was home to deer, squirrels, raccoons, opossums, groundhogs, beavers, rabbits, bear, and bison. Its hills, streams and lakes were teeming with ducks, turkeys, geese, swan, partridges, grouse, and pigeons in flocks of thousands.

Fish were trapped in submerged baskets made of oak. Shad swimming up unpolluted and free-flowing streams during their annual runs were easy prey to even the most unskilled fisherman. They were smoked and cured and added to the family table.

Fruits and nuts of every type, herbs and vegetables were readily available. Peaches, apples, pears, plums, chestnuts, walnuts, chinquapins, hazelnuts, grapes and berries, wild greens and honey were all part of their diets.

But even with all the richness of the land, the families still struggled. No amount of work and good weather resulted in surplus goods or money for the families, and with each passing year of unfruitful labor they grew more and more frustrated with the colonial government and legal system. After a time, they recognized that their problems were caused in part by their own greed. They had wanted cheap land, but in obtaining it they had placed their families in the middle of a major land feud, the one between Henry Eustace McCulloh and Earl Granville.

Henry Eustace's father, an Ulster-Scot from London, and his investors were granted 1,200,000 acres of land in North Carolina. The grant consisted of twelve tracts of approximately 100,000 acres each, and was acquired in 1737 through action by a Privy Council in London. The body of dignitaries and officials chosen by the British monarch as an advisory council functioned, sometimes secretly, through its committees.

Once the grant was made, McCulloh's father sent agents into other colonies and to Europe to promote his lands. Between 1750 and 1760 droves of settlers from Pennsylvania, Virginia, Maryland and Germany bought land and established permanent homes in North Carolina.

At first, McCulloh took great care not to encourage backcountry Scots-Irish to buy his land; they were known to be footloose people of the lowest morals, and troublemakers to boot.

Bolstering that opinion were the writings of Charles Woodmason, an Anglican preacher. After taking his holy orders in England, he had returned to the colonies to ride the tortuous trails from coastal Charleston to the piedmonts of the Carolinas preaching his sermons to a despicable disorderly crew. At some stops he was offered food but he couldn't touch their provisions because all their cookery was exceeding filthy and most disgusting.

He wrote to friends that the Scots-Irish were a set of the lowest vilest crew breathing, and that many hundreds live in concubinage swapping their wives like cattle. He noted that he spent his time marrying free of charge rogues and loose women and baptizing their brats.

At one North Carolina settlement he was insulted and threatened by lawless hooligans who saw his presence as an affront to their backcountry freedom. They told him they wanted no black-gowned worthless preachers among them, and they threatened to lay him in the fire, and when he tried to preach they brought coon and bear hounds to his service, and yelled and whooped like Indians.

Other clergy complained that men in their congregations couldn't keep their eyes on the preacher, for the women, many very pretty, came to church barefoot and bare-legged, without head coverings. He commented that they were literally in a state of nature for nakedness counted for nothing in a region where ten to fourteen people or more lived in the same tiny cabin.

Woodmason knew that the poor wretched settlers had been allowed to inhabit the backcountry as a barrier between the Indians and the rich plantations of the east; theirs was a land without laws, government, churches or police. They had been offered cheap land for that very purpose, and now they fought every day against the gangs of villains on the western frontiers. He witnessed first hand groups of outlaws, sometimes numbering in the hundreds, who conspired to move stolen horses, fence goods and sell slaves. He wrote that these ruffians possessed regular communications with each other from the back settlements of Georgia, the Carolinas and Virginia.

The backcountry was infested with squatters, runaway debtors, freeloaders, good-for-nothings, crazies, slackers, criminals, speculators, rustlers, thieves of the worst breed, and women marginal in both morals and character.

The Whitakers and Collinses, along with their neighbors, good family men, religious and productive, were forced to coexist with the scum of mankind. Huge gangs spilled out of the Georgia and Carolina backcountry, polluting the land with their vile, taking over farms, raping wives and kidnapping young women.

Five of McCulloh's tracts fell within the territory previously granted to Earl Granville, which in effect created dual grants. Tract Eleven, the tract in which Cager and Vardimen bought land, was squarely within Granville's claim. As a result, Granville filed suit against McCulloh's group. Counter suits followed counter suits and the litigation went on in British courts for years.

Granville had strong political connections with the governor, and he instigated the forming of several new counties. Among them was Orange County in which Vardimen and Micager lived. Granville and his friends placed the new county seats outside the tracts claimed by McCulloh. Hillsborough promptly became the Orange County seat, thus any registration of land had to be finalized in that courthouse, a town miles from the landowners in Tract Eleven, and a court controlled by friends and lackeys of Granville.

Many settlers, after paying McCulloh for their land, paid Granville's agents for recording the sale in the land office, paid once again to record the sale at Hillsborough, and finally paid quitrents. The exorbitant fees were illegal and extortionate, and that helped to fuel unrest and distrust of the government.

When McCulloh realized he could lose in British courts, he transferred huge acreage to his son Henry Eustace. In an attempt to establish legal title, Henry Eustace began to quickly buy back previously granted lands. Granville eventually won in the courts, but died in 1763. His land office was quickly closed. The estate was in constant litigation; therefore, no new land grants could be made. Sensing cheap land, settlers began making tomahawk surveys, marking trees for establishing property lines, and squatting on the land, waiting for the land office to reopen.

McCulloh's empire collapsed and at a sheriff's sale in 1765, with only one day's notice, the seven tracts of one 100,000 acres each were sold at auction. Each tract was bought for five pounds. The governor of North Carolina, William Tryon, was one of the buyers. In the meantime, Henry Eustace was rapidly selling the land he had bought and that transferred to him by his father.

This was the backdrop against which Cager and Vardimen toiled daily. It was in this mix of confusion, fear and frustration that the Whitaker and Collins families survived. And although they never knew when thugs would fall upon their families, they were prepared to deal with such threats. Preparation, vigilance, and good muskets could ensure their survival against this scourge on humanity.

The settlers understood violence and would-be terrorists, but what they couldn't comprehend was the workings of judicial and bureaucratic systems forced upon them by Granville and the royal governor. They were systems rooted in sleaze and corruption, and the settlers couldn't understand how their own colonial government could allow scurrilous court and county officials to continue to operate so openly. They never knew when county agents would come to demand more money, or confiscate their harvests or livestock, claiming nonpayment of trumped up quitrents and exorbitant fees and taxes.

It was common knowledge that Granville's agents regularly paid corrupt lawyers in Hillsborough to write fraudulent indentures with dates that predated those land agreements made by settlers, and then they demanded higher payments from the already poor farmers, or forfeiture of their property. Many times, deeds inexplicably disappeared from the courthouse and land offices; mysteriously, new ones were often found in their places.

It was a sheriff's notice that his land would be confiscated for underpayment of land taxes that brought Cager Whitaker to Hillsborough in the spring of 1768. He had received the notice the week before. Upon reaching the courthouse, a lawyer accosted him on its stone steps, offering to be his representative for a highly inflated fee. Cager pushed him aside and entered the courtroom. He was just in time to hear the judge say, "The court finds against you, John Steiner. You have ten days to vacate the property."

Steiner screeched, "You can't take my land. I paid my taxes. You've trumped up the fees. You're stealing people's land. Me and mine will fight to the end."

"You're in contempt of this court!" The judge screamed. "Get this scum out of here. Take him to the whipping post, and after you've lashed him throw him into a cell for ten days and," the judge snarled at Steiner, "I guess when you get out of jail your time to vacate will be up, so I'll send a couple of deputy sheriffs to impound your personal property and livestock. That way you won't have to delay your departure from this county."

The clerk chuckled and whispered to the deputy sheriff, "I want to see his horses before you get rid of them."

Steiner cried out, "But what about my wife and daughters?"

"They'll be okay. We'll take care of them," the deputy blurted, grinning.

As the poor man was taken away, the judge slammed the gavel down. "Read the next case!"

Cager, not yet noticed, moved toward the front of the courtroom. He stood alone, at attention, straight and proud, obviously out of place in the courtroom. He held his big, black slouchy hat with both hands, pressing it to his heart. His shiny black hair lay pasted almost flat against his scalp, and one could still see little particles of white lard here and there along the run of his mustache and beard. He wore bulky, pull-on boots, evidently handmade; his thick black belt held a dark cowskin whip and a long hunting knife. His eyes were dark yet twinkly, and seemed to dance, taking in every movement in the room. He stared at the judge for long seconds before finally announcing, "I am Cager Whitaker. Why have ye sent me dis notice?"

The judge, a skinny, nervous man with rotten teeth and a twitching right eye, bolted straight up in his huge brown leather chair, surprised and shocked at the intruder. "Who are you? Can't you see that this court is in session and that official business is being carried on?"

"I see whut kind of biznus ye're carryin' on. And I don't like hit none neither."

The judge, noticing the huge dark eyes staring at him, pacing his every move, felt a twinge of fear spread over his body. He paused for a moment, slightly shrugged his shoulders, turned to his clerk, and whispered, "Do you have this man, Cager Whitaker, on the docket?"

"No, judge, this man is not yet scheduled. We have many other tax derelicts scheduled ahead of him."

"This notice says I am. I rode thirty-five mile from Alamance 'cuz of this hyeh paper, and I ain't leavin' 'fore it gits clhered up. I don't owe no taxes."

The judge pointed to Cager, "Whitaker, you have no standing in this court. You are interrupting our ongoing proceedings, and if you don't vacate this courtroom and indeed the town of Hillsborough immediately, you will be in contempt of court."

Cager stood his ground, staring with great contempt, his gaze boring into the judge's eyes. "I sed I ain't leavin' till I git me jestis. I paid me taxes."

"Get this...this...ignorant groundling...person out...out of here!" Screamed the judge, his voice thin, high-pitched, breaking in alarm, his thoughts still captured by Cager's dark, ominous, lingering eyes.

The sheriff moved across the room toward Cager. He reached to grab his shoulder as Cager turned toward him. "Ye tech me and ye'll regret hit. Iffin ye do, that'll be the laihst thang ye do."

The sheriff rotated his body to punch Cager, and as he thrust his fist forward it stopped in mid air, held fast by the iron grip of a powerful Whitaker hand. A fleeting glance into Cager's dark eyes was enough to immediately weaken the sheriff. Terror spread across his face, and he knew he had seen great danger, deep danger rooted in eyes of retribution and contempt. Cager released his grip and the sheriff skulked away, eyes pleading with the judge, silently warning him of the danger.

"Uh, Mr. Whitaker," the judge, clued-in now, said softly, "there must be some mistake. Let us look at the records in the next few days. I'm sure an error has been made. If you say your taxes are paid, then we'll give you the benefit of the doubt. Clerk, mark Mr. Whitaker's taxes as paid for now."

"Okay jedge, ye look over 'em papers, and ye'll find that 'em taxes are paid. That's Whitaker werd! Colonel Warshington knows Whitaker werd! Ye hear me now, that's Whitaker werd. Ain't nobidy takin' me land. But ye 'member now, I seed whut goes on in this hyeh court." Cager tapped his dark cowskin whip against his thigh, "I seed the way ye treat me neighbors, and I don't like hit none. Ye'd better stop this hyeh or ye shall suffer great konseequences. Ye'll know Whitaker wrath and Whitaker jestis. Do right, now, or know air wrath. Iffin ye take not heed, ye'll see!"

Cager's giant eyes flashed fire; he turned quickly, rushing with great purpose to the back of the courtroom. He could hear the chatter of the slick lawyers as he stepped through the big oak doors, never breaking his stride as he headed down the stone steps to the hitching posts. He mounted his mule and headed back to Alamance.

During the 1760s, in the coastal cities of America there was growing anger with the British government. It nurtured American resentment by passing the Stamp Act of 1765 and the acts of 1767 imposing import duties on glass, paper, printers' colors and tea, and the arrival of British troops at Boston the following year.

Soon, resentment became annoyance, and annoyance became irritation, and irritation became anger, and anger became fury, and in 1769 culminated in rage and the seizure and subsequent scuttling of the armed British sloop Liberty, off Gravelly Point at Newport, Rhode Island.

Throughout the early 1760s men of the Piedmont feeling alone, unprotected and without power rebelled in quiet ways against the royal government, its corrupt bureaucracy and courts. But by mid decade, the seeds of rebellion were growing rapidly, budding and flowering in a climate of suspicion, corruption and oppression, until finally the settlers had had enough. In 1768 a committee of North Carolinians, calling themselves *Regulators,* drafted a petition and dispatched it to the Governor and Council of North Carolina, William Tryon.

The petition stated the Regulators were neither disloyal to the Crown, disaffected by the constitution nor dissatisfied with the legislature, and the disturbances were due to the "corrupt and arbitrary practices of nefarious and designing men, who being put into offices of profit and credit among us, and not satisfied with the loyal benefits which arose from execution of their offices, have been using every artifice, practicing every fraud, and, where these failed, threats and menaces were not spared."

They further stated, "How grievous...must it be for wretches to have their substance taken from them by those monsters of equity, whose study it is to oppress and steal..." and, "The sheriffs grew arbitrary, insulting the populace, making such distresses as seldom ever known, double, treble, nay, even quadruple the value of tax was frequently distrained, and such seizures hurried away to Hillsborough." The letter went on to say that a group of "twenty-seven men, consisting of sheriffs, bombs, tavern-keepers, and officers" took several men not even remotely associated with the Regulators into custody, thus alarming "the whole country."

Tryon answered their grievances "by no means warrant the extraordinary steps you have taken in assembling yourselves together in arms, to the obstruction of the courts of justice, to the insult of the public officers.... and to the injury of private property." He went on to say that, "it is my direction that you...desist from any further meetings, either by verbal appointment or advertisement; that all titles of Regulators or Associations cease among you; that the sheriffs and other officers are permitted to execute the duties of their respective offices."

In August of 1768 the Regulators answered, "...since the iron hand of tyranny has displayed its baneful influences over us with impunity, how has dejection, indifference, and melancholy, and chagrin diffusively spread themselves far and wide among us; and, unless... you use your united efforts to extricate us out of our present misery, and secure our rights and property, the sullenness and gloom with which we are already seized, will sink deep upon our intellects and general disregard to everything below ensue as a consequence thereof; nor shall we strive any more than barely to keep then, our tottering frames from falling to pieces, until death, in compassion of our sufferings, and in commiseration of our wrongs, shall kindly appear in shape, and remove us from this spot of dirt, about which, and its products, there is so much contention and animosity."

Tryon took the petition and answer to his letter as a direct threat against the royal government, but did nothing of any consequence to either appease the Regulators or confront them. While his inaction was meant to effect no change, others inside and outside North Carolina steered the colonies farther along toward rebellion.

In March of 1770 soldiers of King George III fired on his American subjects. It was called the Boston Massacre. Five colonists were killed, including a seaman named Crispus Attucks, who was half Negro and half Native American. His death would be remembered as the first of the Revolution.

In North Carolina, Regulators armed with cudgels and cowskin whips attacked lawyers and a judge at Hillsborough, and drank damnation to King George and success to the Pretender—toasts that referred to the Prince of Wales, who took for himself the title of King James the Third after the death of King James, confronting openly and directly the legitimacy of the rule of King George.

They chased several county officials into stores, and they assaulted them with stones and brickbats, and once court opened they filled the house, saying they had come to have justice done, and they insisted their cases be tried, and the court continue to do business without lawyers. The judge refused and they escorted him home with great parade. That evening, a disturbance began and they fell upon two lawyers in a furious manner. Within hours the mob of 150 tripled in number. A riot ensued, and culminated with the tearing down of one lawyer's house.

The next day they left Hillsborough and moved west. One informer reported that Regulators had spoken against the Governor, Assembly, judges and others in office and "Many of them said the Governor was a friend of lawyers. The lawyers carry on everything. There should be no lawyers in the province." Later, some threatened to fight and kill a company of the King's soldiers.

By early 1771 there had been riots at the Anson, Salisbury and Hillsborough courthouses. And when authorities tried punitive measures, the Regulators and their sympathizers refused to pay taxes, and further terrorized administrators and disrupted court proceedings.

Prompted by years of ongoing anarchy, Tryon assembled a group of little more than a 1,000 troops, and marched westward.

Many battle-seasoned former soldiers, including Vardimen and Cager, hurried toward Salisbury, thinking that Tryon's intention was to force a confrontation either there or somewhere along the Yadkin. Others of lesser experience stayed in the general Alamance area.

By the middle of May, Tryon's army had made camp on the banks of the Alamance. A little farther to the west 2,000 poorly armed and untrained Regulators camped raucously—singing, dancing, wrestling, joking and firing their few weapons, unaware of the danger of their situation.

Tryon sent a letter to the leaders of the Regulators at Alamance: "...I lament the fatal necessity to which you have now reduced me by withdrawing yourselves from the mercy of the crown and the laws of your country, to require you who are assembled as Regulators to lay down your arms, surrender up the outlawed ringleaders, and submit yourselves to the laws of your country, and then rest on the lenity and mercy of the government. By accepting these terms in one hour from delivery of this dispatch you will prevent an effusion of blood, as you are at this time in a state of war and rebellion, against your king, your country, and your laws."

When the offer was rejected, in full uniform, hat cocked, sword drawn, Tryon ordered the militia to attack. It was May 16, 1771.

The rebellion was crushed. It was called a military defeat, but it was simply and unequivocally a rout. Of the 1,100-member militia, only nine soldiers were killed and sixty-one wounded. The uncoordinated and unqualified Regulators suffered severe losses, but the exact numbers went unreported. Later, Tryon executed seven Regulators, tried twelve others for rioting, and put forty in chains and paraded them through the Piedmont just to make his point.

Tryon reported to the British government "...The action began before twelve o'clock, on Thursday the sixteenth instant, five miles to the westward of Great Alamance River, on the road leading from Hillsborough to Salisbury... action was two hours. But after half an hour the enemy took to tree fighting, and much annoyed the men who stood at the guns, which obliged me to cease the artillery for a short time, and advance the first line to force the rebels from their covering. This succeeded and we pursued them a mile beyond their camp, and took many of their horses, and the little provision and ammunition they left behind them. This success I hope will lead to a perfect restoration of peace in this country. Though had they succeeded, nothing but desolation and ravage would have spread itself over the country; the Regulators had determined to cut off the army had they succeeded..." He added a postscript: "General Wadell, with two hundred and fifty men, was obliged, on the 19th instant, about two miles eastward of the Yadkin, to retreat to Salisbury. The Regulators surrounded his forces and threatened to cut them to pieces if they offered to join the army under my command. I shall march tomorrow to the westward, and in a week expect to join the General."

Vardimen and Cager returned to their farms amid the mourning that followed the defeat of their comrades at the Battle of Alamance. For all practical purposes, the War of the Regulation was over. But the undercurrent of disgust and suspicion of the Crown continued to boil to the surface in every colony.

Finally recognizing the gravity of what was happening in the colonies and due to the intensity and widespread hatred of the Crown, the British Parliament in the mid 1770s, in an attempt to warn her other colonies, declared "the existence of a state of rebellion in Massachusetts." Soon after, followed the Declaration of Independence and the long bloody war of American independence.

It was a personal war for Vardimen and Cager, and later Micager and Vardy. About twenty percent of the total population participated. Casualties were heavy—how heavy will never be known, as death was a lonely friend in the backcountry.

4

The Spigoting

The Piedmont of North Carolina—1776

When they were alone together, they talked constantly of Bat Cave and The Clear Fork. How someday they were going to go back there to set up a mine.

Vardimen's plan was to bring a train of pack mules to The Clear Fork, load them, and then strike out for Blackwater Creek, and the narrow ridge that he called New Man's Ridge, because he would be the *new man* there. "Only man thar," Cager mused. It lay between the Clinch and the Powell, a short distance from the Virginia border. He would acquire the land with all its valleys and ridges—the beautiful country from Mulberry Creek and Little Ridge to Big Sycamore Creek and Short Mountain; and all the land to Washington County, Virginia would be his.

Cager also had plans. He had made up his mind that he would settle in The Clear Fork, that he would live in Bat Cave until he had built a fine cabin. Then, he'd fetch his family.

He dreamed of the happy times they would share, the abundant game, the fish that could be seen through six feet of clear mountain water, the cool and fresh breezes that raced up the valley and over the ridges; and he dreamed of the great glare of yellow light that every morning burst through the eastern sky; its rays burning off undulating blankets of high fog and white valley mist that trailed just above the blue mountains—limitless waves that humped and stretched towards the mounting sun; and he dreamed about the warmth of the new cabin he would build on the flat that overlooks the clear little stream that flowed into the Tug.

Cager's mind spilled over with images of a happy mountain life, and the peace, safety and tranquility his family would know there. He loved that valley, and someday he would have all the things that he remembered about it. He and his son would own it someday, and the ground would become more and more sacred with each passing generation of ancestors—a valley consecrated with the blood, tears, joy and toil of generations of Whitakers. That was his dream—a new beginning in The Clear Fork.

But it was not to be. Events were unfolding that would change their lives and their plans forever. Out of the East, South and North came accounts of discontent. Turmoil abounded in the Colonies. Everywhere, there was talk of the battle at Lexington and Concord, and as a result the British Parliament had sent thousands of troops to New England. Rumor had it that General Washington's infant Continental Army had begun a siege of Boston; that people of Mecklenberg had severed their ties with England; and now, the colony of North Carolina had declared itself independent.

Central North Carolina had become a cauldron of hatred and violence. Loyalists raided, killed, raped, stole and tortured, while rebels returned the favors; "two eyes, an ear and a tongue for an eye" was their slogan. Farms burned, women wailed, babies cried, and men died in lonely places. War had come to the peaceful red rolling hills of the Piedmont, and privates Cager Whitaker and Vardimen Collins were part of it.

It was spring of 1777, when delightful fragrances of a young year began to sweeten the air. The flowers were in full bloom, and the magnificence of dogwood was painted throughout the rolling hills of central North Carolina. It was at that time, a time of renewal, that the war had taken its nastiest turn.

Cager tuned in his saddle as the sergeant rode up.

"Whitaker, ye scout to the southeast. See if ye can round up some livestock from one of them Tory farms," Sergeant Leach ordered Cager and Vardimen, then added, "Ye might as well do some rooting along the way; the other boys didn't do so good." Leach had referred to "rooting parties," squads sent out to search for wild sweet potatoes, a particular favorite of the troops.

"Okay, we're on air way," Cager replied, grabbing his musket, and nodding to Vardimen. They kicked the flanks of their mules and rode steadily into a huge, red rising sun.

Two hours of cautious riding brought them to the first Tory farm. It lay near the banks of Haw River, its fertile fields gently rising and falling into the horizons. It was a beautiful farm, rich with whitewashed buildings and fences, corn cratches, out-barns, fertile earth, and tall fescue and cedar trees that confined great stands of young tobacco, cotton and corn.

They dismounted behind a stand of cedars and began a cautious walk over the last few hundred feet to the house. They had closed the distance by some three-quarters when a terrible piercing scream broke the heavy morning air. They stopped behind a fencerow, looking at each other, perplexed as the screams intensified and quickened.

"Lut's go!" Cager whispered hoarsely. Maybe, hit's one of airs."

Running low, hiding behind trees and bushes, they quickly negotiated the field, finally stopping, falling to their knees when they had a clear view of what was causing the commotion. They saw a man hanging by his wrists bound by a single rope wrapped around a stout limb of an oak tree. He was being turned around and around by two husky men, mountain men dressed in deerskin.

"This'll teach ye. Ye lying Tory traitor! I'll bet ye won't burn any more of our cabins. Ye won't come up on me mountain agin, will ye?" The burley Irishman growled as he butted his musket into the side of the poor man, pushing his body into another half-turn. The man shrieked in pain, praying, begging his tormentors to stop.

"Ye pitiful, crying, slab of cow dung! This'uns for me woman, my good and true Lorraine!" The Irishman struck again, this time with the end of his musket barrel; he shoved it head-on into the man's groin. The poor man screamed in agony, losing consciousness just before the big man slammed his rifle butt into his side. "And this'uns for me little Johnny, and this'uns for me purty little baby, Sally." He pounded the hanging man's left shoulder, driving him down farther onto a sharpened piece of wood.

"My, God, Cager, they's spigoting that man," Vardimen's throaty voice broke their silence.

"Spigoting?"

"Yeah, hit's an ol' Ahrish trick. They dangle a feller from a tree, jest high 'nough to lut his naked foot touch a long sharpened wood spike. Hit's anchored through a board. When the rope stretches and the man's body gives 'way, his weight makes the spike jab into his foot. Din, they turn the poor soul 'round and 'round, corkscrewing 'im to the spike. Hit's a long and awful death—hit only comes outta slow bleeding, a blowed up heart, or a shot to the haid."

"We gotta stop 'em. Only men would...critters are kinder than that," Cager blurted, not really knowing what to do.

They stood up, their courage fleeting as they walked closer to the mob of raucous men. When the men saw their advance across the last few feet of field, they raised their muskets almost in unison. One fired a booming shot and shouted, "Who be ye? Answer or be laid out!"

Rocking from the deafening blast and acrid smell of gunpowder, Cager yelled, "Militia from Alamance." He watched their fingers, itchy and wanton fingers that could pull triggers at any moment.

"Well, ye will enjoy this. Ye can see the last blood flow from this piece of garbage. Wanna take a turn?" mouthed the big grinning man holding the Tory.

"We got orders to look fer livestock. Any hyeh, boys?"

"None here and none around," spoke up one of the grisly men, a man who was now curiously eyeing Cager and Vardimen. "Maybe ye wont to eat this Tory. I doubt he would make a good stew. Even the worms and beetles would pass him till last. Dirty, no-good, rotten Tory, he be!" He slapped the poor man again with his musket, causing another half-turn, and another piercing scream.

"Lut's git out of hyeh," Vardimen nudged.

"See ye 'round, boys," Cager looked directly at the big Irishman. "I trust ye'll lut his fam'le pamper 'im a bit now that ye've had sich fun."

"Maybe we will, maybe we won't. Maybe, we'll hang him like a dog, and sun bake 'im like the gutless knave he be." He replied gruffly, hoisting tobacco juice from deep within his throat. His huge jowls tightened just before his breath spurted the brown liquid through his teeth. The powerful stream found its mark—Cager's left boot. The glob splattered onto Cager's pant leg. He looked down at his stained boot, looked at the burley Irishman now staring inquisitively at him, menacingly moving into his space, grinning and daring him to retaliate. That's when Cager pulled the trigger.

The shot tore through the man's chest. Surprised, he looked at Cager, staring blankly, before he pitched to one side, dying almost instantly. The mob scattered as Cager and Vardimen turned and ran. They crossed the field and just as they were in calling distance of their mules, shots rang out; Cager stumbled and fell.

"Git up, Cager! Cager, we gotta run. Can ye run?"

"I'm dun fer, Vardimen. He got me good. Tell me youngin,' Micager, 'bout Bat Cave and The Clher Fork. Tell 'em how to git thar. Promise me, now! Promise me!"

"I promise, Cager."

"One more thang, Vardimen. Make shore me dry gray bones are buried in The Clher Fork. Come back fer 'em, an' take 'em thar, Vardimen. Double promise me, now, Vardimen.

"I double promise. I do right hyeh and now. I'll make shore ye bones are buried proper-like."

"Now, leave me. Leave me hyeh. Nothin' ye can do now."

"I ain't leavin' ye!" Vardimen replied as he cradled Cager's head in his arms, "Git that through ye stubborn Whitaker haid, Cager!"

"Leave me now. They'll kill ye. Nothin' left of me now but a dead carcass anyhow. Go, now!"

Those were Cager's last words. He was hit squarely in the forehead by a shot meant for Vardimen. Stunned, Vardimen jerked away. He ran panicked toward the mules, leaped over the haunches of his big black mule, landed on the saddle, and wildly flailed the flanks of the spooked animal.

Cager's body crumpled; a moan escaped his lips; his body relaxed; his eyes opened widely and his mind responded with a clear vision of the beautiful mountains of The Clear Fork. His last thoughts were that he would never see his green valleys and ridges again; he would never build his cabin and bring his family to the mountaintop. He would never walk the tunnels of Bat Cave again.

His business in The Clear Fork had to be completed. His son would have to finish it; Micager would have to do it. A tear formed at the corner of his eye...and then...and then life left him. Cager was dead...his body rigid, at last free of war and violence, his restless spirit now set loose to wander about the red rolling hills of the Piedmont.

5

Micager

South Carolina—September 1781

Micager Whitaker had turned sixteen only one month before. He had joined the North Carolina militia on that very day at the Trading Ford near the village of Alamance. The call had come and he had answered it, just as his father, Cager, always had answered his.

No family had been more patriotic than the Whitakers; no family had supported the cause of freedom more than the Whitakers; and he was ready to prove that his generation could maintain that tradition. He was proud to be a soldier, just as his father had been. His father had died in the Service, and he figured that if his time to die came on the field of battle that he would die just like his father, a courageous, lonely death.

Someday, he would retrace his father's steps. Vardimen had told him about the field on which Cager had drawn his last breath, and how he had died quickly in his arms. He had gone there, to the place where he thought Cager's body lay, but found nothing. He had gone without Vardimen. Vardimen was lame, injured in battle, unable to go. Long and hard searches had not found Cager's bones, his body or his grave. In fact, no sign of any kind had been found.

He would search again after the war, if he survived. He would find his father and give his remains a Christian burial—a burial that would take place in the land his father called 'The Clher Fork.' Someday he would go there; someday he would keep his promise to his father. It was the same promise that Vardimen had given, but Vardimen was too sick now; the Tory slug that ripped into his leg was still with him, and he was in constant pain, too sick to ride alone over the harsh trails of the Piedmont in search of Cager's grave.

Besides, Vardimen talked of nothing except the valley between the Clinch and the Powell. Vardimen would go there soon. It would be his last exploration, his last adventure. He deserved it; he deserved to die in the place of his dreams.

No, Vardimen couldn't help him. He would not ask. It would be up to him to follow his father's wishes, and he would. After the war he would begin a new search, alone, without Vardimen, and if he couldn't find Cager then his descendants would search for all time until Cager's remains were found.

When he was called to arms just a few days after his birthday, he and young Vardy Collins joined with others as they marched over the countryside and through Salisbury, finally becoming part of a large force of North Carolinians. They marched at record speed to join Green on the high hills of Santee Creek, where his army had camped since his withdrawal from Ninety-Six.

Green was well respected by state militiamen and Continental troops. Washington, himself, had placed him in command of the southern armies, replacing Horatio Gates, who was despised by his men and slighted by Washington.

Green had shown exceptional leadership and ability, and it was well known that he was Washington's favorite. The men liked him and trusted him. He would get them through the battle with the least number of casualties possible. The battle would begin soon, they figured, and they were glad to fight under such a man.

Major General Nathanael Green had lined up the North and South Carolina militias first, forming up his Continentals and cavalry in a line behind them. The militia had advanced with great steadiness, finally closing with the British Army commanded by Lt. Colonel Alexander Stewart.

Gentle breezes softened the morning mist that lay low against the banks of the Congaree River into whirling designs that moved and twisted around the men. Micager hated the cold, clinging fog that seemed to creep every morning along the banks of Carolina's rivers, sneaking into the surrounding fields and valleys. He watched impatiently; his eyes, dilated and extended, hinted of his confusion and anticipation. They probed the alternately thickening and thinning masks of murky vapors.

Suddenly, his eyes fixed on the ghostly mass moving silently through the fog and into range. He could hear the tramping, tramping of hundreds of soldiers marching scores abreast over shiny, dew-laden fescue.

Gusting winds shoved the fog aside, fully exposing the enemy army. Musket, rifle and cannon shots rang out from what seemed to be every imaginable spot: to his left, to his right, behind and forward of him. Thunderous booms deafened him, thick blue smoke obscured his vision, percussion shells shook his body, awful screams of pain and terror from the dying pierced and inundated the field, and sickening smells of body parts attacked his senses. Reeling from fear and the horror of battle, he froze!

He was frozen in time. Ghastly images of the battle floated around him. His hands waited for a command, but there was none to give. His mind, suspended in its stupor, catatonic in his panic, refused to contribute, to be part of his body. He stood there, exposed, while mayhem and chaos filled the battlefield.

Micager! Micager! Fire...fire your rifle! A command from some unknown source burned through his confusion, jolting his brain to act. Suddenly, the command was heard, and he realized that he was to die, that day, that hour, that moment, unless he acted quickly. He squeezed the stock of his long rifle, his tight grasp forcing the blood from his fingers. Finally, he shouldered his rifle. Staring through the dense blue smoke, he took aim at the unearthly legion of soldiers marching toward him. He fired and some poor soul cried out, and somewhere in the fog slumped the body of a man that he knew he had killed.

He could hear the zing of shot whizzing past him, see the flashes of bayonets moving steadily toward him, and feel the heavy air choking him. Two men in his wavering rank fell withering in pain; another moaned grotesquely as a musket ball passed through his neck. Blood was everywhere; the ground was covered with it, from side to side, from front to back. For as far as he could see in all directions, men cried, reaching out for help as they died in bizarre twisted horrible positions.

On one knee, he tried desperately to reload, feverishly pounding the ball into the small rifle bore. He kept dropping the slug. He felt a sense of gloom and hopelessness; a curtain of dread and terror descended over the battlefield, and Micager knew he would die.

Suddenly, the makeshift army began to run. Like scared animals they ran through the thick smoke, away from the glinting bayonets and away from certain death. Mass hysteria settled over the battlefield; the undisciplined and undrilled army had become a mob, moving away from confrontation; parts of a whole, separate and unattached, chaotically moving in the same direction, controlled by no man, yet with a single purpose—to escape the horror of the battle and seek safety in the Santee Hills.

Micager watched in disbelief. It was a surreal ghastly vision; weapons thrown into the pungent air; panicked men stumbling and tripping over the dead and groping wounded, rushing headlong to save themselves.

Micager began to run! And as he ran, he grew more and more frightened. As his courage retreated, his speed increased proportionally, his legs pumped faster with each long stride and with each foot of ground left behind.

Micager neared a small spring that bubbled up from cypress knees. Tall trees draped in thick moss overhung its cool clear waters, and small scrubby oaks called blackjack completely surrounded it, forming an almost impenetrable border. "Nobidy can see me thar," he thought, "Nobidy! That's whar I can hide."

He lunged forward, dropping to his knees, and began his frantic crawl through the barrier of bushes. Mad with fear, neck stiff, head down, he plowed his knees and elbows deep into the sandy soil as he moved his body forward in a frenzied crawl for safety.

Suddenly, he stopped! He felt a shroud of coldness cover his body—a shadow moved over him. He was not alone. He knew now. Someone was there with him. He looked up into the harsh sun, behind the intruder. Its rays spilled over and around the visitor and his mount. A horseman was there, a rider watching his every move, between him and the spring. He could see him now—not plainly, but enough to see him wave his long rifle above his head as his black steed snorted and reared skyward on strong hind legs.

The man turned toward Micager, and just for a second the shadows drew back, and the sun dulled, and their eyes met, and he felt the strength and calm of the rider; and his mind, his being, accepted the stranger's gift. His body relaxed and his courage returned as the rider broke his gaze and rode on, disappearing into the smoke and fog of battle. Micager regained his feet, slowly turned and walked resolutely toward the advancing wide red line of British soldiers.

As he advanced, other retreating militiamen turned, marching with him. All through the woods and fields, militiamen stopped running, picked up rifles and turned to face the British. As more men joined, Micager marched faster; finally he began a slow trot and then a full charge toward the British. They laid down a withering fire, but Micager and the men kept running, closing quickly. Screams of "Attack...Attack..." filled the air as Micager and the men wildly scrambled, stumbled toward the British in a screaming, cursing, knife and bayonet-waving surge of fury that climaxed in a relentless fervor of cruelty and brutality. That's when Green, sensing his advantage, ordered a general charge, throwing the Continentals into the battle.

From the front and flanks, Green's men charged full-force into the British lines. Bayoneting, kicking, clubbing, fist-fighting, stomping, they rammed the wavering line of Redcoats.

The British gave ground, and Micager and the militia overpowered them. Viciously, they dispensed with the few troops who had the courage to stand and fight. They continued their charge even as the British retreated in all-out flight. They stopped only when they had reached and overrun the British camp. Had the militiamen not begun to loot the camp and drink what spirits they found, it would have been a great victory for Green.

With Stewart's army in shambles, Green broke off the engagement and retired to the Santee Hills. The bloody action resulted in six hundred casualties. It was the last significant battle in the Carolinas—the British were finally driven out.

Micager marched quietly in the militia's shabby ranks. He hoped that his action that day had made his father proud, no matter where his spirit might be. His father would know, somehow he would know.

But, who was the rider? The rider had saved him. Who was the rider? Was he on a black horse or a black mule? He remembered only the man's eyes, nothing else, just big dark staring eyes; eyes full of strength, calm and resolve. They seemed familiar but he couldn't be sure.

"What's your name, son?" A loud voice heavy in New England brogue hammered against his wall of thought.

"Huh?" Micager replied in a matter of fact manner, still in deep thought.

"I said, 'What's your name?'"

Micager finally tore himself away from his thoughts, and looked toward the speaker. It was an officer mounted on a striking white horse. Its mane flowed and rippled in the warm breeze. "Me name is Micager, son of Cager Whitaker, sir."

"Micager Whitaker, we know of your father, Cager. He was a good man, a good soldier. His passing was a great loss to our cause. But you, young man, also deserve the appreciation of our infant country. I saw what you did today, how you turned the militia forces. Because of you, we won the day."

"But sir, whar ye the man on horseback at the small spring?"

"Man on horseback? Oh, no, there were no cavalry troops anywhere near you or that spring." The officer paused, looking curiously at the young private, then added, "Private Whitaker, I wish to personally commend you to General Washington. Good luck our young hero." The rider spurred the horse, riding quickly away.

"Micager, don't ye know who that wuz?" Vardy yelled from two ranks back.

"No, but—"

"—That wuz General Nathanael Green, hizzelf!"

"But who wuz the rider?" Micager mumbled again.

6

The Decision

On the Alamance and in the Virginia Hill Country—1793

Vardimen Collins hadn't slept a wink that night. He had tossed and turned as the thoughts of western North Carolina raced through his mind. Finally, giving up trying to sleep, he dressed silently, stoked the fire, and slipped toward the door, looking back at his small sleeping family. "I have to go. I jest have to go, an' soon," he thought.

He crossed the threshold, and gently swung the heavy wood door shut. His body tensed from the sharp sting of wintry air. Slapped awake, his mind cleared, and he stretched his upper body, relieving strained muscles as he pulled in his first dose of chilled morning. Yanking his collar tight against his neck, he limped and pained down the hill, footsteps squishing as he drew closer to the Alamance.

The river was clear, almost glass-like after the storm. "Unusual," he thought, picking up a small flat stone and skipping it across the gleaming flatness of the river.

Before the rhythmic ripples could find their way to the bank, he studied the face of the man clearly contrasted in the water's stillness. "The yers've took ther toll," he thought, not believing that he had journeyed so quickly through his youth. "Not much life's left to live now. Hit's time to go to me valley."

The ripples, one behind the other, smoothly rolled from the middle of the Alamance, undulating through the shimmering portrait that his eyes still strained to see. Between the ripples, he stared into the deepness of the water, now seeing a smiling young man returning his gaze. He looked closer. "Yep, hit's him!" It was Cager, "A trick of the worter," he thought. He smiled to himself, wishing that his friend could really be there beside him. His mind groped for memories of his old friend, and it found them quickly—the pleasures of their rides into the mountains, the fighting, the laughing and crying, the sorrow they had endured, the companionship, the solidarity, and, yes, the mysteries of discovery.

Suddenly, he remembered The Clear Fork and Bat Cave. "Yep, Cager, I know I can't look fer ye an' take ye thar now. I grow feeble and ol', me friend, too ol' to keep me promise to ye. But, ye boy will. Micager is a good lad and he'll find ye. I told 'im and me Vardy all 'bout The Chler Fork, and yer youngin's already took up a homestead thar. Vardy'll go thar right shortly 'fore he goes to the Clinch fer good. And someday 'em youngins 'll know air secret.

"Cager, I gotta haid fer the Clinch dierectly. I wanna die on that ridge 'bove the Clinch. Say ye werd t'me, Cager. Say ye werd."

Vardimen's eyes strained. They searched the stillness of the river, probing beyond its flat surface, farther into its depths, searching its elusiveness, until finally they recognized the vague specter—a pale face of death. Cager's apparition rose through the water, hovering just below the surface. His voice muted from another world, the ghost of Cager seemed to mouth, "Hit's okay, Vardimen. See ye soon when ye cross over. Go ye now to the Clinch, me ol' friend." Slowly the formless face receded into the deepness of the water.

Vardimen stared longer into the river. He tried to tear himself away from its hypnotizing translucence, but his eyes somehow remained, still grasping for one last picture of his old friend.

"Thank ye, Cager, me friend, thanks. Ye know how much hit means to this ol' bidy."

Vardimen turned from the river, and began his slow walk back up the hill, retracing his steps. He stopped on the path from time to time, turning to look down at the Alamance. It was a fine river, a fine river, indeed. But it was not the Clinch; no river he had ever seen compared to it.

Just before it met the Powell, its waters grew large and deep, and the valley beautiful. From the moment he first saw it, the deep greens of the surrounding hills and rolling valley meadows had struck his heart, giving him feelings of pleasure and hope. Feelings that he one day would know again. Soon, he would own good farmland, great stands of timber, and he would stand on the ridge and count the myriad colors of leaves in the fall of the year. He would know each of his trees, their different hues and the shapes and patterns of his oaks, walnuts, maples and beeches. He would know each silhouette of every one of his trees, even if they numbered in the thousands—he would know them all; he would love them all. And the valley would return his love, protecting him and his family, and providing for their health and happiness. Soon, the valley of the Clinch would be *his* valley. He would go there in spring.

It was supposed to be a farewell get-together before Vardimen and Vardy left for the Clinch. It had only been a slight inconvenience for them to stop at Mouth of Wilson. It lay near the state line just into Grayson County, Virginia.

They had wanted to say farewell to all their friends and relatives, so family could see them off. Nearly all their former neighbors had come to wish them luck. Many had ridden for hours from Ashe and Wilkes counties to be with them. They had brought food and drink for the social, and the Virginia Collinses had made sure they were welcomed with the best they had to offer.

They drank and ate at the long tables until their bellies stretched, and the men smoked their corncob pipes and side chewed and passed among them bottles of medicinal alcohol, while the women dipped snuff and sang gospel songs until they were exhausted. "Old Ship of Zion" and John Newton's "Amazing Grace" and "How Sweet the Name of Jesus Sounds" were the three sang most often. While the men smoked and listened intently at the long tables, the women sang "Amazing Grace" to end the singing. It was a touching finish to the religious aspects of the gathering. The sweet sounds floated throughout the narrow, sun-drenched valley, bringing warm, spiritual peace to each of them.

Amazing Grace! (how sweet the sound)
That sav'd a wretch like me!
I once was lost, but now am found,
Was blind, but now I see.

'Twas grace that taught my heart to fear
And grace my fears reliev'd;
How precious did that grace appear,
The hour I first believ'd!

Thro' many dangers, toils and snares,
I have already come;
'Tis grace has brought me safe thus far,
And grace will lead me home.
The Lord has promis'd good to me,
His word my hope secures;
He will my shield and portion be,
As long as life endures

Yes, when this flesh and heart shall fail,
And mortal life shall cease;
I shall possess, within the veil,
A life of joy and peace.

The earth shall soon dissolve like snow,
The sun forbear to shine;
But God, who call'd me here below,
Will be forever mine.

After the hymns, a fiddler scratched out several mountain songs, ending with a tune that sounded remotely like "Sourwood Mountain."

Mostly, though, it had been a quietly festive gathering. That is, until the children started doing what children usually do when they become bored.

They were everywhere, running in and out of the log house, teasing chickens, swatting the rumps of hogs, chasing dogs, yelling and screaming at one another, and just plain misbehaving, like scores of little whirligigs spinning further and further out of control.

There were four or five playing under the long table at which several men huddled. On one side sat Hare-lipped Jim, Black Lige and Skinny John Mullens. Erby Gibson, White Lige, Vardimen and Vardy sat on the opposite side. The kids were rubbing the ground and loudly repeating over and over:

Doodlebug, doodlebug!
God bless ye soul
Doodlebug, doodlebug
Come out of ye hole
Doodlebug, doodlebug,
Ye house is ohn fahr
Ye chillun are burnin' up
Come out, wharever ye are!

Other children were a few feet away, near the spring, turning rocks and singing:

Craw-ded! Craw-ded! Ye'd better go deep
Or I'll eat ye 'fore I sleep.

Peggy could see the frustration building in the eyes of the men, men who appeared to be hostages to swirling and reeling heads. She was always the first to notice when they were becoming aggravated with the children. She smiled quietly, turned quickly and walked into a sloping field. Waist high grass only recently spotted and colored with the first flowers of spring partially obscured her body.

She was a pretty woman. Vibrant, full of energy, and rambunctious just like the kids, not at all hampered by her adult years. When she was in a playful mood, she infected everyone near her with gentle yet passionate energy. She had a mischievous streak in her, too, and the children sensed it and loved her for it. She commanded their full attention whenever she spoke to them, or as in this case, beckoned them to come. They knew that whatever she had to say or do would be fun. They all ran to her like a litter of piglets chasing their mother at feeding time.

"It's time to play *Go Sheepy Go*!" She yelled at the gang tripping and stumbling through the grass, disappearing then appearing as they scrambled to pick themselves up and began the run anew. "You too, come on now, Sally Joe and Sally Jim. Stop your lollygagging!" She called to the two little Sallys who were still playing *Doodlebug* under one of the long tables. It was common practice for popular first names of children to be followed by their fathers' first names so they could be identified more easily—wives with identical names sometimes followed the same tradition, taking on their husbands' first names.

"Here's the base!" Peggy announced loudly, pointing to the flat rock at her foot.

"Yeah! Yeah!" Screamed the youngins, all the while jumping up and down enthusiastically. "Ye're hit...No, ye're hit...No, no, not ME!"

"Okay, let's find out who's *it!*" Peggy ordered to a bevy of cheers. "I've got thirteen straws in my hand. The one who draws the shortest is *it!* Everybody line up right here...Polly, you draw first!" Polly drew, then each child down the line...each exhaling loudly after drawing a long straw.

"Oh, nooo!" Cried little Enoch Collins to the screams and laughter of the other children. "Why's hit always me?"

Enoch stood on the base and turned his back and yelled at the top of his lungs, "Go Sheepy Go!" The children, with Peggy leading the way, wildly scattered throughout the tall grass, giggling, tripping and falling on their way to their hiding places.

"One...two...ten...twenty-five...fifty...SIXTY! Ready or not...Bushereee...Busheriii. Who all's out, holler Aye!"

"AYE!" Came the reply from the hiding children, now seeming to be everywhere in the field. Little Enoch, figuring that most of the 'Ayes' came from his right, ran as fast as he could through the tall fescue, trying to tag at least one before they all could sneak past him and touch the base. If he could tag just one then the whole process would start over and he would do the hiding.

Vardimen shook his head, smiled, and said admiringly, "That Peggy shore knows how to handle 'em chillun. Shame, she don't have a dozen or two. In fact, that woman ought to be a school marm. Ain't never seed nobidy like her b'fore."

The men all agreed, "She be an amazin' woman, all right," and Vardimen was once again proud that Peggy was his daughter-in-law.

"Yes, sirree, she's a fine woman fer me boy, Vardy." He sighed proudly, and then they got back to their quiet now uninterrupted chatter, subjects that only men talk about.

Night fell rapidly in the mountains of Virginia, and the children and grown-ups all gathered around a leaping bond fire. The burning hickory and oak logs gave off a sweet pleasant aroma, smells that calmed the nerves of adults and stimulated their children's imaginations. That sat quietly and expectantly under a dark blue airy blanket of fresh mountain sky brightened by millions of sparkling stars. Vardimen was to tell the story—he was the best.

Without a sound, he slowly moved to the center of the inner ring of big-eyed children sitting cross-legged around the fire. The young ones peered nervously at one another through the crackling yellow-red flames that alternately leaped and retreated against wispy images of young faces shimmering behind bright excited eyes.

From time to time, a fast wind skipped and darted through the valley, whipping the smoke into thick, twisting clouds. The haze obscured each child's vision of the other across the fire-circle, making their frightened eyes dance, searching for familiar faces. They squirmed anxiously; their minds racing with thoughts of monsters and ogres of Old World wonder tales. "They's ready fer me story," Vardimen chuckled to himself.

Vardimen's eyes grew larger and brighter with every step he took toward the fire. Palms down, his eyes fixed on the flames, he slowly raised his lean muscular arms, willing them to float atop the invisible layer of heat being thrown up by the swirling blaze.

Peggy was enjoying herself immensely, watching little Enoch and the other children. She smiled at their incessant fidgeting and nervous anticipation. "All this," she thought, "with not a word, and not one looking away from Vardimen." Vardimen's big bright eyes and gaunt wrinkled face drew them...drew them all to him, locking their bright young eyes to his, just as she, also, had so many times been transfixed by them.

Vardimen abruptly spread his arms and looked at the children with a long, grave stare. He turned slowly, looking around the ring, section by section engaging their eyes. "Now, I will tell ye a story! I know not whether hit is myth or occurrence. Ye must make that jedgment, but 'member that skeptics and non-believers from the heart have suffered much misfortune."

He told his story slowly and with much feeling to the motionless children, their eyes glued to his every gesture, hanging on each word. He told of a group of boys—mischievous boys who were unkind to chickens, and to slippery things that live in the small waters of mountain springs. They particularly liked to do away with water dogs and salamanders, and torture them by holding them up to chickens before dropping them inside the chicken yard. They sat on the shake roof of the chicken house, teasing the chickens, ruining the peacefulness and happiness of their chicken lives.

Once, one of the boys held a water dog high above his head so all the chickens could see it. It squirmed and twisted and finally slipped from his hand. It fell on the low bird in the pecking order, and the low bird was hurt badly by the frenzied onslaught of the other chickens; chickens that had every right to chase after the water dog, to remove the intruder from their home in any way they could. The low bird died, and every chicken knew the boy had caused its death.

The boys laughed when the low bird screamed in pain and took its last breaths. They enjoyed this as great fun, so much so that every time they saw a water dog they would do the same thing. They were always kneeling along the springs, searching for small, innocent water dogs to throw into the chicken yard, causing great consternation, anxiety and fear within the hearts of all chickens.

The chickens of the chicken house were extremely alarmed by the wickedness of the boys, and they held a chicken council of war. Their great chief, the big white Leghorn rooster, spoke loudly and clearly. He said the entire chicken nation had been challenged, and they must respond in kind with the full weight and force of the great Rhode Island Red, a rooster of enormous ability to make war. First, though, he would make every effort to scare the boys enough to change their ways. The warrior rooster would wait for his chance to trick them into entering the chicken yard, and then their chicken revenge would be taken. There was much clucking, "booking" and crowing, signaling the chicken nation's agreement with the great chief.

It just so happened that one of the boys had been hunting water dogs nearby, and had seen the chicken gathering. He dashed back to the other boys and told them everything he had seen. Disbelieving, a tall skinny boy called Trench, who had short blond hair and long legs that looked like large trenchers on two stilts, along with another boy called Dev, went to confirm what had been reported. They rushed back, terrified at the great congregation of chickens...a gathering the likes of which had never been seen before or since in the shadowy hollows and high ridges of the great Appalachians.

The boys decided they would catch the warrior rooster and do away with him. There was even a suggestion by a chunky boy with prickly hair that stuck out evenly from his head. He had an overly wide mouth on his big porcupine-looking head, so he was called Jar Head. He had intentions of becoming a famous chef, and he cruelly insisted that chicken soup should be made with the carcass of the hated rooster. Everybody agreed that Jar Head had a great idea.

They thought about many ways to bring that big rooster's life to an early end, but none seemed to be a good plan. Frustrated with their own thoughts, they consulted an old farmer's widow from Montgomery County, Virginia.

After hearing their story, she was horrified by their treatment of water dogs and chickens. Knowing all about chicken-war tactics, but loving their peaceful ways and appreciating what God offered through them to humans, she sought to teach the boys a lesson. She told them that roosters have a special rooster gene that lets them guard their flocks continuously, a gene that allows them to sleep only in short intervals, sporadically over a twenty-four-hour period, and the only way to catch one was to find him sleeping and throw a burlap sack over his head. She said the rooster would have to be watched constantly, day and night, if they were to capture him.

Armed with this new information, the boys decided they would strike first. One night they sneaked into the hog pen that was adjacent to the chicken yard and cut a hole in the fence that protected the chicken house from outsiders. They hid the cut so they could use the opening later, when their trap would be sprung.

After weeks of lying in the mud behind the rumps of two big sows, late one night, they thought they saw the big Rhode Island Red fall asleep. One of the boys on lookout ran to report to the others. He said that if they would come quickly they could capture him. They hurried to the chicken house, and they saw that he was asleep!

They charged, and the big warrior rooster let one of the determined boys throw a bag partially over his head. Faking surprise, he clawed and pecked and lurched past the boys, stopping in the middle of the chicken yard. He slowly turned, his face glowing with faked anger, contempt and vengeance. He looked mean; and there was a supernatural air about him that sent cold chills down the boys' spines.

They were scared, really scared, but they knew they had to do something. So they decided to surround the rooster. And when they finally found the courage to encircle him, he began to spin. He twirled around on his two legs until he became just a blur. The faster he went around, the taller and thinner he became, and the bigger his eyes; his body got thinner and thinner and taller and taller until he towered over them—just one skinny spindle of fluff holding up two huge, bulging, pulsating red eyes, eyes that were as big and bright as a full moon, but real mean-looking. He was a whirlwind of thin vague shapes and huge brilliant eyeballs.

He spun like a top, so fast that his eyes stayed in one place; and no matter what place in the circle a boy stood, the warrior rooster's big staring red eyes looked down at him through a smear of feathers. The boys yelled at one another about his eyes; each boy in the circle around that spinning chicken swore the rooster's eyes were looking at him; each swore at exactly the same time that his strange eyes danced with theirs—in lockstep, never leaving them.

The big Rhode Island Red warrior rooster had managed to stare at each of them all at the same time. Each begged for mercy, each crying piteously and pleading for forgiveness. "Please, please, don't harm us. Please don't lock us in ye chicken spell and peck us to death all at de same time wit ye gigantic beak, or stab us all wit ye razor-like spurs. We'll leave ye and ye chickens and the worter dogs alone, we promise!" But their crying was to no avail. The rooster had other plans.

The great chicken warrior with a wingspan wider than the widest river and a body taller than the highest mountain scornfully looked down upon the pathetic, pleading boys. His big, bright, bulging eyes surrounded the boys and hypnotized each of them at the very same time.

Without sound or movement, his thoughts filled their heads, "Ye will never tease thangs wit feathers and wings agin. Ye will always 'member this night in ye dreams, and ye and one of ye youngins and one of his youngins and all the way down the line will dream 'bout this night ever night of ye lives. Ye will always suffer great fear of chickens, but ye will always brang us the best of worter dogs. So be hit. I have spoken!"

The boys awoke from their trance, seeing nothing of the strange scene they had all witnessed. The big Rhode Island Red rooster stood on his perch, both eyes covered with a huge red comb; it drooped over his face and looked like a big red hand, a hand he used to block moonbeams. The chicken house was quiet with sleeping chickens.

It was frightening for the boys. Their minds couldn't believe what had happened. Just for a moment, they froze in place, but once one of the boys started running, it fed itself, the mob growing bigger and faster as shrieks of terror sliced the air around the chicken house. In sheer panic, the boys scrambled wildly away, stumbling and screaming back to their homes.

The old woman from Montgomery County, Virginia lay in her bed listening to their screams, and she smiled to herself, knowing that as long as they lived the boys would never again hurt chickens and things with feathers. She had done a good thing.

Still trembling from Vardimen's scary story, the younger children unhuddled and followed their parents back to the tents and wagons, holding their hands tightly. As night fell deeper into the valley, their imaginations filled the dark tents and covered wagons with delusive appearances—figments of chicken ghosts with huge dancing eyes.

Vardimen, preparing a last smoke, sat at the long table with the other men. He smiled as he listened to the thin voices coming from the wagons and tents, "Momma, stay right hyeh wit me 'til me fall 'sleep, please," and he knew he had told a good story.

7

The Cabin

Between the Clinch and the Powell—1794

Vardimen decided to build his temporary cabin on a high ridge that overlooked a long narrow valley. The valley stretched northeast from extreme upper East Tennessee and overflowed into newly formed Lee County, Virginia.

He and his eldest son, Vardy, had arrived at this place in late spring after the floods had passed. They would raise the cabin on the long, skinny ridge that looked east over the Clinch River onto the slope of Clinch Mountain. Powell Mountain lay to the west, and past it meandered Powell River.

He had picked this particular ridge because it shadowed the valley. He could see all comers and goers, enemies and friends, Indians and white men; he could see them all from its high reach.

Later, he and Vardy would build a fine cabin for his family. But, by first building a temporary shelter, he could take his time in finding just the right spot for his family to live. He could look for a vibrant spring for drinking, and a stream that he could divert toward his house so a dam could be built and a small pond created for his livestock. He'd dig a well later. Spring water would do for a time. In a couple of years, he and his family would have the best homestead in the valley. But right now, it was important to make a shelter for Vardy and himself, so they could survive the winter weather that surely would tear through the small valley in a few months. The shelter would provide space for storing edible roots, herbs, potatoes, wild apples, nuts, and bark for tea; and its fireplace would offer accommodations for curing wild meat and drying fruits and vegetables.

Once their temporary cabin was erected, they would scout for the perfect location for the new house, cellar, corn cratch and barn. Vardimen would make sure that it would be a fine home for his family. It would be a cabin that Vardy would inherit; one that would remain in the family for generations. Even the temporary cabin would be useful. It would become a place to store grain and earthenware, and myriad other necessities.

They started marking trees on the morning of the second day of their arrival. By the end of the fourth day, they had felled close to eighty trees, and using only an ax and an adz they had built the sixteen- by twelve-foot cabin in only eight days.

Its walls, raised over a dirt floor, were chinked with clay. They collected creek rocks for the fireplace, and used clay to secure it at the northwest end of the cabin. The chimney was a mixture of creek clay and sticks. One by one, with mallet and froe, they rived the roof shingles from chestnut. Later, they chinked against bad weather by stuffing a mixture of moss and mud into the cracks.

An unventilated sleeping loft was built, accessed by a notched log stair. Finally, they made the single door, and shutters that swung on wooden pegs for the one small window. Such a small cabin needed the window only for ventilation. In fact, such adornments, although attractive by some standards, could be extremely dangerous in the backcountry. Animals, thieves and ruffians found easy prey behind them.

It was a great relief to have finished. All was finished except for the lean-to they would attach to the side of the cabin. It would be for curing and storing meat. It could be built easily once they returned from their hunting trip.

They sat on a cut of log, smoking and staring reverently at their new cabin, appreciating their work. They had little time to enjoy it, though. As with most backcountry settlers, they had to prepare for the coming winter. Fodder for their mules, cords of wood, kindling, hides for clothing, food, grain and fruit for brewing alcohol-based elixirs and drinks for medicinal and social purposes all had to be found, gathered, prepared and stored.

The next morning they left their new cabin unlocked and unguarded and headed northwest toward the mountains, mounted on mules and followed by a packhorse. They crossed over the hump of the small narrow ridge that sheltered their new cabin and headed for Powell Mountain. After descending it they forded the Powell River and headed for the Cumberland Mountains. There would be plenty of game there, and it wasn't more than a three-day trip at hunting pace. They went to the Cumberland range because they preferred not to hunt in the vicinity of their cabin—at least not during fair weather. Scaring off local game before winter came could affect their very survival if the weather were unusually harsh, or if something or someone raided their meat house. Untouched local game was their ace-in-the-hole. Only the Indians and the best and most rugged hunters understood the necessity of leaving local game alone. Many settlers delighted in their easy harvests until a severe winter set in. Then they were forced to trudge miles over unfamiliar terrain just to find enough game to keep themselves and their families from starving.

Early fall was a good time to hunt the vast hills and long narrow valleys of the Cumberland range. They would not want for water or food. Neither would they suffer from the heat or the cold of the past summer or the coming winter. It was just cold enough to preserve the game until they could properly dress it. Yes, it was a perfect time for a hunt.

They crossed over several high narrow ridges and splashed through the Cumberland River, and finally trailed into a hollow that backed into the main run of a huge pine covered mountain. It looked to be a particularly good place to hunt since there was sufficient cover and food for big game. In addition, the high mountains to the west afforded protection from the chilling north and west winds that soon would be tearing through the countryside.

They trailed up the mountain following an active deer path until reaching a small natural bench. Vardimen topped onto the bench, and suddenly whispered his mule to a halt. Vardy stopped immediately, guessing that game must be ahead in the bushes.

"I thank I can git hit," Vardimen coolly whispered. He shouldered his long rifle and squeezed the trigger; a sharp crack shattered the stillness.

Hearing the rustle of leaves, Vardy spurred his mule forward just in time to see a huge mule deer crumple to the ground. Its carcass lay not more than sixty feet away, shot cleanly through the heart.

They approached it cautiously; making sure it could be of no danger. Satisfied, they field-dressed the animal and covered its body with leaves and brush, so as to protect it from predators. They would make camp close by and return the next morning to do the butchering and begin the curing process.

They selected a small flat about halfway up the ridge where there was good protection from the elements, animals and humans. They hitched their mules to a line of trees, made a small fire and boiled some dried vegetables and meat. The meal went well with a swig or two of applejack. They talked awhile, banked the fire, and retired to the distant howls of the ever-present mountain wolves.

Vardy awoke to the warmth of sunlight streaming through the branches of a huge pine that canopied high above the small flat. He had slept well on the thick mat of dry pine needles that blanketed the forest. The fresh crisp air was exhilarating. He stretched, relaxing his muscles; his blood slowly warmed his chilled hands and feet. He rose on one knee, inspecting the spent fire from a distance. Something wasn't right. Snapping his head quickly to the right, he realized that Vardimen was nowhere around.

"He must've gone fer the deer," he thought as he walked toward his still-tethered mule. He saddled it, adjusted the rope bridle and smoothly swung onto the mule's back, reined him to a slight turn and gently kicked his flanks, setting off in the direction of the small creek they had past the day before.

He negotiated the trail with ease, swinging the reins from side to side as he followed its winding path down the hill toward the spot where the deer lay.

Suddenly, the mule reared and bolted to one side, away from the path and down a steep incline toward the creek. Vardy pulled hard on the reins but the mule moved faster and faster, jumping downed trees and stumbling over outcroppings of rocks. It brushed low-hanging branches that whipped and slapped against Vardy's face and body. Amid constant shouts of "whoa, boy, whoa big boy," he tugged the reins with all his might. Panting hard, frothing at the mouth, his body thick with lather, the powerful mule, now completely out of control, rampaged down the mountain.

Vardy knew if he didn't jump he would be either dead or badly maimed. Just as he positioned himself for the jump, the mule tripped, swiped a tree a few feet from the creek, and rolled heavily onto one side. The momentum of the mule's fall threw Vardy clear far to the mule's flank. He crashed against the flat rock scattered along the creek's red clay bottom.

Stunned, waves of nausea coursing through him, he crawled slowly from the cool mountain water. He clawed a few feet up the bank, and began to inspect his body. He knew he was hurt, but how bad? After moving each limb, he determined that his bruises and cuts were not serious. His lip was bleeding and there was a large gash on his left knee, but nothing more, although the back of his head pounded from some sort of injury. He noticed that his vision blurred when he turned his head; maybe he had fallen backwards, headfirst against one of the rocks. The mule had righted itself and was now splashing down the creek at full gallop.

"Whut made the mule to—," He heard something above him. "Whut is hit?" He mumbled to himself, all the while looking up the narrow path, his eyes following the trail farther up the hill.

He peered into the thick overgrown vegetation. *Something moved!* He focused his eyes, making a triangle around the spot of the movement, *and then he saw it!* Moving down the trail and straight toward him, he saw the tawny brown coat of a huge mountain lion. Behind her followed a yearling cub.

Vardy lay quietly, hoping the cats would stop; he knew that almost always they would not attack. Generally, they were scared of humans and would retreat at the first sight or smell of a human being. But the big cats kept moving toward him.

"Oh, no, they's still a-comin'!" He looked around for a tree to climb, but there were none small enough, and no low hanging branches upon which to hoist himself, to make his body appear bigger. There was nothing, nothing to help. The mountain lions kept coming.

"Me rifle! Whar's me rifle?" He realized that it had been thrown far down the creek, out of sight. "Knife, git the knife," his brain screamed, "the knife." He pulled it from its sheath, his hand firmly clenched around its handle.

He scooted his body closer to a large beech that towered from the creek bank, thinking that at least his back would be protected.

The enormous mountain lion splashed into the creek, and immediately turned toward Vardy. He crouched, feet pushing the ground, pinioning his back against the tree as the powerful cat moved into his space. Their eyes locked in a spellbinding dance of fear and hate.

The cat swung a giant powerful paw, ripping and slashing the flesh of Vardy's shoulder. He cried out in pain, swinging his knife wildly. The cat, undaunted, charged closer grabbing Vardy's arm, thrashing it back and forth, from side to side. It clawed at his chest and sides, and bit violently along his forearm.

He could smell its stench and feel its hot breath as the big cat crouched and snarled, ears laid back, black-tipped tail twitching, readying itself to lunge for Vardy's neck. He positioned the knife for one final thrust.

It was his last chance for survival. If it didn't work he would have to play dead, putting his life fully at the whim of the cougar.

He readied himself. A second later he saw the tawny and buff blur, and felt the lion's weight. Drawing every ounce of strength from his body, he swung the hunting knife and buried its nine-inch blade into the cougar's chest.

Reeling, screaming in pain, the cat dropped to the ground, pulling its body from the knife still locked in Vardy's grasp. Moaning and squealing, it scampered up the hill toward its cub.

Vardy crawled under a heavy stand of bushes farther down the bank. Not trusting his thoughts, he steeled himself for the cat's return and its final and deadly attack. It would return and there was nothing he could do. The cat would take him without a fight. It would play with him, and with its powerful jaws drag him into the dark forest, and hide him yet alive under a grave of leaves and brush, coming for him from time to time, and uncovering him; playing with him, it would drag his body from grave to grave until he died a slow painful death. Once the end came, Vardimen would find his mangled body hanging in a tree, or in the back of a cave—if he found him at all.

Vardy's life ebbed from him, each beat of his heart foretold the end; each beat brought him closer to death. He could see about him no more; only a small tunnel of dim light remained. Near death, Vardy fainted.

Vardimen returned to the campsite just in time to see a huge bleeding brownish-yellow mountain lion and her cub run wildly up the path. Instantly, he reined the mule in the opposite direction of the big cat's flight, spurring his mule quickly down the path toward the creek. He broke through the heavy brush, immediately spotted Vardy, jumped from his saddle, and carefully inspected his son's wounds.

Vardimen retrieved his pack from the mule, pulled out a strip of cloth and quickly wrapped Vardy's arms above the wounds, cutting off the blood supply to his mauled arms. He washed, packed and bandaged the terrible gashes and slashes. Afterwards, he didn't move Vardy; throwing his trail blankets over him, he made sure he would be as comfortable and as warm as possible.

His son's wounds were now under control, not life threatening—at least the ones he could observe. His great fear was the ones he could not examine. Many times, internal injuries were the worst. If Vardy had been hurt badly inside, there would be little hope for his survival. Vardimen built a fire, heated some water, and waited for Vardy to regain consciousness.

Sipping a cup of lukewarm sassafras tea, he squatted quietly on the bank staring into the creek's glass-like waters. Rocks of all sizes and shapes covered its sandstone bottom. It was there, not ten feet away, that he saw a small glittering lump of gray ore. He waded into the creek and searched the rocky bottom through the water's quivering translucence. "Whar's hit at? I knowed hit was close." He thought, becoming more and more frustrated with each passing minute.

Finally, it showed itself again. It had settled behind a dark flat rock, under a foot of water. Vardimen squatted to pick it up, but as he did he slightly slipped, almost losing his balance. As he caught himself with a stiff right arm, his eyes involuntarily jerked away from the creek bottom and came to rest on an unusually dark spot in the steep bank of the far mountain.

"Whut's thar? Whut do yer ol' eyes spot, Mr, Vardimen Collins?" He said to himself as he slogged toward the bank. Nearing the edge of the water he stopped. He saw it for sure. It was exactly what he thought—a rockhouse. It stood not fifty feet up the side of the mountain.

He scrambled from the creek and hastily ascended the steep bank. Out of breath, he entered the rockhouse, taking in everything about it—its rock columns, its single flat rock roof and its smooth sandstone floor. At the back of the rockhouse was the entrance to a cave; its mouth was about the size of a hogshead and it dropped almost straight down for about ten feet and then made off flat. Where it leveled off, he could make out an old pick, a canteen and what looked to be several small moulds spilling out from sheepskin aprons.

Vardimen tied his cowskin whip to one of the rock columns and shimmied down into the narrow opening. Once his feet touched the cave's crusty soil, he twisted forward into the shadowy space of what he imagined to be a gigantic cathedral-like room. Vardimen's body stiffened, his nerve shrinking from the foreboding darkness before him. Shaking away his dread, his attention returned to the artifacts he had seen.

He nudged the aprons with the toe of his boot, not wanting to reach with his hand for fear of a rattler or copperhead. There seemed to be nothing more than what he had first seen. "Reel strange hit is. Who left 'em?" He glanced again into the dark void, "That's 'nough fer me," he thought, "ain't no use in me a-goin' on in thar right now, ain't no use at all."

Hand over hand, testing the strength of his whip, Vardimen hauled himself up the steep passageway, and as he strained to weasel clear of the opening his eyes made contact with a small round object wedged between a large flat rock and the floor of the rockhouse. Once on the level sandstone, he pried it loose. Turning it over and over in his hand and rubbing it between his thumb and forefinger, he chuckled, "Hit is...hit is.... hit's one of 'em silver coins like me great-grandpappy had over on the Alamance. Hit's a French crown fer shore." He inspected it more, grinned and shoved it into the pocket of his hunting shirt.

Vardimen noted his general location—about thirty miles as the crow flies, west northwest of New Man's Ridge, and a few miles north of the great gap in the Cumberlands and just below the saddle gap of an eastward running ridge. "We goina come back....we goina come back with Hare-lipped Jim and the rest of 'em Mullens boys. They'll know 'bout seein' to this stuff fer shore. Yes, sirree, we'll come back to the ford of the Cumberland, to this crick," he thought, "as soon as Vardy heals."

It was the morning of the third day when Vardy awoke. He thought about opening his eyes but feared he would see leaves and brush over him, and he would know the mountain lion had taken him, and would return to torment him and eventually kill him. He strained to hear, but heard nothing except a distant bubbling sound. "Was he dead?" Heart pounding, dreading the worst, he opened his eyes knowing that he would see heavenly angels flying about. Instead, his gaze caught the very earthly eyes of his father.

"Pappy, ye be the best angel me ever saw." Vardy muttered weakly.

"I'll betcha I do look a dang near sight better'n that big ol' yeller cat! I thank we'd better git back to air cabin soins I can look after ye a little better."

Vardimen found Vardy's mule grazing shamelessly in a small meadow a short distance from the sight of the attack. It stood happily in knee-deep bluegrass, chewing slowly and calmly as if nothing had happened.

Two days later they were back at the small cabin. Vardy healed quickly; his youth and vigor easily fought off pain and infection to which older men would have succumbed. In three weeks his strength had fully returned, and the hunting began again. It was then, on their next hunt that Vardimen told of what he had found at the little stream near the ford of the Cumberland—the stream that he had named *Straight Crick*.

8

Vardy's Valley

Upper East Tennessee—1796

Every day brought more and more progress; the rock foundation was in place, and the timbering continued uninterrupted. They had begun the cutting immediately after Vardimen chose the building site. It was a perfect location for their house, their "mansion," as they called it. It would be built near the site of a Sulphur spring, a location that afforded them a view of the valley, yet a spot naturally protected by the mountains, and one with easy access. Vardimen had chosen well, and the timbering had commenced with excitement and anticipation.

Vardimen had moved the cutting site to a stand of tall virgin pines that grew on a bank that overlooked a small creek called Blackwater. Its waters bubbled noisily over a small falls.

Because of the steeply sloping bank and dense undergrowth, it was difficult to judge how tall the trees towered, making it almost impossible to select the next to be cut.

Although they had worked together for most of the timbering, Vardimen decided that he and Vardy would do better in the selection process if they split up. Also, since they were now cutting pines for the ceiling, wood that was soft by oak standards, it was logical that if they worked separately more could be harvested. After all, just their movement between trees required time, and because of dense undergrowth only one man could chop at a time. So, it made perfectly good sense to split up, especially since Vardimen's bad leg always slowed down the both of them.

They labored up the hill, each carrying a straight handled ax over his shoulder. Halfway up the hill, Vardimen picked a medium-size pine to down, while Vardy continued his climb until he spotted a huge pine, its trunk anchored just under the ridgeline.

"My goodness sakes," he muttered aloud to himself, "we can git enough boards outta this'un to finish!" After inspecting the girth of the trunk, he sighted his father's position with the handle of his ax, and began the initial notching. He made the notch cut on the opposite side from where the main cut would be. This would ensure the angle of fall would be away from and far to the right of Vardimen's location.

High on the ridge the breeze was gentle, gusting at times but mostly steady light winds filtered sporadically through the thick underbrush. It was a hot day and the thin currents did little to relieve his misery. Sweat rolled down Vardy's face, and he felt the wetness in his armpits and on his bare chest. He continued his chopping figuring that he would take a long rest after the tree fell.

Each downward slice of his ax, followed by a powerful upswing, sent large pieces of the pine spewing. He had been at it for a little more than an hour, when he realized that only a few more forceful swings of the ax would bring down the tree. He chopped enthusiastically, for a few minutes. "One more," he said out loud, "jest one more!"

He steeled himself for his final onslaught, grimacing on the backswing. Shoulders tense, muscles taut and anxious, back stretched and slightly twisted, without command or hesitation, his arms recoiled, springing forward, slamming and driving the ax deep into the teetering pine. It swayed defensively, slowly leaning in the direction of the fall line.

Suddenly, without warning, an intense gust of wind forcibly smacked the tree, throwing and twisting it in a different direction. Its flesh cracked and popped violently under its own wrenching pressure. The tree swayed a final time balanced momentarily, then tilted toward Vardimen.

"Pappy, pappy! Look out! Look out! Git out of the way," Vardy shrieked behind the pitching tree. The huge pine, now grabbed by gravity, parted the heavy air in a thunderous scream, throwing its full weight hard against the steep bank, and ripping away its weak tether from the huge stump.

Vardy dropped his ax and ran hysterically down the hill toward the fallen, now-sliding tree. He thought he had glimpsed his father trying to move away just as the tree smashed into the bank and plowed partially into the creek. He stumbled, falling forward, and slid feet first into a slick chute of vegetation, propelled on his backside into the creek, just below the falls, overshooting the fallen tree.

He lay stunned in the shallow creek; his back bruised and cut by sharp river rocks. Momentarily, his head cleared, and he heard nothing, saw nothing; and as he looked into a deep blue summer sky, he knew.

He raised his body from the creek, crawled up the bank and staggered toward the huge tree. He called out for his father; again and again he called his name, and as he rifled through the huge tree's limbs he prayed aloud for his father to be alive.

Abruptly he stopped, stood rigidly, hands locked behind his neck, arms cradling his temples. He began to moan and sway. Suddenly, desperation overcame his grief; turning, he dashed back to the creek. Kneeling on the gravelly creek bottom, he dipped his scarf in water, and returned to his father. "Oh, pappy, oh pappy," Vardy whimpered as he bathed his father's face and forced drops of cool water between his lips. There was a deep wound in his father's head, and Vardy could see that he had been knocked completely senseless. Both legs were crushed hopelessly beneath the huge tree; his father was beyond the reach of human skill to save. His father was dying.

Vardy cut away the crumpled branches and pulled the nearly lifeless body from beneath them. Gingerly, ever so carefully, he cradled his father in his arms and carried him to the cabin.

Never leaving his side, Vardy nursed him for days, knowing that nothing could save him. Not once did Vardimen open his eyes or speak. It was hard to give him up, but he did. He knew he had to. He buried him in the valley below the ridge, in the land of the Clinch, as he had always wanted. Now they were both gone; Cager and Vardimen were gone. Cager fell dead, his body still lost somewhere in the Piedmont. And Vardimen fell in his beautiful valley...in his own valley...he fell in the valley he loved...in Vardy's valley.

In the late fall of 1796 Vardy returned to North Carolina. He stayed near Alamance only a short time before removing to the familiar hills of Wilkes and Ash counties. His family had subsisted in that area for generations, living, farming, hunting and fishing on both sides of the border.

Originally they had come from the low country along the coast of North Carolina and Virginia. He had never learned for sure why his ancestors left that area, but he knew that his family had been in the Appalachians for several generations. Many of the old folks claimed a Portuguese heritage, while others were sure they were of English stock. He had concluded they both were right; the two groups had met almost two centuries before.

They met in the Piedmont of North Carolina. The Portuguese, shipwrecked sailors, had followed Pee Dee Creek from the coast of South Carolina, and by chance the Englishmen and their Indian friends from Roanoke Island had crossed their path. They had stayed together, believing that numbers would ensure safety against their enemies. They chose to speak English because the Portuguese and Indians were illiterate. Generations of intermarrying evened out their differences and blurred their physical distinctiveness. Time, ignorance and hardship obscured their history, heritage and true identities.

Many of their descendants claimed their Portuguese and Indian ancestry in an attempt to reconcile their dark skins, and to ward off discrimination, but others hid their bloodlines, choosing instead to live and walk apart from white people.

Vardy was born in Augusta County, Virginia (later Grayson County) in the early 1760s. He didn't know the year. His mother had only guessed at the year, and she didn't know the exact day; but she was positive that he was born in March. So, he took the first day of the month as his birthday. It didn't matter to him. He figured that he was in his thirties.

When Peggy asked his age, he told her that he was born on the first of March in the year 1763. That satisfied her. Before they married she had wanted to make sure that he wasn't too old for her, she being born in 1773. She was a Gibson, and, like Vardy, had smooth copperish skin, a straight narrow nose and raven-black hair. There was a striking contrast, though. Vardy was a big man; although lean and muscular, he was tall for the time. Peggy, on the other hand, was thin, small and elegant, graceful and poised. She had small hands and feet; a smooth, beautiful, goddess-like face; and dark and mysterious eyes that had a faraway look. She was educated and spoke properly and sensibly, acquired skills that were virtually unheard of in the backcountry. Yes, Peggy Gibson was perfect when he met her, perfect when he married her, and was still perfect, and she would always be perfect in his eyes.

Peggy was the one who pushed him. She wanted him to go back to the valley. She wanted to raise their children there. Her idea of uxorial duties would involve her entire family. She would support and defend her husband and family in spiritual and physical ways. And whether it was following the teachings of the Bible, cleaning, cooking, gardening, making soap or spinning, quilting and knitting, she wanted them all involved, however many children she and Vardy would have.

They would be a family that would do things together; they would be a family that would feel for one another. They would share each other's happiness and sadness; and together they would overcome all life's obstacles. They would be a happy family wherever Vardy took them, because it would make no difference to her, as long as she could be with her husband and their children—wherever their home, she would make them happy.

And even though she had never seen the valley and the beautiful mountains that Vardy described, she recognized his love for them and his longing to return, and she understood.

One evening after supper, she spoke softy and sympathetically. She told him that she knew he wanted to go back to the valley, and she recognized that it would be difficult for him to see the place where his father had died, especially knowing the circumstances. But she said, "Vardy, your father would have wanted nothing more from you. You must fulfill his dream and yours. We'll go together. I'll be with you each step along the way."

Vardy was touched by her kindness, her insight and her support. He would go back. They would go back together. His family would at long last settle in Vardy's valley. His father would smile down from the heavens.

How he loved Peggy. Looking deeply into her eyes, he told her of his plans; that before they could go together, he had to do something; he had a task to complete. It was an undertaking that had been on hold for many, many years—a mission that was meant for his father. Now it would be up to him. "Soon," he told her, "I go to visit Micager to talk 'bout hit." She knew by his look and his voice that he would go soon. She could deny it no longer. She would not be with him. Vardy would go alone to The Clear Fork. Only then would her family settle between the Clinch and the Powell.

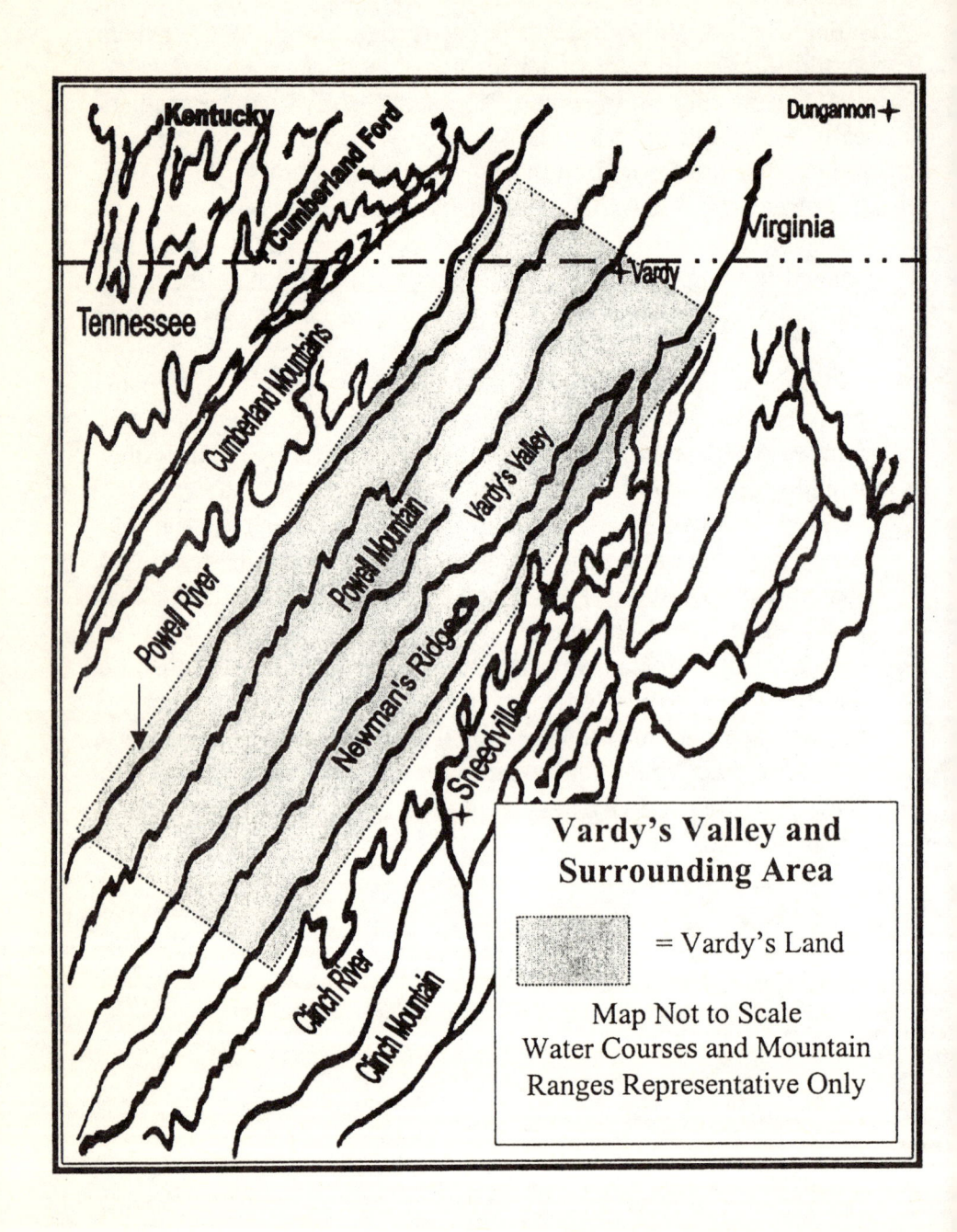

Vardy's Valley and Surrounding Area

= Vardy's Land

Map Not to Scale
Water Courses and Mountain
Ranges Representative Only

9

The Finding

Alamance County, North Carolina—1963

Rufus Edward Whitaker dug his heels into the flanks of his mule, urging him farther up the steep rise. The mule was tired from two years of constant searching; and with each long day of hunting, his body had grown weaker from the weight of Rufus. He hesitated, reserving his strength, then as always he responded, struggling to the top of the ridge.

Rufus reined the mule to a sudden stop. He gasped as his eyes adjusted to the openness, marveling at what lay before him. Open-mouthed, he sat straight, still and stiff in the saddle. His brain reeled from the panorama.

Below him stood a high, grassy knoll. It rose above a small stream that coursed along the contour of its base. Farther down the valley, a narrow wagon trail sprang from the curve of a dark hollow and meandered to the base of the knoll. The trail was worn and scarred, its surface exposed rich, red soil, sharply contrasting the greenness of the fescue-covered hill. It crossed the small creek, snaking its way up the steep hillside to a narrow footpath that led to the crest of the knoll.

Far down the hollow he could see a funeral procession led by a dark curtain-wrapped hearse. A glistening black horse fitted in silver studs and polished leather quietly pulled it. A long line of mourners, dressed in Eighteenth Century funeral clothes, trudged slowly behind the wagon; they walked one after the other, heads down, silent in their grief.

The procession crossed through the shallow waters of the small creek, and then ascended the steep, rutted trail that led to the footpath.

Reins untouched, outside human dominion, the horse stopped. Six male mourners left the procession and slowly pulled a black wooden box from the hearse. Silently, they carried the box at shoulder height to an open grave.

Rufus knew this place. Yes, he knew it. All his life he had known it; every night this scene had come to him, and its ghostly presence had given him no respite and no peace. And now he was here at last. He had found it! He had found the place of his visitation.

He spurred the mule forward, riding solemnly and resolutely toward the open grave. The mule's pace neither slowed nor quickened; steady in its purpose as it approached the procession. A powerful confident gait carried Rufus along the path toward a mound of red soil; and without a verbal command the mule stopped between the grave and the six men.

Looking down, he hailed them. "Who are you burying, old men?"

A white-haired, black-garbed preacher moved to the front of the gathering. He held a ragged leather bound Bible; pressing it tightly against his breast he answered, "We bury the bones of this poor man. Gray and dry we found them in the Haw Fields. He be an old, old soldier. He left only two letters carved into his musket. We know not his name, and not the meanings of the letters. It is carved 'C. W.'"

Rufus took the piece of musket stock offered by the preacher. Lost in another world, oblivious to the curious around him, he gently traced the letters with his finger, cleared his throat, and twisted in his saddle. He reverently placed the old scrap of wood into his saddlebag. Moving to meet the eyes of the old preacher, he said, "I am Rufus Edward, son of Ezekiel, son of Erasmus, son of Nimrod, son of Oxendine, son of Micager, son of Cager

Whitaker. I have come for my ancestor's bones. These bones be those of Cager Whitaker. I take his few remains to bury them in The Clear Fork, granting his last wish."

"You do a good thing, Rufus Edward Whitaker. Take the bones of your kin. Bury them whar he asked. Only then will his spirit rest. Take my wagon yonder in the holler. Take it and this box of bones. The old man looked at the rough wooden box and whispered, "Farewell, old soldier. Farewell. Sleep in peace now." Turning, the preacher motioned for the box to be returned to the hearse. The horse retraced the path down to the stream, crossed it, and pulled the hearse down the narrow road toward the old preacher's wagon as the procession slowly filed behind it.

"Therefore, brethren, we are debtors, and when this passing world is done, when has sunk yon glaring sun, and when we stand in Christ in glory, looking over life's finished story. Then, Lord, shall I fully know—not till then—how much I owe. Praise the Lord."

"Amen, Brother, amen," mumbled someone from the graveside congregation. "Our brother's dry gray bones are at last in the Lord's arms."

"Yes, yes, Brother Cager's bones have rejoined his spirit."

"And the angel said to the people, 'Cager is not here; his spirit has risen to his room in the house of God. He has left all and he has followed the Lord.' And the Lord sayeth, 'Come to me all who are weary and burdened. Return unto the Lord ye who are weary from wandering.

"Cager's weary soul has wandered wide and long over the lands of the Alamance. After his long search, Rufus Edward has brought his remains to us. Now, we place his bones in this grave on this knoll in Whitaker Graveyard at the mouth of Mankins Hollow along The Clear Fork, just as Cager wished."

The preacher stood grasping his Bible in one hand, as he pointed to the heavens with the other.

"Be proud, be proud of your Brother Cager. His toils are partly responsible for this great land. So, wipe away your tears;

he has gone to the Lord. Isaiah 25:5: 'The sovereign Lord will wipe away all the tears.' Let us sing, *When They Ring The Golden Bells*. Yes, yes, let me hear its sweetness. Let me hear it now, let me hear it for our new-found brother Cager."

> *Don't you hear the bells now ringing?*
> *Don't you hear the angels singing?*
> *'Tis the glory hallelujah Jubilee.*
> *In that far off sweet forever,*
> *Just beyond the shining river,*
> *When they ring the golden bells for you and me."*

After the end of the short graveside service, Pappy, Rufus Edward, Hobe and all the other Whitakers and their relations who had come from near and far filed solemnly past the lowered casket. They dropped nosegays of red roses and yellow daisies into the grave, and then continued down the ridge and onto the mine road that tracked around its base. At last, Cager was at rest in The Clear Fork.

10

The Walking Man

McDowell County, West Virginia—1963

Greenwalt **Christian had been** a member of the McDowell County Court for years, a squire and lawman. He carried a badge and a pistol, and kept a rifle at the ready during the few times he rode a horse. He was the people's choice, because he had never lost an election. He was the "legal man" who quoted law the same way a fiery mountain Baptist preacher might when he picks apart the Holy Book for his stubborn flock.

He was called the "Walking Man" candidate." He worked the entire county of McDowell in his usual fashion, walking and talking everywhere he went. Hardly ever did he ride his horse; he preferred to "jest go a-walkin." He wore heels and soles off his shoes, tore his shirts scurrying through brier patches, and split his pants jumping gullies and climbing split rail fences.

He loved animals, and during every step of his daily walks he talked to squirrels, grouse, deer and his trusted black-and-tan coonhound. With unforgiving eyes and terse language, he dressed down men who were mean to animals, telling them that if he saw them mistreat them again they might suffer the same as their poor critters.

Greenwalt Christian did not deal from the bottom of the deck. He was a man not capable of deception; he spoke clearly, forcefully and honestly to his friends, neighbors and foes alike.

He stomped and snorted his way down the halls of county courthouses, and he was known as an honest and caring broker of the people's business. Corrupt judges in all the counties of southern West Virginia dreaded his courtroom presence. Many with the power and backing of county commissioners and coal barons tried to bully him, but he feared no man; not even cadres of county bureaucrats could intimidate the "Walking Man."

He once said that to learn the ways of their elders, and to teach them how not to act, children should sit a spell in Domestic Relations Court, and listen to the lying God-fearing Christian men and women. He'd say, "Them youngins would soon learn just because people are grown up and claim to be religious that it doesn't mean they tell the truth. That would teach 'em to be on alert."

Greenwalt was a fierce competitor when it came to campaigning for office, and he used every opportunity to do so. He met eyeball to eyeball with every voter in the county, making sure they understood his positions.

He was a man of above-average height, thin with lean long muscles. He wore a small tufted beard, a bushy charcoal-color mustache and thick, dark gray hair. His face suggested kindness and humility. He was quiet and patient, yet he had a powerful presence. When he spoke, people listened, and they understood him. He knew the mountains and he knew mountain people—he was one of them, and they loved his straight talk and his deference to a higher authority, a power much greater than corrupt politicians and sleazy lawyers could muster.

He passed out flyers and loudly condemned the corruption that plagued county politics, and he spoke and wrote movingly. One flyer he ended:

"But as I have told you before, I would like to have the Office of Sheriff, and in order that the people of McDowell County may have rest and ease, I throw my body upon the alter of Abraham, Isaac and Jacob that the fire may be kindled in the minds of people that corruption and mismanagement of our county be destroyed, and *that* without any strong drink or white lightning."

It was rumored that Greenwalt's family originally came from Upper East Tennessee, but no one knew for sure, because he chose not to speak of his ancestry. He wasn't a talkative man, except when it came to politics. But many said that if you found him on Christian Mountain late at night at a gathering, and if there were a few bottles of good whiskey around, he'd be in the right mood to talk about himself.

At one such get-together he opened up and told about his trip to Texas. He said when he was just a young man in the spring of 1915 he left McDowell County, and landed a job in Oklahoma with Wells Fargo, riding "shotgun" on a stagecoach. The driver was a fellow from Texas. "That man talked all the way from Oklahoma to Texas telling me about how good Texas was. His ranting continued for a couple of hundred miles and became an intolerable tirade as we crossed the Oklahoma border and headed for 'Cow Town'—how rich the state, how wonderful the terrain, how big the bison, how tall the trees, and how powerful and intelligent the men, and how beautiful the women. On and on he went, on and on!"

Finally Greenwalt had had enough. He looked ahead and saw nothing but dry and windy terrain—just tumbleweed rolling with the wind, no mountains, no streams, and no green trees as far as the eye could see. So, when the man said, "Why, if people wanted, I'll bet that puny little state of Tennessee would fit—*plop*—right down here in a little tiny part of Texas. We sure have plenty of room, Greenwalt!"

Greenwalt answered that there was no question "Tennessee would fit—size-wise, it would fit," he said, and then he thought a moment, and looked the driver in the eye, and said as thoughtfully as could be. "Why, the way I see it—sure God would be an improvement!" He never heard another thing about Texas from that day to this—from that fellow.

Greenwalt had a particular loathing for braggarts, especially Texans. He always said that, "Texans are like the Rio Grande—a mile wide at the mouth and only four inches deep." And he figured that some of that Texas arrogance had found its way into the confines of the McDowell County Courthouse. Whether county officials were indeed empty-headed loudmouths made no real difference, but when they turned the corner and became sycophants and braggarts for coal companies, cockily spouting their cases, it infuriated him.

So, when Judge Lucas called him into chambers, he was particularly irritated to find himself sharing the room with one J. Frank Hutson, CEO of Champion Sheet and Tube. Hutson grinned as Judge Lucas explained that he wanted Greenwalt to serve Ezekiel Whitaker with a Non-Payment of Tax Notice, and to summon him to court.

Hutson had interrupted, his sharp Northern accent cutting through the thin almost apologetic tone of the judge. "Christian, you do this and Champion will make you a rich man, just like we've done for so many others in this county. I'll see to it that you and your family have whatever you want. New cabin, car, or mule, whatever—it makes no difference. I'm prepared to offer you, right now, nine hundred dollars. Christian, you haven't ever seen this much money before, have you?" He waved the stack of fresh green bills in front of Greenwalt, whose face quickly changed from a soft flesh color to a bright scarlet, sharply contrasting a set of dark narrow eyes."

Greenwalt looked Hutson squarely in the eye, "Mr. Hutson, if you try to bribe an officer of the court again, I will arrest you and throw you in my jail for a long, long time."

"Now see here, Christian—"

"—Call me Sheriff, Mr. Hutson," Greenwalt snarled.

"Sheriff," the judge broke in, "this is a legal summons, and you must serve it. It's the law, Sheriff, whether you like this man or not, it's the law."

"I'll serve it, Judge, but I know that all you are is just a rubber stamp for the coal companies and one day you'll get what you deserve. That money you've been taking ain't worth the trouble you'll have someday."

"Don't you talk to—"

"—Yeah, and you'll see what Champion can do, too! We know about your piece of land; the one they call Christian Mountain! Our land is all around it. Maybe we'll block it off so you Christians can't get in or out."

"Mr. Hutson, are you ready to meet your Maker?"

Hutson turned paper white, suddenly realizing that Greenwalt had moved his hand to the butt of his pistol. He stammered, avoiding dark eyes that hinted of grave danger. "Oh, now, hold up, now. No need to get all fuzzed up, Sheriff Christian, sir. I shouldn't have spoken so quickly. Champion Sheet and Tube, and certainly I, want nothing more than to see the free exercise of all citizens' rights in this county. Even if that exercise runs contrary to the mission and policies of Champion. The citizenry of McDowell should have their rights protected, without question, and Ezekiel Whitaker is no different. Right, Judge Lucas?"

"That's right, Sheriff. Mr. Whitaker will have a full hearing, unbiased and thorough."

Greenwalt stared, eyes lingering disdainfully at the two. He snatched the paper from the judge's hand, turned and slammed the door behind him.

Pappy Ezekiel Whitaker saw the rider on horseback coming at a gallop up the trail leading to his log house. Dropping his kindling ax, Pappy reached for his long rifle. "Could be anybidy," he thought.

As the rider came nearer, the path turned, placing him directly in front of a low hanging morning sun. Trying to identify the intruder, Pappy strained through squinting eyes shaded by a raised and flattened left hand.

The shadowy silhouette approached without the loud customary greeting. Pappy's hand tightened around the grip of his rifle just as his arm began a smooth steady hoisting of the gun barrel along his right side, stopping at his belted waist. He swiveled the barrel to a spot that would allow an unobstructed line of fire toward the trespasser.

Suddenly, out of the sun's glare, appeared the rider. It was Greenwalt Christian. He was dressed in loose black trousers; a brown sagging hat cocked to one side, partially covering sad eyes and a contorted mouth; brown Wellington style boots rode the stirrups; a bright silver star stood out from the breast of a dark maroon-colored wool shirt. He brought the chestnut-color mare to an abrupt halt with, "Whooooaa, girl! Whoooa, now, girl!"

"Jumpin' Jehoshaphat, Greenwalt! Ye ain't a-walkin' today! And I seed ye ridin' up wit yer chin on yer chest—like ye wuz thinkin' deep 'bout somethin'. How come? Must be a mighty heavy reason fer not a-walkin'?"

Greenwalt, with clinched jaws and narrowed eyes, sighed loudly, "I had to get here fast, somethin' mighty substantial, Pappy. I hightailed it up here to warn you of what the county court ordered. I've come to say that Judge Lucas wants you in open court for prosecution of non-payment of taxes. Pappy, they want to force you off this ground so Champion Sheet and Tube can claim it."

"I ain't a-feared of the court or that stil comp'ne. This hyeh land is mine. Me many great grandpappy, Micager, wuz give this land by General Warshington, hizzelf. Ain't nobidy takin' hit from me fam'le."

"Well, I just thought I'd warn you. I've got to bring you in for court on the fourth Monday of August. That's next week, Pappy. Will you come with me? I don't want no trouble. Just doing my job."

"I'll come wit ye. Us Whitakers ain't never run from a fight yet."

"Pappy, do you have the papers?"

"Whut papers?"

"The papers that say this land was given to Micager."

"No, ain't never laid me eyes on 'em, but I know fer shore this is Whitaker land. How else would we've stayed hyeh all 'em generational years?"

"Well, Pappy, I hope you're right. I'll see you next fourth Monday. Just remember, I'm with you, Pappy." Greenwalt drew lightly on the left rein and gently spurred the horse to a slow trot back down the path.

11

Whitaker Werd

McDowell County Court House, Welch, WV—1963

Curious onlookers from all over the county milled about in the courthouse yard gawking as Pappy Whitaker rode his mule up the street toward the front of the huge stone building. What made the crowd curious was that Pappy was a man out of time with the world. He was an anachronism in an age of automobiles, televisions and corporate jets. He dressed, spoke, and acted as if some mysterious time machine had transported him from the end of the Eighteenth Century to Twentieth Century Coalwood.

His small, lean body seemed to slide over things, never touching leaves, twigs or rocks as he glided through, over and around them. Some said it was because his ancestors were some of the very first settlers in West Virginia, and they had acquired the habit out of the necessity of avoiding Indians and ruffians who roamed the backcountry in huge gangs. They said that Pappy had merely inherited his ancestors' characteristics. Whatever it was, Pappy could walk through thick layers of dry leaves and never make a sound, a track, or break a leaf or twig.

He was in his late sixties and sometimes he could be seen riding that mule up and down the roads. It was a huge mule and Pappy looked small and strange on it. He rode back straight, knees relaxed and unbent in low stirrups, lightly moving back and forth above the saddle to the rhythm of the gait. His butt seemed never to touch the saddle, nor did his thighs and calves rub the flanks of that mule—only his big black boots appeared to be riding that mule.

For all practical purposes, Pappy Whitaker was not on that mule—only his boots in the stirrups and two little fingers lightly under the reins were all that mule ever felt. He rode like he walked, real ghost-like.

Pappy had big, dark, glimmering eyes, and copper-color skin drawn hard over a thin muscular body. He stood nearly five-foot six, weighed about a hundred and forty pounds, and sported a dark mustache, cascading beard and long, straight black hair pasted under a slouchy black hat with a rounded top. He wasn't a bad looking fellow at all, but he had a real backward streak in him. It was said that his standoffish ways were inherited, because his ancestors learned not to trust strangers, so they just stayed away from them, silently watching them pass by from secret hiding places.

He eased the mule to a slow walk and then brought it to a smooth stop with a soft "whoa, big boy." Slowly he dismounted, and with the naïve wonder of a child he stood motionless before the huge stone building. Finally, the spell lightened its hold and his eyes broke away. Dropping the reins he murmured, "Stay right here, big boy, right here," and without hitching the mule to the rail at the edge of the courtyard, he walked along the stone retaining wall that encircled and guarded the courthouse.

Pappy looked good in his freshly washed and ironed black trousers and white shirt; his black hat had been blocked for days over its rounded mold, and was not quite as slouchy as usual. He had done it all himself. His precious wife, Mammy Whitaker, would have wanted him to look good. He had lost her some years before to tuberculosis, and ever since he had lived with an empty heart. He resigned himself to being too old to go looking for another wife, but, "Maybe, someday, maybe," he thought.

That morning he had taken meticulous care to make sure he would look respectable, honorable and honest like the descendant of a Revolutionary War soldier and a man who had personally helped his dearly loved country with many good deeds over his own lifetime. He was proud of his heritage and that every Whitaker generation had done its duty and patriotically supported America.

His ancestors had fought the French and Indians, the Hessians and the British twice, the Mexicans, Spaniards, Germans, Italians and Japanese, and the Koreans. It was for his ancestors that he had dressed so well. He would fight in court for them. He would overcome the charges and objections, and the court would recognize his claim, and set all right. He had great confidence in the country's justice system—it was a citadel of righteousness and fair play, a fortress of decency, a protector of the rights of all people, and especially a defender of the cause of patriots. He knew that a basic premise of American jurisprudence is that a person is presumed innocent until proven guilty in a court of law. That no man had to prove himself innocent; that whoever brought the charges would have to prove his guilt.

Yes, Ezekiel Whitaker was a self-assured man, thankful that he was born an American, yet knowing that he and his ancestors had done much to secure their own freedom, and the nation's as well. He confidently negotiated the long, steep, cut-stone set of steps, swung the huge, thick oak door to his left, stepped across the threshold and entered the sterile confines of a poorly lighted McDowell County Court House.

The Clerk read, "Hear ye, hear ye! All rise. Court is in session. The Honorable Judge Lanceford Paul Lucas of the Court of Pleas and Quarter Sessions presiding." The judge slipped into the courtroom, and took his seat smoothly. "Take your seats, please," instructed the Clerk.

Lucas raised the wooden gavel with his right hand and brought it down sharply, slamming it hard against the huge oak desk. "My court is now in session. Contending parties please stand. Clerk, read the case."

"Docket 241; Case number 2034 dash 21; 24 August 1963; Champion Sheet and Tube on behalf of McDowell County versus Ezekiel Whitaker, also known as Pappy Whitaker; Non payment of real estate taxes."

Judge Lucas looked at the two sides in the case. To his left stood the Plaintiff's six lawyers, all dressed in black pin-striped suits, white silk shirts, red ties sporting double Windsor knots, red handkerchiefed breast pockets, and shiny black wingtips and matching black socks. To a man, they had medium-length, well-groomed dark hair, thick gold- framed glasses, and pencil thin mustaches. Even from the bench he could smell the aroma of fine after-shave and spray perfume. A smiling J. Frank Hutson stood beside them; he winked as their eyes met.

The defendant, Pappy Whitaker, stood alone, at attention, straight and proud, and obviously out-of-place in the courtroom, awed by its grandeur and his own respect. He held his big black slouchy hat with both hands, pressing it to his heart. His shiny black hair lay pasted almost flat against his scalp, and one could still see little particles of white lard here and there along the run of his mustache and beard. He wore bulky black pull-on boots, obviously homemade; his thick black belt held a dark cowskin whip and a long Bowie hunting knife. His eyes were dark and twinkly, and seemed to dance, taking in every movement in the room.

Some chatter erupted in the room as a few tardy spectators took their seats. "Court, come to order! I said come to order!" Judge Lucas banged the gavel; its sound reverberated throughout the courtroom. "If I hear the slightest commotion again the bailiff will remove you all. This court will proceed without further disruption."

The judge began his summary of the case even before either of the parties had had a chance to speak. He glanced at Pappy and then quickly shifted his eyes to Hutson, keeping them there for the remainder of his little speech.

"This case is a simple one. No taxes have been paid on land owned by the Whitakers. We carefully checked the records of the three county seats. The first was the 1867 seat designated by the West Virginia legislature. Some say it was on the old Philip Lambert land at Daycamp; others say it was Snakeroot, now part of Coalwood. Makes no difference, I guess, and " Lucas continued, "in 1872 Peeryville, now English, was voted the new county seat; and after a contested ballot issue, Welch became the third in 1892. Peeryville accused Welch of paying temporary workers to vote. Later, trying to avoid violence, all county records were secretly moved in wagons to Welch, and they've been here ever since.

"So, no one can accuse me of being derelict in my historical research. My staff and I took great care to investigate all possible repositories—we explored all leads but found nothing of importance or anything germane to this case. Anyway, no taxes have been recorded since tax accounts began to be kept—since 1858 when McDowell was erected from Tazwell County, Virginia.

"The defendant, Ezekiel "Pappy" Whitaker, claims this land. The plaintiffs have brought the case on behalf of McDowell County, and those who pay taxes and those who use the services provided by the county at taxpayers' expense. How do you plead, Mr. Whitaker?"

"I...I say I ain't so much as a little bit guilty, ye Honor," Pappy answered confidently, holding his thumb and index finger up so Lucas could get a good look, and realize just how innocent he was.

"Do you have proof of your claim?"

"Yeah, show us the proof, Whitaker!" J. Frank laughed under his breath as he elbowed his lead counsel.

"Well, *do you*, Mr. Whitaker?" Lucas screeched and winked at J. Frank.

"Yes, sirree, I do! I give me werd that the land wuz give to me ancestor pappy, Micager Whitaker. Me own pappy's little brother, Garfield Whitaker, lost the paper pappy sent 'im. He wuz a-bringin' the paper right hyeh to this courthouse, right hyeh to Welch. He wuz goina enter hit reel 'ficial-like when he wuz overcome by that Great Coalwood Flood; it wuz way back thar in the year of air Lord, nineteen hundred and twenty-three. He wuz hurt reel bad; it wuz hiz heart and he had to go, poor man had to go to Aunt Susannah's place, way up at Hootmocker Hospital in Penn Yan, up in that big state of—"

"—*I don't care about your uncles...or your uncle's problems! Don't waste the court's time*," the judge callously interrupted. "You mean to tell me that you only have your puny word to show...to give me...*that's all you have?*"

"Yes, sir, that's *Whitaker werd!* Whitaker werd hit is," Pappy raised his chin and stood a little straighter, a little taller, as he said 'Whitaker werd.' "Yes, sirree, Whitaker werd is as parful a bind as ever bin. Gener'l Warshington, air great president...air foundin' father, he knowed Whitaker werd. An...an...Captain Big Aron an...Nathanael Green knowed hit, too. They knowed Whitaker werd is good. Hit's good as gold, hit be. Ye can count on—."

"—Your Honor, this is ridiculous! These are ravings of a lunatic. This poor man is clearly harebrained." The immaculately dressed attorney in charge of the plaintiffs' team stepped forward, interrupting Ezekiel. Pointing at Pappy, he spoke mockingly, "This ignorant man obviously has no claim to the land," The lawyer stared at Pappy disdainfully, then continued sarcastically, "Are we to take that thar Whitaker werd?"

Pappy's face returned a minatory look, a gaze so threatening and menacing that loud gasps were heard throughout the courtroom. "Ye respect the good name of *Whitaker!* Ye hear me now, youngin?"

The lawyer turned to the spectators and yelled derisively, "The only *thang* the 'good name of Whitaker' means around *hyeh is chawing toobakki, moonshine and ugly old black mules and—*"

"—In fact," J. Frank stood up, cutting in, "I'll bet if we put this chawbacon in the driver's seat of a car he'd run over half the people in McDowell County and knock down most of the buildings, all the while yelling, '*Whooa, car! Whooa, car, whooa!*'"

Astonishingly, the spectators showed no outward signs that they found anything the two had said funny; just quick gasps followed by shaking heads and shocked wide-eyed looks. They obviously didn't share in the attempt at humor. In fact, to local court observers, their stunned looks gave the impression they had heard something ominous, something foreboding and portentous.

Only the entourage of corporate lawyers seemed to find the remarks funny.

Eyes bulging, bushy brows jammed together across the bridge of his nose, angered by the pompous bully of a lawyer, Pappy exploded, "Ye kwite down now, right now, or ye'll come to know air wrath. Kwite, me sed, kwite!"

"Don't tell me what to do, you ignorant hillbilly!" Screamed the lawyer.

"Ye off sourin' of the earth." Pappy slapped his cowskin whip against his thigh, and, like distant thunder, his voice rumbled through the thick air of the court room, "Ye'll know the same fate as 'em way back in Hillsberri—the ones me own great-great grandpappy hepped run off."

The lawyer dismissed Pappy's threat. Turning away from Pappy's huge, luminous, dark eyes, he addressed the court, "Your Honor, we at Champion Sheet and Tube on behalf of Olga Coal Company and McDowell County will pay the back taxes on the land for simple and clear title. This is the best course of action since the taxes now calculate from 1858 to present to just under $200,000. This would be a great windfall to the people of the county, and in addition it would remove another derelict from the delinquency sheets."

Judge Lucas nodded, looked sternly at Ezekiel, "Mr. Whitaker, I'm afraid that if you have no proof of ownership you must forfeit your claim and vacate the land. The court will give you forty-five days to remove whatever personal property you may have. At that time, and after the collection of the back taxes, a firm title will be given to Champion Sheet and Tube on behalf of Olga Coal Company. Enter my judgment." He slammed the gavel down. "Court is now adjourned."

"Ye...ye can't do...ye didn't let me talk. Ye didn't prove nary a thang. General Warshington hizself gave that land to Micager, and Micager to hizzin, and hizzin to hizzin, and all the way down the line to me. Mr. Jefferson and Mr. Madison done signed hit, too. Pappy told me so! That land is Whitaker land. Blood, sweat and toil of me ancestors is in that land, and me own are buried thar—Cager, me great ancestor Cager, is right thar, happy under Whitaker dirt. Me own boy, Rufus Edward, searched fer his dry gray bones. He found 'em in the Piedmont, and brought 'em back right thar to Whitaker land, whar they belong, and this is whar his bones will stay. And me own Mammy, she's buried two rows from Cager right thar under a big shagbark hickory, behind 'em blackberries. Right thar, they's buried right thar wit all me other kin. Cager and Mammy and me blood will stay right thar!" Pappy shook his fist and yelled at the judge, *"The Clher Fork is Whitaker land forever!* Whitakers ain't never goina leave air land! Ye'll see!"

"Mr. Whitaker, justice has been served. You are to leave this courthouse immediately or you will be confined!" The judge yelled over the chattering crowd, taking full note of the huge, staring eyes of the defendant. They seemed to bore into his body, hot yet cold at the same time. It was a sight he would not soon forget, and as he felt a gnawing fear settle throughout his body he knew that he was in danger.

He knew what Pappy Whitaker had meant when he spoke about what happened at Hillsborough in 1770. "Off scourings of the earth" is how a group of North Carolina settlers, calling themselves *Regulators,* labeled Orange County lawyers before they attacked them with cudgels, cowskin whips, stones and brickbats, and destroyed their houses. It was the prelude to the War of the Regulation, when two thousand Regulators battled eleven hundred royal troops under William Tryon, royal governor of North Carolina.

The battle that took place on May 16, 1771 was fought near Alamance in Orange County and many believe it was the *real* first battle of the Revolutionary War. The Regulators were defeated and a hated Tryon soon left North Carolina to become the royal governor of New York. "Could it be? Lucas thought, "Could it be that a Whitaker ancestor helped instigate—" The harsh, determined, threatening voice of Pappy Whitaker interrupted his racing thoughts.

"—Now, I seed the jestis of this hyeh court. Now, ye'll see Whitaker jestis! Ye'll see hit reel up close-like. Ever time ye look at the mirror or stare ye eyes in a pond, or in a winder, or ogle ye'self in ye woman's eyes, ye'll not see ye own reflection. No, sirree, ye'll see me and me Whitaker ancestors lookin' back at ye, straight at ye wit air blazin' mean eyes. Ye'll know Whitaker eyes. Yes sirree, ye'll know 'em fer shore. This hyeh...and thar ain't no doubt 'bout hit...this hyeh coun'e is a kack...kees...tok...krasee. Me ancestors' land ain't never to be stole by the likes of ye, by that thar comp'ne or by Mack Dal Coun'e. *The Clher Fork 'll stay Whitaker land, free forever! Ye'll see!*"

Pappy's giant eyes flashed fire; he turned quickly, rushing with great purpose to the back of the courtroom. He could hear the laughs of the slick northern lawyers as he stepped through the big oak doors, never breaking his stride as he headed down the stone steps to the hitching posts. He mounted his mule and set out for the backcountry of Coalwood. He knew what he had to do.

12

The Posting

Coalwood Main—4th Wednesday of August 1963

They sat quietly on the steps of Olga Coal Company's Big Store. To a boy, they were drinking bottles of Coca-Cola and Pepsi filled with *Tom's* peanuts. All looked basically the same—mid teens, bean-lean and lanky, short hair, faded blue jeans and shirtless. They were always together, or at least a group of them was invariably somewhere around. They were high-spirited and a little mischievous—and some people in town were openly calling them Coalwood's misfits.

Hub, a tall boy with dirty blond hair, was sometimes the group's leader. He sat on the top step peering over several flattops brushed to "Class A" presentations. He stared trance-like at the Post Office while occasionally one of the boys turned his pop bottle straight up and banged his hand against its thick glass bottom, trying to persuade the last peanut to drop into his mouth.

Coob, a boy with a slightly large head and two bulbous eyes that shifted much too easily above a short, lean body, sat on the top step with Hub, behind all the other boys. He was the first to mention it, the unusual activity at the Post Office.

All morning, Whitakers had been going in and out of the big white building. They came at irregular intervals. First Hobe, Pappy's eldest son, had come, his big black mule's saddlebags bulging with letters. Then it was Pappy, then his youngest son,

Rufus Edward, and then other members of the family. Each and every one of them carried a bag of letters to mail.

Even Elmer Clarence Whitaker evidently had come from his home near Meadowview, Virginia. They watched him as he talked quietly to Rufus behind the big circular flowerbed that colored and broke the yard of green grass in front of the Post Office. At times Rufus became quite animated, but on each occasion Elmer Clarence seemed to settle him down with whispers and hand movements.

What surprised them all was that Rufus was there. Nobody in Coalwood had seen Rufus Edward for at least two years. He had just disappeared one day. The entire little town of Coalwood had been awash in rumors of the cause of his disappearance and his whereabouts. Many believed he had been killed; that he had been tracked over toward Wallins Creek by two jackleg Kentuckians; and somewhere in the high mountains he had been bushwhacked and his body done away with. "He's probably buried with his mule in a shallow rocky grave on one of the high lonely ridges of Black Mountain," they supposed.

Others said word had come that he had been seen riding his big black mule through the red rolling hills of the Piedmont of North Carolina; near the town of Alamance, they believed it was.

But, he was back. He was definitely back, and now the fence line rumormongers would have to come up with new tittle-tattle to pass along. The actions of the Whitakers this day "should cause a buzz for weeks," Burrhead figured.

Hub fidgeted from buttock to buttock. That meant he was intently curious; that his curiosity would soon overcome him. He was a boy who had to know everything that went on in Coalwood. And he almost always did.

"Wha...what'll you...you think it is, Hub?" Muss, his grass-blade-thin crew cut brother asked. He, like the rest of them, had been silently speculating.

"Don't know, but it's somethin' big," Hub replied, lifting and rubbing his chin, "I've never seen the Post Office this busy."

"Me neither, and it's only the Whitakers doin' it, too!" Burrhead offered.

The boys were so preoccupied with the activity they didn't notice that Jack and Norm had pulled up in Jack's red and white Metropolitan, and parallel parked near the Big Store. Only when Norm slammed the car door and yelled something about "...all the people at the Post Office" did they notice the pair of smartly dressed, flattopped boys.

"We don't know, but it looks like the whole Whitaker clan is mailing letters today," Coob answered rather coolly. In the past, none of the boys had been very fond of Jack and Norm. They once considered them to be part of the social elite of Coalwood. But over time, as they themselves passed into their teens, the added maturity brought a better understanding of the two. And with that understanding came empathy and respect, and eventually true friendship on the part of most of the misfits.

"That's funny, I never thought they could write," Jack answered.

"You're wrong, a couple of 'em can write. Elmer Clarence's got to be writin' those letters, and maybe Rufus. I know they can read and write. And come to think of it, Hobe can write some, too," Pearman answered, proud that he had remembered seeing a crude note written by Hobe a couple of years before.

"I wonder if it's got somethin' to do with what happened Monday at the courthouse in Welch." Jack blurted.

"Wha...What happened at the courthouse?"

"Yeah, what happened?"

"You haven't heard? Judge Lucas took Pappy's land. He had never paid taxes on it. Somebody said he was $200,000 in the hole. They'd have never been able to sell enough moonshine to pay it off. Some slick Yankee lawyers from Ohio and Pennsylvania got it all done."

"Slick lawyers? Why would they get involved?" Hub asked, suspicious now.

"Don't know. They represented Champion Sheet and Tube, and Olga Coal."

"If Youngstown is that interested in the land there's somethin' of value on it. You can bet your butt on that. If not, they wouldn't give it a second thought

"Must be a lot of coal and gas on Pappy's land, or maybe virgin timber. His land's never been cut, except for the little bit that was done by Top Notch Timbering. Pappy got so mad at 'em, he threw 'em off his land—said they were ruinin' his mountaintop with their roads and collection point, and had cut too close to where he works. Remember?"

"Yeah, that's right," Pappy, Hobe and Rufus almost scared 'em to death; ran 'em right off the mountain. Nobody ever figured out what scared 'em so bad. I remember seein' that big convoy of loggin' trucks speedin' out of Coalwood. They were too scared to even look out of their windows; they kept their eyes to the road and stared straight ahead!"

"Hey! Look over there!" Burrhead pointed toward the side door of the Post Office.

Brownlow Bean, general superintendent of Coalwood, stood close to Sutt, the postmaster. The boys figured that something was obviously up, so with Hub leading they hurried en mass to the opposite side of the Post Office, sneaked through the passageway between it and the barbershop and peered around the corner a few feet from Sutt and Brownlow. They were just in time to hear the conversation.

"Brownlow, I don't know why but the Whitakers have brought in over four hundred letters today. I've done nothing but research and cancellations all day. I figured you should know. It's quite unusual; besides one by Hobe, the Whitakers haven't mailed a letter since I've been postmaster. That's over fifteen years. I thought they just didn't know anybody outside Coalwood, or they couldn't read or write. Come in here. I'll show you what I mean."

A perplexed Brownlow Bean followed Sutt through the side door, and the boys moved closer, listening to every word. Inside, Bean inspected the letters. "My God, Sutt, these things are going all over the country. Look at these! To the Collinses of

Vardy Valley, Tennessee, the Gibsons of Lynch, Kentucky, the Mullenses of Dungannon, Virginia, and—"

"—You think that's something, look at these," Sutt interrupted. "This one's to the Wins of the Blue Ridge, and these to the Jackson Whites of New Jersey and New York. Here's one to the Over-the-Hill tribe of the Cherokee. And...and look at this one, it's—"

"—Wait a minute! Did you say 'the Jackson Whites'?"

"Yep, that's what I said," Sutt confirmed proudly, "They're supposedly a different clan, maybe even a different race, and some call them 'blue-eyed high yellows.' Apparently, migrated from somewhere in the southern Appalachians. I just read about them."

"I see. I don't think they're high yellows, though. Maybe they're...what? These are addressed to the Tuscarora of New York and Ontario and the Mohawks. Northern Indians? How could they be connected?" Bean asked, watching Sutt through knowing eyes.

"Yes, sir. I looked it up. Strange as it might seem, the Tuscarora were run out of North Carolina 250 years ago. They lived in eastern West Virginia before they went north to join the Iroquois Confederacy.

"The Mohawks have their home—they call it a castle— along the Mohawk River in New York. In the 1700s, they as part of the Iroquois League controlled this whole region, all of what is now West Virginia. And that's not all," Sutt continued, "here's two letters to the Mingo and Canoy—they lived here, too. That's where the word 'Kanawha' comes from. You know—from the Canoy Indians. They used to call West Virginia that.

"But look at this, Brownlow. There's a ton more. These are to the Ridgemanites of Campbell and Anderson counties in Tennessee, and these to the Indian Browns and Joneses of Kentucky, the Ramps of Wise and Scott counties of Virginia, the Blackwaters of the Blackwater Swamps, the Collinsworths of Brushy Mountain, the Meros of southwest Virginia."

"My, my, this is unbelievable," Bean mumbled to himself, shocked and worried at the scope of the action the Whitakers had taken, "and here's a slew more...the Brass Ankles, and the Rivers and Lumbees of the Carolinas and Baltimore, the Weremos of the Powhatan of Virginia, the Wesorts of Southern Maryland, the White-Browns of Coon Mountain, Virginia, and the Yuchis and Croatans of eastern Virginia."

"See what I mean! Nobody could come up with all these obscure clans and tribes unless they're friends or related! I think we have trouble brewing. That's why I called you."

"I think you're right, Sutt."

"Oh, I'm right for sure. I've done a lot of research today," Sutt pointed to a set of encyclopedias that he had evidently brought from home. Here's one last one. It says 'To the Melungeons of Sneedville, Tennessee.'"

"Sneedville?"

"Yes, it's across the Virginia border from Dungannon. You know, a lot of these letters are going to addresses that are between the Clinch and Powell rivers, and along New River. These clans have to be closely associated. Some sort of meeting is being called, for sure."

"Is there any way to know what those letters contain?" Brownlow looked quizzically at Sutt, asking, but not really.

Sutt thought it was a good way for Bean to deny involvement. Brownlow didn't overtly ask him to do something illegal, but he expected it. It angered him, and a mask of crimson spread over his face. "I don't know of any. I'm sure not going to break the law." Sutt hesitated then said forcefully, making sure his point got across, "No, no, there is nothing that can be done. There is nothing *I will do* in that regard, for anybody, for any reason!"

"Okay, I understand; I wouldn't either. Just thought I'd throw it out. Don't blame you. The only reason I alluded to it is that the higher-ups in Youngstown will surely ask me, *and you*. I wanted you on my side."

"Good! By the way, there are several letters posted to Morocco, Portugal, Turkey, and Old England."

Brownlow Bean's brow furrowed; he paused, slightly nodded at Sutt, and then turned and quickly walked through the doorway. Bright sunshine momentarily blinded him just as he came face to face with Hub and the boys. Rubbing his eyes, he asked, "What are you...what did you hear, boys?"

"Nothing sir, Mr. Bean. We just got here. Saw the door open and that's when you came out. Wanted to ask Sutt if he was going to Grundy for the race next weekend. Thought maybe a couple of us might go with him."

"Oh, yes, he does like those stock cars, doesn't he?" Bean asked rhetorically, satisfied with Hub's answer. He moved past them without waiting for a reply, and headed for the company offices across the street.

Brownlow Bean knocked once on the oak-stained office door, opened it quickly without waiting for an invitation and locked it from the inside as he stepped over the threshold. He hurried across the room to the huge drafting desk and a surprised Marty Messer.

"Oh, hello, Brownlow! What's the occasion?"

"Marty, we've got problems. I was just at the Post Office and Sutt is pulling his hair out. The Whitakers have mailed letters to clans all over the country. Evidently, they're calling for a gathering. Even the out-clans are being asked to come. I saw them all."

"A gathering! The out-clans were called?"

"Yes, they called them all, and Marty, we're being asked to help, too!"

"You sure?"

"Yes, look at this!" Brownlow pulled an envelope from his coat pocket. "I had to take it, Marty. Sutt would have seen it for sure." He handed the letter to Messer and intently watched for his reaction.

Marty paused, studying the outside of the envelope, then read softly, almost in a hoarse whisper, *"The Beans and Messers up on Log Mountain, Kentucky,' the Beans and Messers up on..."* and as he realized the gravity of the letter, "Oh, boy! Oh, boy! What'll we do? Should we read it? We don't have a choice; we have to attend. It's a direct call for us both—all Beans and Messers."

"There are no options. We have to help them. It was an agreement written in the blood of our ancestors. We Melungeon clans are committed to help, just like we were committed to help Hobe when he asked us to lend a hand to the boys for building their rocket. This looks serious, though. I'm positive it's to do with what happened in court the other day."

"Yep, that's for sure. They might be calling for some kind of intervention."

"God, I hope not!"

"Yes, but, from what I heard about what went on, I wouldn't blame the Whitakers."

"Well, let me study on this awhile longer—whether we should open the letter or not. If we do, we can always send it to our cousins from the Welch Post Office. That way Sutt won't be involved."

"He's a good man, Brownlow, as good as any man in Coalwood. He's honest as a country preacher."

"True, he is." Bean paused, then tapped the desk several times, obviously frustrated. "Ahhh, heck, Marty," he slapped his palm against the desktop, "there's no use waiting. We don't have a choice. We've got to open it." Bean pulled his *Old Timer* from his knife pocket and ran its blade along the seal of the envelope. He unfolded the letter and read:

Out-bloods and In-bloods!!
Our blood is mixed. Mixed by ancestry and mixed by brotherhood, and mixed by history. Blood must follow blood. Blood must defend blood. We of your own blood call for you to defend your own blood. Gather now at The Clear Fork.
Ezekiel Whitaker

"Oh, my! Oh, my, Brownlow! All In-bloods and...and even Out-bloods! Oh, my! This hasn't happened since 1861. The Whitakers...they're calling for...you don't think—"

"—An all out show of force? Yes, that's exactly what I think. An all-out show of force!"

"Yes, but for who? Who do they want to send the message to?"

"I guess we'll know for sure pretty soon, but it's got to be the—"

"—It's the land, Brownlow. They're calling for the defense of Whitaker land. I'm certain of that!"

"Yes, and we've got to answer their call. The Whitakers and the Collinses have kept our families safe and secure and financed for years. The In-bloods know they paid for your education, and also mine. We owe them."

"Yes, but why is Whitaker land so important that we have to go to this—"

"—Shhhh!" Bean held his finger across his lips, suddenly seeing the cracked window. "Shhhh!" He whispered and quickly walked to it, glanced outside, saw nothing, and closed it.

Outside the raised window, Hub motioned with a quick wave of his hand for the boys to duck as Bean slammed down the window. With a nod of his head, the boys scurried back into the nook that lay perpendicular to the alley between the offices and Big Store.

Breathless, Muss sputtered, "See...see...I knew...I knew somethin' big was goin' on. I told you guys. Didn't I? What...did you hear all that Out-blood and In-blood stuff?"

"Yeah, and what kind of show of force are they talkin' about?"

"And... and, who are these people?"

"Okay, we don't know anythin' yet. Just keep everythin' we've heard secret," Hub whispered through a raised finger, "No talkin' about anythin,' except to ourselves." He noticed the younger boys fidgeting, big eyes eyeballing each other, "Understand, Choke Knot, and you Lurch?" He paused, accepting their grim nods. "Good, now you guys go on home, and don't breathe a word of any of this. None of it! We'll meet here tomorrow mornin,' same time. Bobby, you, Square Head, Pearman and Muss stay right here; we need to talk."

"Okay, Hub, what do you think is really goin' on?" Asked Square Head, knowing that Hub had shooed the younger boys away so they could speculate more freely.

"Well, guys, it looks like Pappy's callin' in all his markers. I think he's lookin' to start a war over his land. What I don't understand is just why the company wants it so bad. Why would Youngstown take him to court for a little mountain land? The coal companies own millions of acres. Why the big to-do over Pappy's ridge?"

"Yeah," Square threw in, "and Brownlow and Marty seemed to be sidin' with the Whitakers. Somethin' about 'no options,' and 'In-bloods and Out-bloods.' And what about the Whitakers and Collinses payin' for *their* schoolin' and keepin' *their* families secure?"

"And who the heck's the Collinses?"

"Yeah, there's a lot we gotta find out."

"I know what we can do, Hub!" Pearman bragged. "I know Elmer Clarence and his daughters pretty well, stayed at their house near Meadowview. Since he just showed up in Coalwood, I'll pretend to be surprised to see him and strike up a conversation, ask about his wife, Martha, and his daughters, Millie and Mollie; and see if anythin' can be learned."

"Good idea! But we need to talk to Hobe, too. And how about Rufus Edward? Anybody wanna talk to him?"

"Are you crazy?" Shouted Bobby, "Nobody's goina talk to him; he's too scary. There's somethin' weird about him, and—"

"—Okay, okay, we'll forget Rufus. We'll just talk to Hobe and Elmer Clarence. Bobby, why don't you talk to Hobe?

"Okay, I'll talk to Hobe, but just him; I'm never talkin' to Rufus Edward again, though."

"In the meantime, me and Muss 'll watch Brownlow and Marty. There's somethin' funny there. Think about it! They're the two big wigs for Olga Coal and they seemed to be sidin' with the Whitakers against Youngstown. That's strange and could be quite a mess. So, we gotta watch 'em closely. And as I much as I hate to say it, I think we gotta bring Jack and Norm into this"

"Have you lost it, Hub?" Bobby screeched, "We can't bring 'em into this, 'specially Jack. He's the boy who whipped our butts behind the Post Office that night—karate chopped us all!"

"You think I forgot about that? I'm the one who sat moanin' in pain for days afterward holdin' my seeds, while all you got was your little butt scared off. The fact is, we need Jack. He lives right here at Coalwood Main where the offices are; he has that Metropolitan for getting' 'round fast, and both him and Norm are sneaky just like us. Pretty smart, too. They can do the job, for sure!"

"Yeah, but—!"

"—But what?"

"Okay, I guess you're right, but I don't wanna be around 'em!"

"Let it slide, Bobby. What happened was a long time ago. But, you don't have to be around 'em, anyway. I'll talk with 'em. Besides, they're okay now."

"Sure, and me and Burrhead are the Everly Brothers, too!"

13

The Talking

Coalwood, WV—4th Friday of August 1963

Pearman **waited until** Elmer Clarence Whitaker crossed the small concrete bridge that led southeast from Coalwood Main and up the road toward Coalwood's lone service station. He revved his metallic blue motor scooter and pulled behind Elmer Clarence's old black two-door 1951 Ford, following him toward the station.

The filling station stood at the junction of Route 16 and Main Street. That's where he thought he would honk at Elmer Clarence, at the stop sign. Once Elmer Clarence saw him, he would tell him how surprised he was to see him in Coalwood, and strike up a conversation, asking at first about Martha and his two daughters. After their conversation warmed, he would cautiously embark on his hidden agenda, an attempt to find out all he could about what the Whitakers were up to.

It was a good plan, but nobody told Elmer Clarence. When Pearman honked the scooter's horn, Clarence didn't respond. In fact, he did just the opposite; he floored the accelerator and sped away, leaving the scooter in a wake of blue smoke and flying gravel.

Pearman hunched behind the Plexiglas windshield and twisted the handlebar accelerator to its maximum position. The scooter reared on its back wheel and lurched forward, speeding after the black Ford. He followed it through Substation and stayed behind it as it rolled into New Camp. The car sped over the dirt road between neat rows of silver painted houses once owned by Olga Coal. It crossed an old ball field and turned up a heavily rutted dirt road into Wolfpen Hollow. That's when Elmer Clarence stopped the car!

Elmer Clarence pushed open the car door and in a split second was standing beside the scooter, looking down accusingly at Pearman.

"Why did you follow me, boy?" He growled.

"I...I...I'm sorry. I'll go home right now!"

"You're not going anywhere until you tell me why you followed me." Elmer Clarence circled the scooter's handlebar with one of his giant Whitaker paws.

Pearman's eyes widened in fear as his mind reviewed in slow motion Elmer's big hairy hand wrapping the handlebar. He knew he was in for trouble.

"Let me go! Let me go home! I'll leave right now, Mr. Whitaker! I...I...didn't mean anythin'..."

Elmer Clarence despised it when people truckled to him. "Boy! Stand up for yourself! Don't be afraid to speak up for yourself. I have no patience with namby-pamby people who don't have the stomach to stick up for themselves. All I want to know is why you followed me. Tell me now!"

"Don't be mad now, Mr. Whitaker. Please don't—"

"—Just tell me, and stop your quivering!" Elmer Clarence's face glowed with anger, and he pointed his finger and roared, "I want it now, boy!"

"Okay, I'll tell you! I followed you 'cause us Misfits heard Sutt and Brownlow talkin' about all the letters you Whitakers mailed, and later we heard Brownlow read to Marty what you wrote. We thought maybe we could help you, since Whitakers helped us with our rockets, and you let Bobby and me stay at your house. We figured that I should be the one to contact you since I'd already met you and your family."

"Now, that's more like it, son. You should always stand up for yourself, especially when you haven't done anything wrong, and particularly if you think you're right. Never let other people run over you. My mother taught me that right off the bat. 'Nobidy's better than a Whitaker, but a Whitaker ain't no better than nobidy else,' she'd always say. In other words, fear no man and put fear in no man unless he's your enemy."

"Huh?"

"Now, when I tell you something, and ask your opinion, don't go along with me on everything I say. I want to hear what you think, what you really think. A man who surrounds himself with 'yes men' is a fool and he's doomed to eventual failure. Remember that, son. Now, if we can all be honest, maybe we can figure this thing out."

"Okay, I'm sorry, Mr. Whitaker. I guess I feel kind of uneasy, maybe threatened around you. You're such a big man. Look at your shadow. It covers the whole car!"

"Oh, don't let that worry you. You've heard of the gentle giant. Well, that's me. All I want to do right now is to concentrate on helping Pappy."

"But, how about Brownlow Bean and Marty Messer? They know."

"Don't worry your head about Brownlow and Marty. They'll understand and keep quiet, but don't you and the boys ever mention that those two know anything about what's in the letters. Understand?"

"Yes, sir, I'll make sure everybody gets the message, Mr. Whitaker! But I still don't understand why you came here, to Wolfpen Hollow?"

"I came here because this is where Garfield Whitaker, my father, was hurt in the Great Coalwood Flood. Remember, I told you about it?"

"Yes, somethin' about a mule fallin' fast against a submerged tree and pinnin' your father."

"That's right. He was hurt real bad, and eventually momma had to take him to Hootmocker Hospital. Well, he had a small tin with him that contained the bounty land warrant that Micager Whitaker received for his Revolutionary War service. He was going to have it recorded for his pappy, at Welch, but the flood took him just as he turned his mule to head for Indian Gap. Poor man was pinned against a sunken log. That's when I figure he must have dropped the box in the floodwaters, somewhere upstream of here. That's why I'm here, just trying to visualize what happened."

"But, if he dropped it, it would have been ruined by the water, and it was so long ago?"

"No, momma said it was wrapped in layers of oiled bearskin tied with greased burlap twine. In other words, it was waterproofed. She said he might have kept it in his saddlebag."

"So, you think that if it dropped out, it would've just floated downstream."

"Yes, but only God knows how far."

"But if it didn't fall out where would it be?"

"That's the big question. My daddy would have kept that with him at all costs. He would have died before giving it up. It was Whitaker land at stake, you know."

"Well, then," Pearman speculated, "shouldn't we figure that he did keep it with him, probably under his coat? It was a real small tin box, right?"

"Yes, momma said it was just a little thin thing."

"So, it must've gone with him, wherever they took him, maybe up to New York," Pearman theorized, rock serious, concentrating through squinting eyes.

"That might be so, son. We'll have to check things out with Horace Maynard. I...I...guess it is possible. I never heard anything about it, but it is possible. I'll send him a note first thing tomorrow morning. In the meantime, let's backtrack up the hollow just to get a better idea of what might have happened after the accident."

That evening, Pearman stood on the Big Store's loading dock. The boys referred to it as the Pavilion because in every sense it was an exhibition area, a stage for their nightly performances. There were shows that featured the newest jokes, the most recent revelations in town gossip, newfound expertise in *Shooting the Dozens*, and a range of other individual and collective ways to pass the time away. They loved the Pavilion because it was secluded, far enough away from the busy part of town to mute their wild laughing and hide their clowning around.

Figuring that he was in the catbird seat, Pearman began proudly reporting to the other boys about his day with Elmer Clarence. His eyes reflected a strange smugness, yet he was quite animated as he related his activities.

After Pearman finished, all eyes turned to Hub. He was the analytic one, the one who processed information more rapidly than the rest of them. "Hmmm, I think I got it. Garfield took the paper with him. It's got to be up in New York. And if Elmer Clarence sends the note to Horace Maynard then Pappy's land 'll be saved."

"Yeah, that's if they can find it," Pearman cut in.

"Well, if they don't the Whitakers and all those other people they've been contactin' will fight for sure. Things are goina get pretty nasty in Coalwood, soon too. All we can do now is wait. Keep close to Elmer Clarence. Soon as you hear somethin,' let us know."

"Okay."

"Wait a minute, Hub," Square Head almost yelled, "When we were digging niter in Bat Cave, didn't Hobe tell us that Micager lived in there for awhile after he moved from North Carolina?"

"Yeah, he did. So, what?"

Well, how do we know that Garfield really had the paper on him? It's just a story, you know. No one really knows for sure."

"Good point. We'll look in Bat Cave to make sure. The Whitakers seem to think it's the safest place around."

"Yeah, that's right. I heard Hobe say that, except for one, no man, white, black or red, had ever found either entrance to the cave, so why wouldn't they keep their most prized things hidden in it."

"You're right. Remember, we weren't supposed to go into one of the corridors?" Coob offered, now convinced that Bat Cave held the document.

"We'll ask Hobe to help us."

"Yeah, he'll level with us and help us for sure."

"Hootmocker" Hospital
Penn Yan, N.Y.

14

Hootmocker Hospital

Penn Yan, Yates County, New York—1963

Horace Maynard Whitaker wheeled his 1963 seafoam green Lincoln Continental onto East Main Street, finally stopping across the road from Number 246, the former address of Hootmocker Hospital.

From the curb he looked over the structure, feeling a certain familiarity with it. Being a very young boy at the time of his father's accident, he barely remembered his family coming to Penn Yan, let alone many specifics of the building. But there were certain things about it that were indelibly etched in his memory.

He remembered being fearful of the eight-light windows with the tall thin shutters that seemed to bode ill from the second floor. He remembered holding his mother's hand as they walked along the narrow sidewalk and up the three-step staircase that led to the front porch, and the clop of their shoes as they walked across the huge planked and columned veranda. He hadn't forgotten the massive wooden door, or the darkness and drabness of the front room, or the stench of alcohol, morphine and rotting flesh.

No, some things he would never forget. He shuddered, his soul revolting from the thought that his father had died in the upstairs room behind those very windows.

The hospital was a two-story frame building with finials and verge board, a good example of Gothic Revival architecture. It was painted a light yellow-green, almost jasmine, with white trim. It was Penn Yan's very first hospital, operated and owned by nurse Susannah Hootmocker. She had installed sanitary plumbing, a hot water heating system, and an acetylene gas plant. Doctors of the area used her hospital for over a decade, treating hundreds of patients.

The building had seven rooms for patients, one operating room and an office. In 1924, soon after Garfield Whitaker died, it closed its doors for good. A new hospital was built, and the building sold. Later, it passed through several hands until finally a fundamentalist religious group bought it to use as a meetinghouse.

Horace Maynard shoved the gear into park, turned the key, opened the door and briskly walked away from the car, closing the door with a flip of his hand, not looking back, his eyes fixed on the front door of the old hospital.

There was a shiny gold cross, fairly large, suspended from a single nail set about three quarters of the way up the door. Below the cross was written, "All Sinners Welcome," and "Most Sinners Forgiven." The clop of his stiff shoe leather against the oak planks of the floor of the porch sent his mind reeling with memories. He cast them aside, concentrating on the door. Raising his fist, he slammed his knuckles against the door, rapping steadily against its side frame.

When there was no answer, Horace Maynard nudged the door halfway open and slipped around it into a fairly large parlor. He could hear distinct yet muffled sounds coming from behind a center door. He cracked the door, and stepped softly inside, positioning himself behind the last row of packed pews. Everybody stood facing forward—no one had seen him enter. He tiptoed, straining to see the preacher.

"Not one of you is so worthy as to stand before the Lord. Fall down upon ye knees and do penance for ye sins." The preacher moved his hands down, directing the worshippers to their knees, and continued, "If penance be not the road ye take, then by the hand of God, boils will rise up on ye bodies and He shall let plague scar ye faces for all time. Repent ye sinners, repent! Repent and know ye Lord. Repent or ye shall know His power and His awful vengeance. Cast your eyes away from sin. Do it now! Do it now, and another unrepentant lost soul will take ye place at the devil's alter of fire and brimstone. Repent! Yes, yes, let us all repent! Rise up ye bodies and repent!"

"Amen brother, amen," chorused the congregation. "We repent, we repent in the presence of the Almighty!"

"I saw the dead, great and small, standing before the throne, and books were opened." The preacher answered with Revelation 20:12.

The choir, taking his cue, sang only a couple of words before the entire flock joined in:

When the trumpet of the Lord shall sound, and time shall be no more,
And the morning breaks, eternal, bright and fair;
When the saved of earth shall gather over on the other shore,
And when the roll is called up yonder, I'll be there

It was too much for Horace Maynard. His body swayed with the tune, and his spirit rose with happiness He loved that old song, and remembered the words well; those that James Black, a Sunday school teacher in Williamsport, Pennsylvania, wrote for his congregation in 1893.

The song was born when Black called the youth roll one day and Bessie, the daughter of a drunk, failed to answer. Disappointed, he commented, "Well, I trust when the roll is called up yonder, she'll be there." He tried to respond to his disappointment with an appropriate song, but could not find one in his songbook. His eyes filled with tears of regret and sorrow, and a strong inner voice asked, "Why don't you write one?" The voice persisted during his ride home. Unable to shake the thought, he entered the house and sat down at the piano. The lyrics and tune came effortlessly, and he changed not a word from his labor of love.

It was one of Horace Maynard's favorites. His momma taught him every word, and they sang it often as she played the piano. Spontaneously, unabashedly, from the back of the room he sang loudly, above the congregation's sweet refrain.

When the roll is called up yon-der,
When the roll is called up yon-der,
When the roll is called up yon-der,
When the roll is called up yonder I'll be there!"

On that bright and cloudless morning when the dead in Christ
shall rise,
And the glory of His resurrection share;
When His chosen ones shall gather to their home beyond the
skies,
And the roll is called up yonder, I'll be there.

Let us labor for the Master from the dawn till setting sun,
Let us talk of all His wondrous love and care;
Then when all of life is over, and our work on earth is done,
And the roll is called up yonder, I'll be there.

The congregation turned toward Horace Maynard answering his booming voice in kind. The preacher smiled widely, singing louder with every note, arms waving to the congregation and Horace Maynard to increase the tempo and volume—and they did.

When the roll is called up yon-der,
When the roll is called up yon-der,
When the roll is called up yon-der
When the roll is called up yonder, I'll be there.

Horace Maynard had enjoyed the singing and the preaching immensely, and even though he was a stranger, the entire congregation gathered around to welcome him to their church, and to thank him for participating so openly in their service. They offered cookies, ice cream and apple juice.

He accepted. Later, after much small talk, he followed the man that he now knew as Reverend Jack into a side room.

After the last stragglers closed the door behind them, heading home, he turned to Reverend Jack.

"Thanks so much for letting me share in this wonderful fellowship."

"The good Lord is responsible for all. We are only his servants."

"Yes, I'll say amen to that, Reverend."

"Tell me, son, why have you come to my church?"

"I came to ask for your help and seek your benison for my search."

"Blessed are the meek, my son. If the Lord is willing, I will do all I can to help you. What is it you need?"

"Well, let me start from the beginning," Horace Maynard retold the account of Cager and Micager, and Garfield's accident in the aftermath of the Great Coalwood Flood, and the family's subsequent removal to Penn Yan, how his father languished and finally died in Hootmocker Hospital, and how his mother removed to Stone Arabia, finally remarrying there. He finished with a summary of the court case, and the coming kindred gathering at Coalwood.

Fingertips touching, chin resting on two thumbs, Reverend Jack listened intently, giving no clues to his thoughts. He remained motionless, saying nothing for several moments, as if he were slowly and methodically processing all that Horace Maynard had told him. Then, in a low even voice he said, "We didn't move into the house until '48, after the war."

"1948?"

"Yes, 1948, but I remember some old boxes up in the attic. We looked at them, not closely though. They were old, so we took them over to the Yates County Archives."

"Think they're still there?"

"It's possible. But your paper might not be among them. Look, I know the lady who runs the Archives. She'll do a complete and thorough investigation. Would you like me to ask her to do a search?"

"Yes, please do. Maybe she'll let me help her?"

"Sure, I'll call her right now and fill her in."

Anne Albright extended a limp, pasty hand toward Horace Maynard, "Welcome to the Historical Society, Mr. Whitaker," she said almost automatically as she peered through thick dark-rimed glasses. A gold-colored chain held them in place. "Reverend Jack gave me all the details. Your family certainly has an interesting genealogy."

"Well, thank you, Mrs. Albright. We do have an unusual history, I guess."

"Yes, you do, lots of soldiers in the family. We see very few families that can trace their lines back as far as yours—especially military lines."

"To tell you the truth, we're all pretty proud of the 'Fighting Whitakers,' as we call them." Horace Maynard replied, half grinning, yet obviously proud.

"I must tell you, though, even with all you have given us, your search here is useless. Mrs. Reid and I," she slightly pointed her finger at an elderly woman who was busy filing some document in the "Grantor-Grantee" section of the back wall, "have worked here for over twenty years, and we do not know of any such paper. We have already discussed it at length and checked several files and found nothing. Mr. Whitaker, I'm sorry but the document you seek is not at the Yates County Historical Society, nor is it in any of our courthouse files. We checked there also."

"Are you sure, Mrs. Albright? I was positive that Garfield would have had it brought here."

"I know you're disappointed, but we do not have it here, and we have never had it. But, even so, there is one other possibility. You did say that after Garfield's death the family moved to Stone Arabia?"

"Yes, they did. You don't think that—?"

"—Yes, that's the only other possibility. It might be there. It's worth a try. Let me jot down the address and a person who might help you."

"Thanks."

Horace Maynard gestured to Mrs. Albright and Mrs. Reid, who peered at him, waving behind the huge latticed front window of the old red brick building. He turned the car north as he left the Historical Society's small parking lot. At Waterloo, he headed east. The drive to Fonda would take several hours. More than a few small towns with lots of traffic signals, a busy Syracuse, and narrow windy roads would make sure of that.

At Herkimer, he pulled the car into a parking spot at one of the crystal mines to recheck the note Mrs. Albright had written. "Let's see, I'll continue east along the Mohawk River on Route 5 until I get there. Simple," he muttered to himself, "and then on the right hand side of the road, a block or two over, will be the old Montgomery County Courthouse. 'You can't miss it,' she says."

It was easy to find. Mrs. Albright had given good directions, and as a result Horace Maynard, although a little tired, was relatively stress-free by the time he pulled into the back parking lot of the ornate multi-storied red brick building. A small sign on a door at the back corner of the building offered an invitation to visit the Montgomery County Department of History and Archives.

He stepped through the doorway, and entered a narrow hall that led him a short distance down the side of the building and into a small reception area. A visitors' sign-in log guarded the opening to the research area. The area was long, running almost the full length of the building, and was divided into three sections. Hundreds of books were lined up like soldiers around its walls, and every section of the built-in bookcases was amply marked. Several sizes of neatly placed research tables trimmed its middle. "This library is said to be one of the best stocked in the state, maybe the country," he thought as he signed in, his hopes rising.

"May I help you, sir?" A soft feminine voice interrupted his thoughts just as he finished writing his home address.

He looked up to see a thin woman with natural salt-and-pepper hair. She might have been past middle aged, but she carried herself in such a distinctively proper and self- assured manner that she appeared to be much younger than she actually was. Her cheeks boasted only a blush of powder, and her full wide lips revealed an unoffensive touch of cherry-red. Medium-length curled eyelashes floated above big, bright, concerned blue eyes. Her face radiated a pleasing soft glow and a certain calmness and kindness. He was at ease immediately. "This woman is at peace with herself, and she truly cares about people," Horace Maynard thought.

And he was right. Gail Jacobucci had accepted her maturity with grace, and her attitude toward aging appeared to have stopped and reversed the clock. It seemed the more she engrossed herself in history and the more she learned from the leavings of the old ones, the younger in mind and spirit she became. She was a mellow woman, and beautiful, indeed.

"Yes, I've come from Penn Yan to ask for your help. A lady at the Historical Society told me the document I'm looking for might be here. She gave me a person to contact, a Mrs. Jacobucci, the county historian."

"I'm Mrs. Jacobucci. Was it Anne Albright with whom you spoke?"

"Yes, Mrs. Albright was very helpful. We were not successful, though."

"She's one of the best, you know, but since you're here hopefully we can help. Let's go over to my desk and you can tell me exactly what you need. Mister...?"

"Whitaker. Horace Maynard Whitaker."

"We'll try, Mr. Whitaker, we can't guarantee—"

"—Yes, I am aware of that, but maybe, just maybe we'll find it."

15

Duty Calls

Answering the Call—1963

Roscoe Gibson of Harlan County, Kentucky noticed the return address of Coalwood, West Virginia on the envelope the mailman had just handed him. He tore it open, quickly pulled out the letter, unfolded it, and held it away from the sun. He read it slowly, shook his head, and walked briskly into his house.

"Roscoe, you're white as a ghost. Is there something wrong?"

"I've got to go, Kate. I've been called."

"Been called where, for what reason? You mean now?"

"Yes, right now. Our blood is in trouble. Pack me some jerky, dried apples and pumpkin, and lots of beans, cured ham and some applejack. I'll get the mule ready, and my rifle and ammunition."

"Why the gun? You haven't ever carried a gun!"

"Don't worry now, Katie. It's just to take a few rabbits and squirrels along the way," Roscoe lied.

Samuel Collins of Vardy, Tennessee, also had received a letter. He was a direct descendant of Vardimen Collins and he knew exactly why he had to go. There were no better friends than the Whitaker and Collins families. For generations they had fought together, worked together, prospered together, and done good things together. He pulled his shotgun from underneath his bed, kissed his wife, and headed out the door to join the Mullenses, Goinses, Wrights, Bolens and all the others, including other Collinses. He knew they would all form up at Dungannon, Virginia—it was their meeting place in times like this.

Collins nudged his mule to a measured amble, steadied himself in the saddle, and tied a red bandanna around his neck; it was the traditional way for the Kindred to identify one another. One hundred years earlier in the midst of the Civil War terrified outlanders and upland whites and blacks had seen the huge gatherings of men wearing red bandannas and had quickly tagged them "red necks." And later, during the great West Virginia coal wars, miners borrowed the tactic in order to identify themselves as union men.

Two Dagley brothers, Boots and Vernon, along with Langford Teague, Emmit Wilson and Herman Walden, Ridgemanites from Anderson and Campbell counties in Tennessee, clicked their mules to slow trots and headed into the almost dry bed of Lake Norris. It was the lowest its waters had ever been, exposing the old landmarks, and making ancient roads, trails and streams passable and highly visible.

The Dagleys' big red coon dog led the way, crossing Indian Creek at Hootmocker and continuing east along the ridge to Sharp's Graveyard, where they met other contingents from the area. They headed northeast toward the big band of the Clinch and its junction with Powell River. After a short respite at the old Cora Cooper farm, they waded through the Powell and moved full-force into the Clinch Valley.

That day scores of farmers, miners, mechanics, doctors, businessmen, teachers and bankers all up and down the Goshen, Powell, New and Clinch valleys mounted their horses, mules, cars and pickups and headed north, away from their homes and towns.

A day later, the Casalonys, Ciscos, De Greats, Manns and Van Dunks of the Jackson Whites of Morris and Passaic counties in New Jersey and Orange and Rockland counties in New York were on the move, heading southward.

On the same day the Moors and Nanticokes of Sussex and Cumberland counties of Delaware and New Jersey formed up with the Wesorts of southern Maryland, and headed west for a rendezvous with the Weremos of eastern Virginia.

All across the nation out-clans answered the call. From the Cherokees of Oklahoma to the Redbones, Houmas, Sabines and Cane River Mulattoes of Louisiana, to the Rivers of South Carolina, and the Lumbees of Baltimore, Maryland and Robeson County, North Carolina, to several Mongrel Virginian tribes, they formed into large groups and moved steadily away from their villages.

The Iroquois of upstate New York gathered at the Mohawk Castle near Canajoharie, and quickly began trekking in a southerly direction. Everywhere, there was a general movement of huge numbers of men and teenage boys, armed and well supplied.

Virginia state police stationed at Waynesboro were the first to report large numbers of armed men heading west. Soon after, offices in Roanoke and Buena Vista, and in Ashville and Boone, North Carolina, filed reports of men on mules traveling in both directions along Blue Ridge Parkway, forcing its closure. They seemed to be coming from western North Carolina, extreme East Tennessee and the high mountains framing the Shenandoah Valley.

Lines of communication were opened among state police headquarters in Maryland, Virginia, Pennsylvania, New York, New Jersey, Ohio, Kentucky and West Virginia.

Two days later, the extent of the migration was clear, and as their mysterious destination grew closer and the more times they linked up, the easier it was to determine their numbers, and their probable objective. Their directions of travel were plotted, their numbers counted. And because everyday their numbers increased and their firepower became more concentrated, their possible military strength had to be measured and continuously updated.

Besides, entire towns were now being overrun for short periods of time—they moved through them quickly and confidently. Some groups were dressed and armed like state militias of the Revolutionary War era. Several boasted drum and fife corps, and it was said that each group had elected its own leaders, and that each had its own chain of command.

Other groups were clad in camouflage fatigues, green berets, and carried modern semi-automatic weapons. They wore green and brown jungle boots, canteen and ammunition belts, and carried heavy backpacks. Their faces were masks of smeared paint, green, yellow and black. They marched with precision, and moved in unison with the barks of the non-commissioned officers in charge.

The larger groups followed the main roads. Three massive groups met at Claypool Hill in Virginia. One had come from the east, one from extreme eastern Kentucky, and one from southwestern Virginia and Upper East Tennessee. It was a huge mustering of men. People all along U.S. Route 460 watched in awe, gawking as the giant column of men trained through their little towns.

Bagpipes pierced the air as hundreds of men marched in silence to the beat of the drums. One column split up; one element turned at the Farmer's Market outside Tazwell, Virginia, and snaked along Route 16, over Stony Ridge and through Bishop, and crossed into McDowell County, West Virginia. They trudged through Squire, Newhall, Cucumber, War and Caretta. The other followed the Trail of the Lonesome Pine into Bluefield, picking up Route 52, continuing toward Welch.

Another group crossed Kentucky's big eastern mountains and moved across Tug River and through Williamson, West Virginia, and headed for Iaeger and Roderfield. They had come from Pikeville, Jenkins, Prestonsburg, London and points west.

A mixed group from eastern Ohio and Pennsylvania traveled down Route 19 through Summersville, Beckley, turning at Crab Orchard, snaking through Mullens and Pineville, and on through Welch.

Dozens of smaller groups moved through the mountains, but the one that caught the most attention—at least once they crossed the West Virginia border at Harpers Ferry—was the Jackson Whites of New York and New Jersey. They were driving Cadillacs and Lincoln Town Cars, vehicles that were oddities in a state of farmers and coal miners.

The columns moved on, not stopping day or night. Their goal now was clear to all. The leading ranks of one column, miles long, finally stopped on Premiere Mountain; its tail flanked Wilmore Dam at the junction of Clear Fork Creek and Tug River. The Roderfield side of Whitaker land was now cordoned off.

A few hours later, the column that had passed through Tazwell, War and Caretta crossed Coalwood Mountain and marched through Six, Main Street and Coalwood Main, through Middletown and Frog Level, and continued down Clear Fork Valley until it had reached Wilmore Dam. It extended for miles back through Frog Level and Middletown, a thick human barricade stretching along the Coalwood side of Whitaker land.

A third column filed through Welch, crossed the mountain on Route 16 and took up positions alongside Substation and New Camp rows. Its tail extended along Wolfpen Branch and back past Indian Gap.

Another group tracked along the mountains above Davy. It was robust in size, professional looking and apparently a well-armed company of elite black-bereted soldiers; it took up positions in and around Welch, and cordoned off the McDowell County Courthouse.

The Jackson Whites, who had sped south from the populated East, had arrived earlier. They bivouacked at the Coalwood filling station. Others, small groups arriving over mountain trails by mule train, some from as far away as Prattville, Alabama, filled in the ranks of the main units already positioned.

Up and down the roads of McDowell County, on the high ridges above the Tug and from the darkness of the narrow hollows of Davy and Bradshaw, mule skinners screeched and barked harsh orders at hundreds of stubborn mules, all seeming to howl their discordant brays at the same time—their disapproval and intransigence displayed to all. Yet, the muleteers kept them steadily advancing toward their objective—The Clear Fork.

The groups had come from all points of the compass, near and far, but mainly they had come from the lands along the Clinch and Powell rivers—*from Melungeon lands.*

160

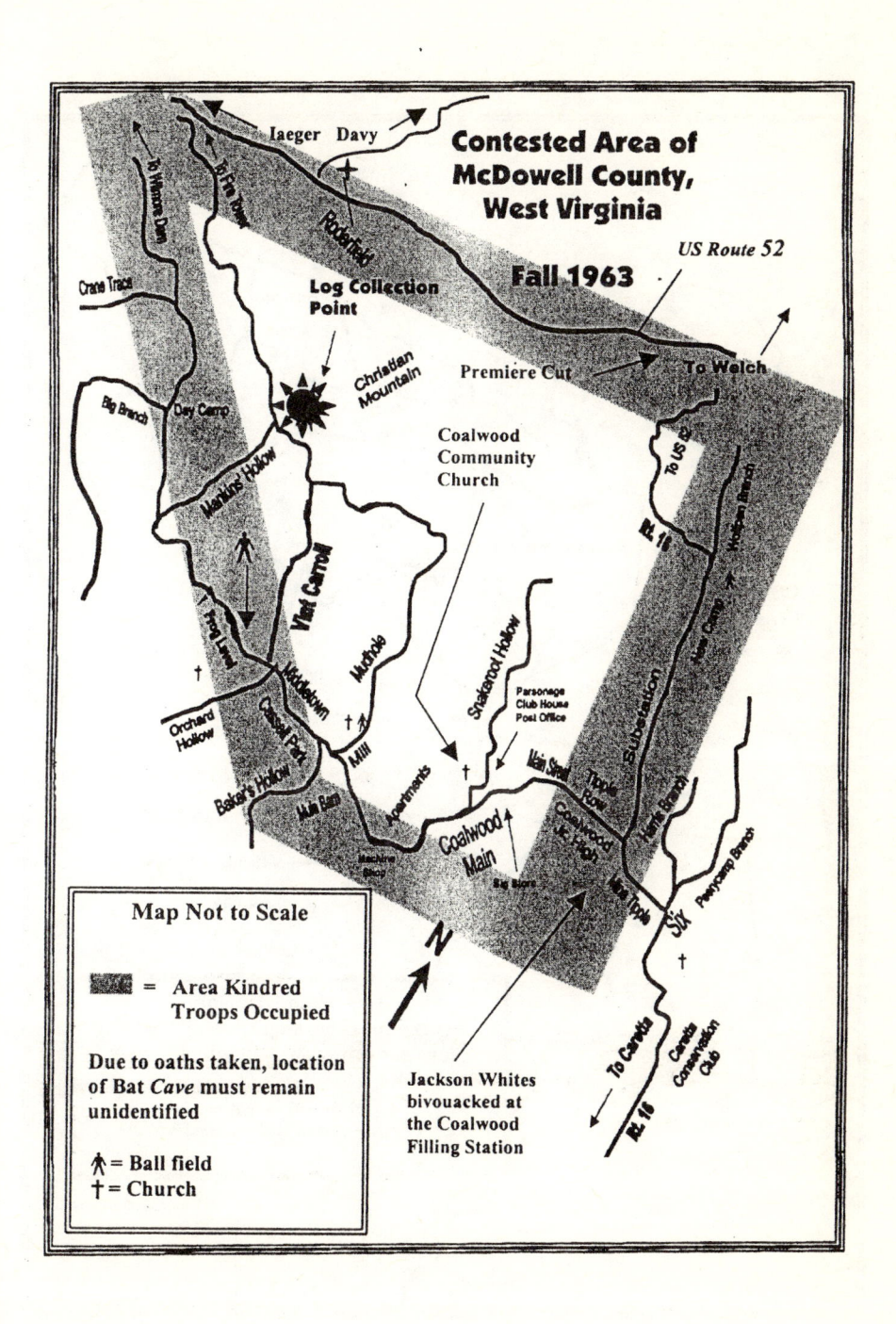

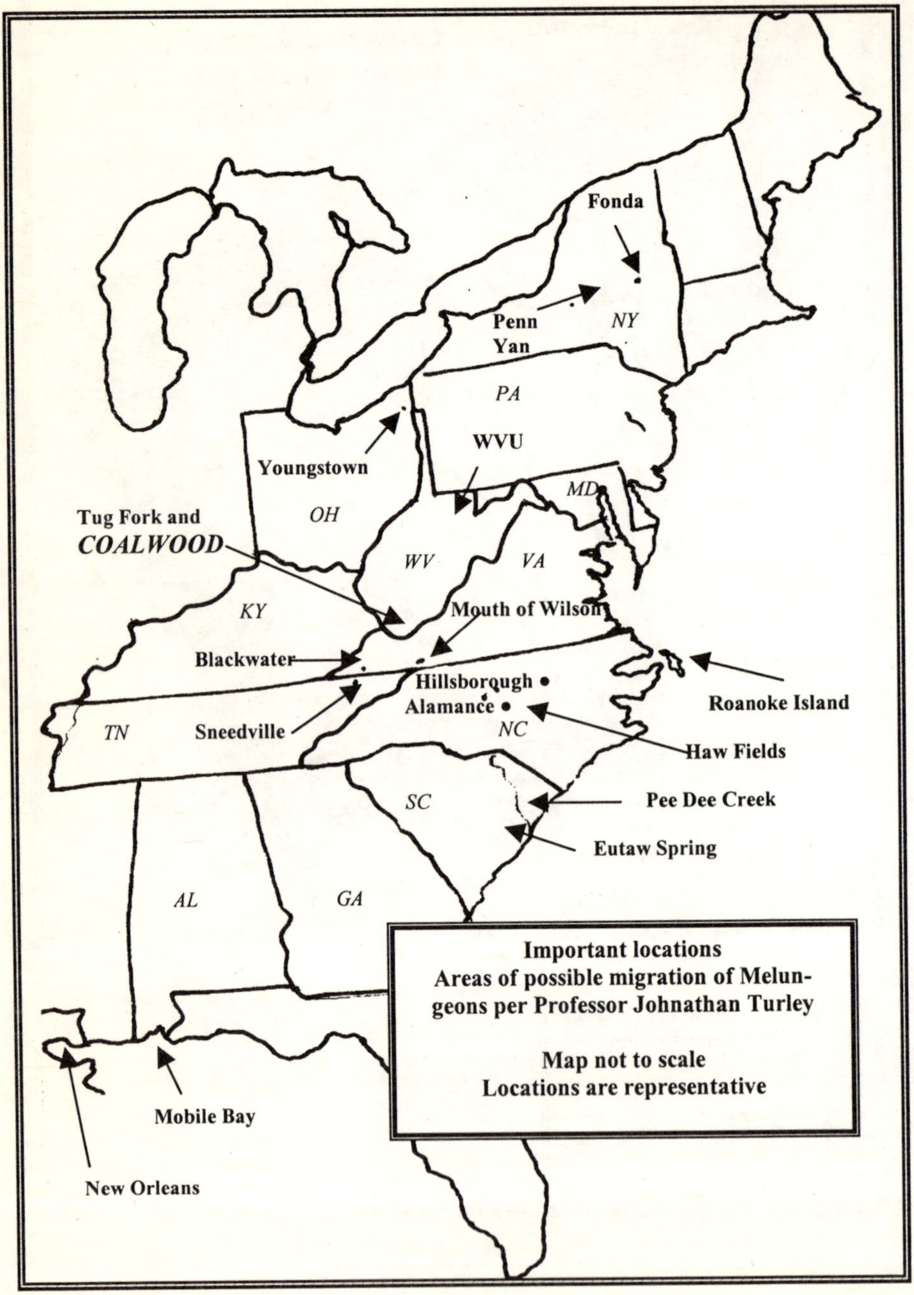
Fonda
Penn
Yan
NY
PA
WVU
Youngstown
MD
OH
Tug Fork and
COALWOOD
WV
VA
KY
Mouth of Wilson
Blackwater
Hillsborough
Alamance
Roanoke Island
TN
Sneedville
NC
Haw Fields
SC
Pee Dee Creek
Eutaw Spring
AL
GA
Important locations
Areas of possible migration of Melungeons per Professor Johnathan Turley
Map not to scale
Locations are representative
Mobile Bay
New Orleans

16

The Professor

J. Frank Hutson stood behind his polished mahogany desk as his administrative assistant led Dr. Jonathan Turley across a wide expanse of deep maroon carpet covering the executive office.

"Sit down, Sit down, Doctor! That will be all," Hutson motioned for his assistant to leave the room, then turned his attention again to Turley, "You have been told of the information we seek?"

"Yes, I have done much—"

"—Good, good, now what is it?"

"Well, let me begin by pointing—"

"—Hubert, get me an update from the Big Board!" Hutson yelled into the intercom to his assistant.

Agitated, Turley tried to continue, "First, you should know that—"

"—Hubert, do you have it yet?"

"No, sir," Hubert replied, his voice thin and anxious.

"Well, get it! Go ahead, Turley!"

"Let me, Mr. Hutson, first say that I don't particularly like it when you keep—"

"—Get to the meat of it, I don't have all day."

"Mr. Hutson, I am a professor of history at West Virginia University, not one of you lackeys. If you want me to help you, I will expect you not to interrupt me, and to treat me with some deference since *you* are of great need of information and I am the only one who can supply it."

"Of course, of course, please continue."

"I have spent my life studying mysterious clans, specifically North American tribes. I have traced almost all of them back to a time long before the very founding of our country. Many of the clans you have questions about are admixtures. That is, they are not pure bloods. Most are a mixture or a combination of three or more common races; those being of white, black and indigenous Indian blood. These mixtures are recent ones. For example, today, the Wesorts, Wermos, Jackson Whites and others are just that—recent admixtures of various races.

"The one group that is little noted in the U.S., and indeed the world in general, is the clan known as Melungeon. They are a bizarre people, kin to no one yet kin to everyone. Their history has never been proven, but many of my colleagues believe they are descendants of Portuguese-Moroccan explorers, Moors, Phoenicians, or Carthaginians. Some say they are descendants of Welsh explorers led by Madoc, who around 1170 A. D. landed with ten ships filled with colonists at what is now Mobile Bay. Supposedly, he left behind, with the Indians, the Welsh language. Other theories range from the educated guess to the ridiculous.

"Some lecturers even believe they are descendants of the offspring of Martians, who they say landed in the New World long before Lief Erickson and Christopher Columbus. As evidence, they point to old backcountry stories of Melungeons having strange looking eyes when they are agitated or in a defensive mode. They seem to 'dance,' it is said. Supposedly, at those times their eyes are large and brilliant and hypnotic, just like the eyes of little Martian people one might see in the movies."

"Bull crap! I don't believe anything those California space heads come up with."

"I didn't say they were from California."

"Well, chances are good they are. Smoking too much of that—"

Turley for the first time cut him off, "—Well, they may be partly right...about the eyes, that is."

That remark went flying over Hutson's head. "So, what else?"

"Another tradition has it that they were Portuguese pirates who survived a shipwreck off the South Carolina coast, and wandered up Pee Dee Creek. Hiding from Indians and soldiers of the Crown, they eventually fled into the safety and isolation of the high mountain ranges of Appalachia."

"Hubert, I said I want that report!" Hutson yelled into the intercom, looking up only after catching the motion of Jonathan Turley walking toward the door with a closed notebook under his arm.

"Oh, Mr. Turley, please!" Hutson extended his open hand, inviting Jonathan to sit down again. "I apologize. Please, please, I will not interrupt again."

"I will not waste more time here if you don't—".

"—You have my undivided attention. Please?"

"All right, last try though." Turley warned, and then walked briskly back and sat down. Momentarily, he stared at Hutson, cleared his throat and began, "Other historians claim that Melungeons are descendants of the survivors of the Lost Colony. It was established in the low country off the North Carolina coast— on Roanoke Island, back in 1587. The English-speaking colonists vanished, and to this day the fate of those one hundred or so settlers isn't known. The only clue was the word *CROATOAN*. It was carved into a log of a palisade, which the colonists had used to fortify their settlement. Croatoan was an Indian tribe that lived in the vicinity of the island.

"Many believe that a series of terrible storms forced the colonists and the Indians to flee from the island and the low country, and that they settled for a short time along Alamance Creek in what would become old Orange County, North Carolina. Eventually, due to an influx into the Piedmont of white settlers, mainly Germans and Scots-Irish, they moved north into the hills of Augusta, or now Lee and Scott counties in southwestern Virginia, and the area of land that is now the North Carolina counties of Ashe and Wilkes."

"Here's your report, Mr. Hutson," a pasty-white, bug-eyed Hubert rolled his head around the door, " The Dow is down three and a quarter, sir."

"Did I say to interrupt us? Get out! I'll call you when I'm ready. Please excuse him, Mr. Turley."

"Oh boy," Turley sighed as the door quietly closed behind Hubert. "All right, I'll continue." Jonathan cleared his throat, collected his thoughts, and began dryly, "A few Melungeon families returned to the Piedmont and settled in Tract Eleven. That was a tract of one hundred thousand acres granted to Henry McCulloh. In the mid 1700s, his son, Henry Eustace, sold the land at fire sale prices; many poor farmers and former indentured servants from Pennsylvania ended up there. They were mainly German and Scots-Irish who couldn't afford the exorbitant price of land in the Middle Colonies. Once settled, along with the English, they discriminated against the Melungeons, believing their dark skins and coal-black hair were due to Negro blood."

"Well, were they?"

"Oh, no, pure-bred Melungeons, and I emphasize pure-bred, meaning there has been no intermarriage with mixtures of blacks, whites or Indians that did not originally make up the bloodline; and although the name itself may connote a mixture, most have distinct characteristics—straight, raven-like hair, high cheek-bones, thin noses and smooth olive-color or coppery skin. Their color is consistent over every part of their bodies, even on their palms and feet bottoms. These characteristics are not indicative of the Negro race."

"I see, definitely not black people, maybe they're dirty, lying, cheating Gypsies? They seem to move around a lot, too."

"No, not at all. They are not a naturally peregrine people. Circumstances, that is, bigotry, intimidation and ignorance have historically forced them to move. Anyway, only two families actually stayed in central North Carolina for any length of time—almost forty years. Those were the Collins and Whitaker families. Most of the rest—Gibsons, Joneses, Messers, Goinses, Mullenses, Beans, and others—had moved on a year or so before the French and Indian War ended."

"Yes, yes, but what do *you* think, Doctor?"

"I believe Melungeons originally were a mixture of three groups—shipwrecked Portuguese pirates, English colonists and Croatoan Indians. It is likely they crossed paths in the Piedmont near the Great Alamance. They probably settled there for a few generations, along with a small number of very early German settlers, and they were still there when French trappers and explorers moved through. That's who named the German settlement *Allemans*."

"What do you mean by that?"

"The French even to this day call Germans *Allemands*, so the theory is the name stuck and through the decades the name was given an English sound and spelling, *Alamance*."

"So, the name has nothing to do with Melungeons?"

"No, nothing, although they were there long before the naming."

"So, why are you wasting my time with things that are irrelevant?"

"Not irrelevant in the least. You see, the first large migration of German and Scots-Irish settlers came down the Great Wagon Road from Pennsylvania, northeastern Virginia, and the Middle Colonies. Many came to join distant relatives already in the Piedmont. Others came strictly for cheap land. But whatever their reasons, the influx forced the Melungeons to move on.

"Another fact to note is that Melungeons to this very day speak some Old English; many say Elizabethan English. And they have a secret vocabulary and idiom peculiar only to them, an argot, so to speak. I believe it is because the English colonists from Roanoke Island far outnumbered the pirates who were probably illiterate, although some Portuguese phrases, along with Indian expressions, survived in the language.

"Melungeons are a strange group, very superstitious. That probably comes from their Indian blood, although vestiges of gullibility and irrationality of the European Dark Ages certainly would emerge from time to time. Some of these people still live two or three centuries behind the rest of the world."

"So, you're telling me this odd throng of intruders who have sealed off our mine and our town are all kindred groups who have come to help the Melungeon Whitakers—to fight us?"

"Yes, that is what I am telling you."

"But why? What possible reason would they have to protect the Whitakers? Why would they leave their homes and take such risks to help this Pappy man keep the land?"

"First, Mr. Hutson, these groups all share some common experiences. I'll use the Melungeons as examples, but the same could be said very generally about the others.

"Many people throughout our nation's history have been suspicious of them. Many Melungeons, as I have earlier related to you, have thin lips, high cheekbones, and copper-color skin; and it is said that pure lines have slightly curved, shovel-shaped upper front teeth. Although they are not exclusively white, black nor Indian, at times they were mistaken for blacks, and discriminated against.

"In fact, when there has been a rare—and I repeat rare—admixture of Melungeons with other groups, many cousins, brothers, sisters and close relatives have significant differences in shades of skin color and facial structure. Recognizing the differences, in the late Nineteenth and early Twentieth centuries many Appalachian cousins were identified as black or white. For example, two first cousins named Elijah, one showing Melungeon characteristics and the other German, might commonly be identified as "Black Lige" and "White Lige."

"So, what does that mean?"

"Well, it means that as generations came and went Melungeons were harder to identify, so people became more distrustful of them, fearing they would infiltrate white and black societies. As a result, the Melungeon myth became even more shrouded in mystery, and with each passing generation whites and blacks alike were more and more leery of the strange clans. And typically, Melungeons with ancient bloodlines grew even more reticent about themselves and their ancestors, which only added more fuel for the suspicious among us.

"Strange, indeed. Any other studies besides yours?"

"Yes, a couple of professors from a southwest Virginia college recently completed a study. The problem with it is they used people who *claimed* to be Melung—"

"—I thought you said the pure bloods wouldn't admit it?"

"Yes, that's the problem with their study; moreover they assumed that one could base conclusions on whatever the blood mixtures are at present. Their theories shed no new light about what the bloodlines might have been in the eighteenth and seventeenth centuries, or even previous to that."

"Just another bogus scam!" J. Frank angrily threw up his hands "Probably got a government grant for it. Thieving academic leeches, mindless bloodsucking eggheads. I'm tired of my tax money being—"

"—Another thing you should know is that Melungeons were never slaves," Jonathan continued, ignoring J. Frank's tirade, "and until the 1834 Tennessee Constitutional Convention they enjoyed all the rights of citizenship. But even so, they were described as being worse off than black slaves, because a Melungeon had to live in a community of white men with whom he had no importance, no kinship, and no equality.

"Newcomers to Tennessee, mostly Scots-Irish settlers, coveted the rich farmlands occupied by many Melungeon families. With typical chicanery, they passed a law which prohibited "free persons of color," meaning Melungeons, from voting or holding public office, and from bearing witness against a white man in court. This effectively left them legally helpless. In many instances, Melungeon land and homesteads were confiscated solely on the word of a white man—if he claimed the land as his own, their only recourse was to vacate the property or be forcibly ejected by officers of the law."

"Well, so what's the big deal about that? Seems to me that unproductive people should pay the price, especially those of questionable origins."

"Unproductive?" Turley asked rhetorically, realizing the ignorance of the man. He continued, "Many Melungeons fought with Washington during the French and Indian War, and again during the Revolutionary War, and they took their ill treatment hard, nursing their hatred of white interlopers. And once the Civil War began, most refused to join either the South or the North. Instead, bands of them roamed the highlands of Appalachia swooping down on white settlers, raiding, bushwhacking, looting, burning and killing. It was a time of sheer terror for the outlanders and upland whites—"

Jonathan paused momentarily after J. Frank's surly grunt of admission that he had heard the truth at last.

"—For generations, Appalachian backcountry children considered *Melungeon* synonymous with *bogeyman*. As they sat before crackling fires and listened to stories, young imaginations, magnified by dark hollows and shadowy mountains, associated the name with the heavy and brutal sounds of monsters and giants of Old World wonder tales. At night when strong winds shrieked and roared against secluded log cabins, whistling above wide-mouthed fireplaces, frightened children shrank under bed covers, expecting at any moment to be gobbled up by dragon-like Melungeons. And if a child did not mind, he was sometimes threatened with, 'I'll get the Melungeons to come for you if you don't straighten up and start minding!'

"As a result of their unfortunate circumstance, Melungeon descendants refused to speak of their heritage, hiding their blood links to their strange ancestors. Trying to distance themselves and their offspring, many claimed to be descendants of various Indian tribes.

"No one knows for certain where they originated or exactly who they are, but in 1887 Tennessee gave Melungeons a separate legal existence. The state officially recognized them as 'Croatian Indians,' lending weight to the theory that they are descendants of the Lost Colony, which disappeared from Roanoke Island, North Carolina.

"Some Melungeons settled in the Blackwater Valley of Virginia, far western North Carolina, southern West Virginia and eastern Kentucky, and even to this day, small close-knit settlements can be found in East Tennessee, such as on Newman's Ridge in Hancock County. Reunions of the mysterious clans have been held in Vardy Valley. Their main settlements are in the area around Sneedville, Tennessee, and although little known, there is also a robust settlement on Log Mountain in Kentucky."

Jonathan abruptly stopped. He had been reading from his notes and explaining as he read, but he had looked up to see J. Frank rolling his eyes, sighing deeply and rapping his fingers against the desk. "Am I boring you, Mr. Hutson?"

"To tell you the truth, you're just like those professors I had a BU. They were the most boring bunch of people I ever met. Had they given more interesting lectures, I would have made better grades—almost flunked out the way it was. The school should have replaced them all, *but they were tenured*, of course. They'll be boring brilliant students for generations, ruining them. I barely escaped."

"Well, I'm sorry to hear you had such a tough time at Boston U. Must have been hard on you knowing more than the professors."

"Brilliance endures, you know."

"I guess so. But, lets get back to this. I'll try not to bore you much longer. Do you understand the plight of these people—the cause of their behavior?

"Yeah, you're telling me these poor, poor Melungeons have been mistreated all these years. My heart aches for them. These poor illiterate half-breeds—"

"—No, Mr. Hutson, not half-breeds and not illiterates. Many Melungeons have college degrees and they have established themselves in every aspect of our socio-economic life—from teachers to bankers to engineers to corporate managers to attorneys. Few groups have done better. No, sir, they are not to be considered half-breeds. Now, that does not mean they were not originally a mixture of two or more ancient races. I believe this group until very recently had been one of the purest on earth, and that few people, even today, can claim blood as pure as theirs.

"Nonsense! Despite your opinion, I still believe they are weak half-breeds, troglodytes who at first sight of real trouble will run into the shadows to hide; and, by the way, my bloodlines are uncontaminated, straight from European royalty."

"Well, if you say so, but I must warn you that Melungeons and their kindred are known for fiercely and proudly defending the United States, and their own property. I hope you understand what I just said. They will not go easily."

"Okay, so what? So, let me get this straight. You're telling me that they along with their kindred have chosen to make a final stand on our Coalwood property. I just can't believe that! There must be more to this than what you've told me?"

"Yes, there is more, much more."

"Like what?" Hutson asked sharply, impatient for Turley to get on with it.

"Well, there is much speculation about their gold."

"Gold! What gold? These people can't have gold. They live up hollows and still ride mules and—"

"—Maybe so, but from the early 1770s it has been rumored that Melungeons were in possession of a cavern with huge deposits of ore and they on occasion minted their own gold coins.

"That's hogwash! Look how they live. Anyway, the West has all the gold, not the southeastern U.S."

"Not so, a German boy named Conrad Reed found a 17-pound nugget on Little Meadow Creek in North Carolina in 1799—it was the first authenticated gold find in the U.S. His family used it for a doorstop for three years—finally sold it for $3.50. Later, a mine was built and nuggets were found in the twenty- to thirty-pound range. Besides Meadow Creek, deposits of oligoclase or feldspar can be found in the Piedmont and in many areas of Appalachia—Floyd County, Virginia, for example. Thus, the extrusive dark grayish rock called andesite is present, and wherever it is there is usually quartz with traces of gold to be found.

"And by the way, Melungeon coins are said to have contained three times the gold of government-minted coins. Supposedly, whoever controls the gold has used it for generations for the betterment of those they call the In-bloods, and often the so-called Out-bloods have also benefited.

"For example, many of their children have been sent to colleges, the most talented to some of the best universities in the world. They have taken care of their poor, and anonymously contributed to many museums, hospitals and schools in their areas. Their gold has been used well and often for over two hundred years. They are reported to have secretly financed a significant part of the War of 1812. Nobody knows for sure who was behind it, but some believe it was Vardy Collins and Micager Whitaker through their sons Shoddy and Oxendine; and that Old Hickory, himself, personally thanked them. The mine has never been found—"

"—Balderdash! I guess they smelt silver, too, huh?"

Turley perturbed and disgusted at Hutson, who he now knew to be a self-absorbed idiot, paused and then replied, "Matter of fact, legend has it they fell in with a Frenchman who with the help of an old Shawnee had mapped the locations of several silver mines. They made their own silver jewelry and coins along Straight Creek, near Cumberland Ford. The Mullenses and Collinses were—"

"I've heard enough of these ridiculous rumors." Hutson, pushing himself up from the desk cut him off. "Get out of here, and when you have some facts come back. Then, and only then, will I pay you for your so-called expertise.

"Mr. Hutson, I think you should—"

"—Get out, you four-eyed, prissy little teacher. Go get a man's job before the rest of your hair turns white."

"Okay, have it your way." Biting his lip, Turley gathered up his research papers. He turned, and quietly left the office.

Hutson stormed after him and foamed, "You academics make me sick. I'll bet if I added up the real-life work experience of you and the whole staff at West Virginia University, I wouldn't get more than two months totally—and that would be from *your daddies'* stores! Collegiate feckless goof balls!"

He kicked the door closed just as Turley, red-faced, turned and glared disdainfully.

Johnathan Turley was still furious as he passed the Star City sign and headed for his office at West Virginia University. "I'll get that crude, miserable wretch," he thought.

All the way from Youngstown, he had planned his next move. He wasn't a vengeful man, but he couldn't stand men who placed themselves above all others. Those who conducted their affairs with a false sense of superiority because they just happened to be born into better circumstances than most. J. Frank Hutson was a conceited bigot. A man whose father had given him everything, his schooling, his money, his connections, his prestige, and yes, his position at Sheet and Tube.

On the other hand, Jonathan Turley had worked his way through school, cleaning tables and digging coal. He was a coal miner in his heart, and by heritage. His grandfather had died as a result of horrific explosions at Cross Mountain Mine Number One at Briceville, Tennessee. Eighty-four men and boys died there—the explosions continued for ten days. His own father had been hurt badly at the Yukon, West Virginia No. Two mine in 1924. The blasts rendered him completely helpless, requiring around-the-clock care until his death in 1927.

At the time of the Yukon tragedy, Jonathan had only begun his higher education, taking a few courses at Bluefield College. Immediately after the tragedy, he began to work fulltime at Bishop Coal Company, helping to support his mother and five siblings. At first, he picked impure coal, called bone, from small carts; later he carried timbers to the miners who shored up the roof. He learned quickly about the dangers of deep shaft mining, and the ruthlessness of coal companies.

Profit was their entire motive, nothing more and nothing less. While sitting in their posh offices of Youngstown, Chicago, Pittsburgh and New York City, they devised ways to rape and plunder the land and people of Appalachia, paying off politicians, threatening law enforcement officials, and taking every opportunity to oppress and manage the coal miners who they controlled through company scrip, houses, stores, constables, lawyers and low wages. The companies were cruel and heartless, and so were their local minions, whom they charged with keeping their mines profitable, making sure miners and their families lived and worked in lockstep with their company's mission.

He had seen and felt the oppression firsthand, and with righteous anger he had joined the union. He had attended every meeting and participated in every strike, and he was proud that he had played his part, however small, in making life better for miners as a whole.

Yes, he had seen the likes of J. Frank Hutson before, and he hated him and the whole lot of them—the fancy-suited, pampered coal executives who hardly ever ventured from their top-floor hotel suites and luxurious offices. Men who had no regard for or attachment to the common men who did their daily bidding in the grimy black holes of Appalachia.

Now, he would do whatever he could to throw up roadblocks to their quest for more and more money—their quest to rob the few remaining private individuals who still owned land in West Virginia. It would be a difficult and dangerous task, but he had made his commitment. He was determined to see it through.

"And I'll bring her in." He thought. "We can fight together, just like old times." He knew she would understand, and that she would try to do something to help. She would welcome the chance to do something good, something necessary.

After all, time and again she had talked about how her own grandfather had died in the 1924 Loomis Collieries explosion at Nanticoke, Pennsylvania. They each found it ironic that her grandfather and his father had been caught in explosions in the very same year. Back then she was bitter that her precious granddaddy had been lost because the coal company intentionally had not spent the money to properly ventilate the mine, even after repeated warnings.

All her college theses had been on the virtues of mine safety, and the long-term negative consequences of absentee land ownership and a vertical economic system. "That system," she'd say, "is, for example, when a steel company dealing in finished metals, not only owns the rolling plants, but the furnaces, the coal mines, the minerals, the timber and the land, and the towns, and the stores, and," she'd finish sarcastically, "by default the miners and their families."

She had it right, too. But she went further than that. "One should equate the parent company of a coal company with communism. They are both equally evil, and equally oppressive, a blight on the face of this great nation. The miners and their families are not slaves to the *State* as in Communist Russia, but they are slaves to the *Company*. There is no easily discernible difference."

She received top grades. The liberal, capitalists-hating professors at West Virginia, and later at Penn State, found great comfort in her submissions. She was a favorite of theirs—and of Jonathan's.

"After all that," he chuckled, "she changed her major to English, and just as quickly to law. She became a defense attorney for street people, barely subsisting for six years, a pittance away from homelessness herself."

He hadn't seen her for years. She had married well, into a prosperous investment-banking family. And since then she had enjoyed a life of comfort, having all things one could imagine. But he was willing to bet that she still would be the same zealous, idealistic person he had met years ago at the university. "Passion like hers doesn't disappear with time," he thought.

He pushed the intercom button and said softly, "Helen, I need you to place a call for me."

17

Marianne's Trip

Marianne stepped past her chauffer, thanking him for holding the door, and asking, "Charles, did you get all the directions?"

"Yes, Mrs. Bretz, I mapped out the route."

"Good!" She slipped into the plush leather backseat as he closed the door and quickly walked around the back of the car and slid under the steering wheel. The engine roared and they scooted away heading toward Route 422 and a quick ride through Youngstown to Route 7 South. At Steubenville the chauffer turned the long black limo east on Route 22—a route that led them to U.S. 19. Its twisting, tortuous path took them south to Beckley, West Virginia, where they picked up Route 16 and followed its steep curves and narrow undulating course into McDowell County.

At the base of Premiere Mountain, near Welch, the first signs of unusual activity became apparent. There was a checkpoint at the turnoff to Coalwood.

"Friend or Foe?" The guard challenged as Charles powered down the window.

"We are friends of Ezekiel Whitaker," Marianne shouted.

"Proceed to the next checkpoint." It was at Indian Gap. There, troops could be seen milling about, some checking their rifles, some marching along the narrow ridgeline in perfect formations, and some just seemed to be quietly talking. Charles stopped the car, and taking the cue from Marianne said, "We are friends of Ezekiel Whitaker." The sentry waved them on without comment.

Another checkpoint was at Coalwood's only filling station. A strange, yellow-skinned man leaning against a Cadillac hailed them, "Nice car there, man. Where ya takin' this fine machine?"

"We're here to see Ezekiel Whitaker."

"Okay." He paused, staring at the limo.

"Nice Caddy you got there. Love the color," Charles, now emboldened, replied.

"Yeah, I like it, too." The strange man proudly patted his Caddy's hood, and motioned them on.

Charles raised his window and proceeded down the road toward the main part of Coalwood, all the while chuckling to himself.

After crossing the small bridge over Clear Fork Creek and entering Coalwood Main, Marianne directed Charles to park at the side of the huge white Clubhouse, directly across from the community church. He did, easily backing the long black limousine diagonally against a sidewalk that lay in front of a waist-high, cut-stone retaining wall that guarded and held back a meticulously manicured lush green Clubhouse front yard.

She waited for him to open her door, and momentarily she stood in awe between the beauty of the gleaming white community church with it towering steeple and the grandeur of the massive Clubhouse. She took a deep breath, released it slowly, and then walked briskly up the stone steps and into the great room of the Clubhouse.

"You must be Mrs. Bretz," Gladys Cox, the unruffled Clubhouse manager, queried in a friendly tone. Although somewhat apprehensive that a director of Champion Sheet and Tube would stay in Coalwood, she managed a wide smile, hiding her nervousness.

"Please call me Marianne. Oh my, this is such a beautiful place. I'll bet you are very proud of your work here. Have you been here long?" Marianne said, immediately putting the manager at ease.

"Yes, I have worked here for many, many years, Mrs. Bretz...uh...Marianne!"

"Well, it is a grand hotel. Would you please take me around sometime?"

"Yes, of course, I will. I have your rooms ready, and if you and—"

"—Charles. His name is Charles, and he has worked with my family since the war. He is part of our family."

"Nice to meet you both. Please follow me," Mrs. Cox replied, and turned toward the stairway.

"Thank you so very much," Marianne closed the door gently as the manager walked quietly back to the great room. She turned the dead bolt, and then hurried to her bed to unlock her suitcase. On top was the large manila envelope from her old college classmate, Jonathan Turley. She had read it quickly before she decided to come to Coalwood, but now she would take her time, sifting every detail. She especially wanted to read again the separate note he had included about Marty Messer and Brownlow Bean.

Brownlow Bean and Marty Messer weren't quite sure why they had been summoned to the Clubhouse, or by whom. They were told only that a director of Champion had requested a meeting.

They walked side by side along the narrow lane that ran between the Big Store and Company offices, and stepped across the lone street of Coalwood Main. Charles walked a few paces ahead of them. After negotiating the stone steps, he turned and motioned for them to follow him along the side of the Clubhouse. Walking briskly, he crossed the road leading them to the back of the Post Office. At the concrete stairway that led to the old Scout Room, he waved an open palm inviting them to proceed without him down the steps.

Brownlow turned the knob, and carefully pushed the door open. He immediately recognized Marianne Bretz. He had seen her several times at meetings in their Youngstown headquarters, but had never had the chance to speak with her. J. Frank seemed to have always kept her away from any contact with seminar participants and company officials.

Marianne sat at a steel office desk in the front of the room. He could see a large manila folder, a small briefcase, and two stacks of papers placed neatly side-by-side on the desk. She held a map and seemed to be engrossed in its detail.

"Hello, Mrs. Bretz."

Her thoughts jolted away from the map, Marianne looked up smiling. "Well, it is so nice to see you, Brownlow; and you too, Marty. It is Marty, right?"

"Yes, Marty, Mrs. Bretz."

"Please call me Marianne. Would you like some coffee or tea?"

"No, thank you, I just had some coffee. Maybe, Marty would—?"

"—Oh, no, I'm already to my limit. Thanks, anyway."

"I asked you two to come over because I have some important things to discuss with you. First, let me say that nothing you say here will leave this room. I am only here to ensure that the Whitakers are treated fairly by the company, and to search for a way to bring this standoff to an end."

"Yes, I just heard that as a precaution Governor Singleton has called out the National Guard and they're beginning to mass along the Mercer and Wyoming County lines. It *has* gotten serious. That's for sure."

"Unpredictable is a better word. If those troops enter McDowell County, there could be a major confrontation. Only today, I heard reports of more men moving this way. This time from northern Alabama and Georgia." Messer offered, shaking his head. "It's a very volatile situation."

"And potentially greatly embarrassing for both of you, I'm afraid."

Marty's expression questioned Brownlow, whose face also reflected concern over Marianne's obviously calculated remark.

"I'm not sure I follow you."

"Oh, I'm sorry, I didn't want to confuse you. Here, read these papers from Dr. Jonathan Turley. He's a professor of history at West Virginia University. He is the foremost authority in the world on extant North American clans and their kindred. His greatest interest lies in the study of mysterious tribes that settled in the Appalachians."

Brownlow took the papers and sat down in one of the borrowed student desks that were arranged in neat rows in the Scout Room. Marty took a seat beside him. Brownlow read the papers quickly, passing each one to Marty as he finished it. Both men fidgeted, heads down; their faces glowed a soft scarlet as they read further into Turley's report.

Finally, Brownlow looked up at Marianne. "That's a very comprehensive report. I've never seen anything like it, or heard of the people he writes about. You, Marty?"

"No, it's all a mystery to me."

"Gentlemen, I have one other document prepared by Dr. Turley to show you."

Brownlow took the paper and scanned it quickly, and then handed it to Marty, who turned a light gray color, and sagged back into his chair.

"I didn't mean to embarrass you or threaten you in any way. I am simply asking you to help me. I just wanted to make sure you are aware of what I know, and you understand that your secret will not be revealed by me. I want you to bring Ezekiel Whitaker here so I can ask him about some things. Will you help me, Brownlow...Marty?"

"Yes, we'll ask Pappy to come, but we cannot guarantee that he will. He's rather independent. Also, due to the clandestine nature of our relationship with the Whitakers and our positions in the company, we'll have to come secretly and alone."

"Should I have Charles pick him up?"

"Oh, no, Pappy, if he comes, will arrive on mule back. He'll just appear with no warning. It's his way."

"I see. Eight o'clock tonight?"

"Okay."

18

Watching and Waiting

J**ack eased his red and white** Metropolitan into gear and followed the limousine that wore Ohio license plates. He maintained a safe distance, one that would not raise its occupants' suspicions. Norm rode shotgun, making sure that Jack kept exactly the right interval.

As far as they could see, there were only two people inside, a clearly visible chauffer and a shadow of a person in the backseat. It was the person in the backseat who interested Jack and Norm the most. That person was surely the one in charge.

They strained to get a clearer look, but the limo's rear windows were darkly tinted, making it difficult to catch a glimpse of the person in the back seat.

It wasn't until the limo backed into a parking space on the church side of the Clubhouse and the chauffer opened the rear door that they realized the person they were following was a woman. Stunned, they watched in silence as she walked smoothly into the Clubhouse.

Pushing his sunglasses up and over his brow, Jack asked, "What d'ya think of that, Norm?"

"Yeah, I saw her," Norm replied shifting upright in his seat. "She looked mighty important. By her clothes, she's got to be a rich widow. Never seen a married woman dressed like that before. I'll bet she's one of them highfaluting big city women. I think we'd better stay here and find out what's goin' on with 'em. Better park this thing on the other side of the Post Office. That way we can't miss 'em if either of 'em leave."

"Yeah, and they can't spot us from there," Jack offered, nudging his sunglasses back over his eyes, once again assuming his P. I. disguise.

Jack circled around the back of the Post Office and backed the Met toward Snakeroot Branch. From that position they could see directly through the windshield across the Post Office lawn to the Clubhouse. Norm fell back in his seat, head bobbing, eyes barely skimming above the Met's dash; and Jack, knowing that their stakeout might be long, gazed low between two spokes of the steering wheel.

It was just before 3pm when they saw Brownlow Bean and Marty Messer emerge quietly from the Company offices and walk across the road to the back of the Post Office. The same man, the limousine driver who they had seen lead the elderly woman into the Clubhouse, walked ahead of them. Once he reached the concrete steps that led down to the Scout Room, he motioned for them to proceed ahead of him. They disappeared down the stairs as he lingered outside.

They watched the limo driver for several minutes before they realized they weren't the only people watching him. From time to time, a blond crew-cut head peeked momentarily from behind the corner of the barbershop, and at other times a different head could be seen popping around it.

"Who the heck is that?" Jack mouthed while pulling against the steering wheel and drawing himself up straight."

"I see 'im, too! Heck, that looks like Hub's head."

"Yeah, that's him. How could anyone not know—?"

"—Hey, there's Muss, too. They're here watchin' Brownlow and Marty."

"Well, if they're goin' to know what's bein' said, we gotta get that limo driver outta the way."

"I got it, Jack. Let's drive by 'im, say somethin' about his limo, and head that way. Maybe make a little noise."

"Good idea." Jack turned the key, revved the engine, and spun toward the driver, who paced and smoked beside the Post Office.

"Hey, Mister," Norm yelled, arm and head hanging out the window, "that's a great limousine you've got parked over there. Mind if we take a spin?"

"Get out of here, punk, and don't get near that car."

"Oh, we didn't say anythin' about gettin' near it. We said we'd like to take it for a spin."

Jack depressed the accelerator, adding a little anxiety to the situation, and rounded the corner in front of the Post Office. He made sure the driver, who had now stepped to the front of the Post Office, realized that the Metropolitan was heading toward the parked limo.

With opportune wisecracks and erratic driving, Norm and Jack drew the driver farther and farther away from what was evidently a meeting between the elderly lady and Brownlow and Marty. As the distance increased, Hub and Muss filled the void, moving into positions at the room's air vents.

The driver walked to the limo, checked its outside for anything out of the ordinary, and then started back toward the far side of the Post Office. Jack and Norm reacted quickly; they scooted back just in time to wave off Hub and Muss only seconds before the driver once again took up his position. They left in a blur of arms and legs, heading toward the Big Store.

Hub and Muss waited at the loading dock of the store, knowing for sure that Jack and Norm would meet them there, and they did. Within minutes, Jack pulled the Metro around the back of the store. Norm flung open his door and asked excitedly, "Did you hear anythin'?"

"Yeah, plenty."

"Plenty? What's the scoop?"

"Well, maybe not plenty, we didn't have a lot of time. But we did hear 'em say that Pappy Whitaker is coming tonight."

"8pm. He's comin' at 8pm," Muss added smugly, straightening his long thin frame, happy to be such an important part of their spy network.

"Wonder why? Why would Pappy Whitaker be meetin' with Brownlow, Marty and this woman...uh—"

"—Her name is Bretz. Marianne Bretz. I heard 'em say it." Hub volunteered.

"Marianne Bretz?" Jack mumbled. "Hey, wait a minute, I've heard of her. She's got somethin' to do with Champion Sheet and Tube. Some bigwig or somethin'."

"Well, there ya go. That's why Brownlow and Marty walked back to the offices like two whipped puppies. Meetin' with the big cheese," Norm said with it all figured out. "We saw 'em leave after you guys left."

"Whatever it is, we gotta to be there. Maybe we can sneak in there before they come in. That way we won't miss anything.'"

"No way, that lady might still be in there. We didn't see her leave."

"Oh, she must have left. Why would she stay until 8pm? We'll check it out first, but I'm sure she's gone. Maybe one of us can hide behind the curtain that's over the wood cuts."

"Wood cuts?"

"Yeah, you know, the cuts of different trees that we use to learn their barks so we can identify them, and count the rings to figure out their ages."

"Oh, I just forgot for a moment," Jack answered sheepishly. He was never very interested in learning the differences between trees. In fact, he had trouble telling apart a beech from shagbark hickory, and spent little time in the Scout Room.

"Okay, Norm, you and Jack 'll have to do the honors tonight. Me and Muss are too tall for this job, plus you guys are pretty good at sneakin' around. Okay?"

"Our job? But what'll we use—"

"—No problem, no problem at all," Jack, pulling on his own huge earlobes, interrupted Norm, "We got all the spy tools we need, right here."

"Wa...wait a minute, Hub," Muss stuttered. He'd been listening intently, and at times shaking his head. "These guy...guys don't listen good, you...you know that. They got too much on their minds."

"That's for sure. Girls and all," Coob answered, almost sadly.

"We...we need someone who...who can sit there like a rock, stone si...si...silent, never movin' as much as a fin...finger or toe."

"You mean someone who has a knack for listenin' and breathes only when he has to?" Hub interrupted, now on Muss's wavelength.

"We need a boy who can place his body in a catatonic state, yet keep his mind and his listenin' ability alert—a boy who'll remember everythin'," Bobby spurted, grinning at the others.

All at once, everybody said, "We need Burrhead!"

"That's right! Burrhead is the best listener in Coalwood. He's like an elephant. He never forgets anything.' He'll soak up everythin.' He's perfect, guys," Hub beamed and gave the high sign to Muss.

"Yeah, everybody knows he's got a photographic memory," Norm threw in, relieved that he wouldn't be the one to do the listening.

"Burrhead it is. He'll do it. I'm sure. He loves the excitement that comes with spying."

"All right, Hub, you bring him by yourself. We'll all be here after the meetin'."

"Everybody stay away from Coalwood Main, at least until Burrhead has completed his mission, okay?

"Okay, we'll meet here around 10 o'clock."

"Okay."

As the clock ticked closer to eight, Marianne was increasingly sure that Pappy wouldn't show. She just had a feeling; moreover there was not a rustle outside, not the sound of a car or the beat of hooves. No, Pappy Whitaker was not coming. She knew it for sure when she turned to see a disappointed-looking Brownlow.

"Well, Brownlow, I guess this has been all for naught. Can't blame him, though. After all he's been through, I wouldn't trust anyone eith—"

A slight movement near the door interrupted her. Over Brownlow's left shoulder she thought she saw a human form. Her eyes strained to focus and when they did, her mouth dropped open. There, behind Brownlow in the shadow of the door, unmistakably stood Ezekiel Whitaker. He was dressed from head to toe entirely in black. A slouchy round-top hat hung over huge brilliant eyes and a sagging mustache and full beard. He had high cheekbones and a thin long nose, both tightly covered in a pleasant-looking copper-color skin. His right hand clutched a cowskin whip, and he lightly tapped it against his thigh.

"Pappy, it's good to see you."

"Happy to see ye, me cuzin Brownlow, and ye, Marty."

"I want you to meet someone who has come a long way to meet you, to help you in your fight against Champion."

"I already seed her. Bin watchin' her fer a long time; pacin' back and forth she be. She's a nervous little filly, but she's a purty thang fer shore. Youngin, too, can't be mor'n sixty-four or five yers ol'. Why, a youngin like that ain't used up at all. Thar's lots of life in her yet, and—"

"—I'm so glad to meet you, Mr. Whitaker," Marianne cut him off, walked toward him and extended her hand, not particularly pleased that her age was being discussed.

Pappy quickly grabbed his hat from his head, and gently took her hand. He held it momentarily, feeling her softness and gentleness. His eyes caught hers and they both felt each other's warmth and energy.

Pappy finally broke the silence between them, "You dun reminded me of Mammy, me good wife of forty yers."

"She must have been quite a woman. Forty years is a long time."

"Yep, she wuz, and we would've bin married longer but her pappy wouldn't let me see her 'cept on the front porch while he watched through the winder. Me courted that woman fer ten yers. Never once got out from under that man's suspicious eyes. Iffin he hadn't bin thrown and kilt by that big stubborn mule he owned I guess we'd still yet be courtin' on the front porch."

A tear formed at the edge of one of Pappy's eyes, "Poor, poor Mammy. She crossed over not too long ago. That woman could milk six cows, split the kindling fer the kitchen stove, and have brakefist fixed b'fore six in the mornin.' I git the foamin' mouth when me thinks 'bout that steamin' hot squirrel gravy, and 'em big fluffy *Martha White* brand biscuits and johnnycakes all filled wit blackberry jam. That wuz her favorite, ye know. Blackberries, she loved 'em. Boy, oh boy, that woman wuz sum gal.

"We buried her right thar at Whitaker Graveyard behind a big stand of blackberries 'neath a big ol' shagbark hickory at the mouth of Mankins Holler. That wuz soins she could smell 'em blackberries and watch 'em squirrels play. Me ol' heart surely misses me Mammy."

Marianne glanced down at the flicker of light that seemed to jump from his hand from time to time. "Why, Mr. Whitaker, I have never seen a wedding ring that big and beautiful."

"Well, when me and Mammy got hitched, we wonted the whole world to know how much love we shard. Hit's a big ol' rang all right. Had to make hit wider and bigger and lots more thicker. That way hit'll laist longer, b'cuz bein' pure gold hit wears away so quick-like. Me gots plenty more purty thangs. Lookie hyeh." Pappy pulled a necklace from his shirt. A huge silver pendant was attached. "Mammy gave me this'un—made hit herself. She had one of 'em Mullens boys to git hit over at Straight Crick, and then a Collins brung hit hyeh, soins she could make hit and s'prise me. Hit's so heavy that sometimes hit's a burden to carry 'round. But, me suffers through hit, and me never takes hit off, or this hyeh rang neither. Hit's fer Mammy, ye know."

"Mammy was a very lucky woman."

"Oh, gosh sakes now, Miss Mayrianne, don't know nothin' 'bout that," he answered, head hanging, blushing.

"Well, I think I'm right. Please sit down so we can go over some things, Mr. Whitaker."

Burrhead pulled the curtain back and positioned a large round cut of log on its end so he could sit comfortably. He checked it out, making sure his butt would be content for an extended period. The big cut of oak seemed perfect. Satisfied, he pulled the curtain closed and waited.

Marianne Bretz came into the room first; Brownlow and Marty followed a few minutes later. After the obligatory greetings, nothing was said. They all seemed to be anxious for Pappy to come. With nothing to do or say, the men fooled around the room, looking at, picking up and handling everything in sight: arrowheads, tomahawks, ant houses, stuffed squirrels, all kinds of knots, and *Boys' Life* magazines.

Once, Marty actually pulled back the curtain a little but looked away before fully opening it. His attention was caught by Marianne's sigh as she rustled the papers she had brought. Burrhead pulled the curtains together smoothly without making a sound. A sloth could not have moved slower and with as much care. All the while, he listened. He listened without moving, without breathing; in total rock silence he listened.

After what seemed to be a very long time, he heard Marianne say that all the waiting had been "for naught," that Pappy wasn't going to show up. At that very moment is when Burrhead felt a rush of cool air move through the room.

It scared him because he had not heard anybody open the door and enter the room, but someone obviously had. He shuddered, figuring that Pappy Whitaker must have just materialized in the room—out of nowhere, he had just appeared. Brownlow's greeting proved him right. Marianne and Marty paid their respects immediately afterward.

They made small talk, then for some reason Pappy started talking about Mammy Whitaker, how she could cook and what a wonderful wife she had been during all the years of their marriage. How he had buried her in Whitaker Graveyard, and how he had never taken off his huge gold wedding ban, nor had he ever removed a silver pendant she had made for him.

It seemed to Burrhead that Marianne was intensely interested in Pappy's gold jewelry. Maybe it struck her as odd that a man, especially one who on the face of it was very poor, would have such large pieces of jewelry. The question became for her, he supposed, "Where did it all come from?" She seemed to be on to something when she inexplicably switched the subject to Pappy's land.

Pappy was quite forthcoming with her, and there appeared to be a satisfaction and trust in their tones that surprised even themselves. Burrhead didn't even have to see them to know that they for some reason had a strange understanding of each other, that they were very comfortable talking, and that both showed great deference.

When Marianne asked about the Revolutionary Bounty Land Warrant, Pappy could only tell her what he had already related to the court. Garfield had it before he was injured, so he either dropped it during the Great Coalwood Flood, or he took it to New York with him. That's all me knows 'bout hit, 'cept—" he added hastily, "—that flood wuz a parful argument between worter and earth." She asked him if there were any other places it could be, or where maybe a copy might be hidden. He said he knew of none. "Even that thar Bat Cave won't give hit up. I bin tryin' to find the secrets of that cave fer yers, but ain't even come close. Me own pappy, Erasmus, wuz goina tell me, but he done died 'fore he did."

"So, you believe the paper might be found in New York?"

"Yep. Iffin hit ain't hyeh, hits got to be up in that way far away place they call New York."

"Okay, we'll have to see what Horace Maynard has found. He's already been contacted, right?"

"Yep, we done rotin him a big letter."

"Well, we'll just see what he's got, if anything."

"I wont ye to know that I ain't leavin' me land. Now, me Cager's bones rest thar whar they's 'posed to be, an they ain't a-leavin.' Me friends and kin will see to that, fer shore. We'll fight, ye'll see."

Marianne Bretz looked at Brownlow and Marty. They shook their heads, letting her know that they were satisfied with her questions. When she turned to say something to Pappy, he wasn't in the room. Not a word, not a sound and not a person followed him—he was gone as suddenly as he had appeared. Brownlow, Marty and Marianne left soon afterwards.

Burrhead waited awhile, then eased out from behind the curtain and quick-timed to the loading dock behind the Big Store. Hub, Jack, Norm, Pearman and the other misfits were waiting.

"*Well*," Hub began, impatient with Burrhead's labored breath, "Come on now, what did they say?"

"They didn't say anythin' worthwhile. Just that woman is goina help Pappy and that they are goina wait to see if Horace Maynard finds anythin' up in New York. Except I heard Pappy say that he's been lookin' for the secrets in Bat Cave ever since his father, Erasmus, died unexpectedly, and that he hasn't ever found anything."

"Soooo, Pappy believes the secret's in the cave."

"That's it for sure. Just like you and Coob thought—you're right, Hub" Pearman chirped. "Bat Cave's gotta hold the secrets."

"That's where we've got to look, for sure. Now we know, somethin' is in there somewhere. We'll all go. Hub, have you asked Hobe yet?" Jack offered, then asked.

"Yeah, Hobe agreed yesterday,"

19

Bought and Sold

Youngstown, Ohio and Charleston, West Virginia

Howard Mills had seen his kind before. The same smooth-talking cookie-cutter executives that seemed to hatch like crocs from the high priced universities of New England. They were spoiled, manipulative users—degreed brats who only differed by the measure of their ignorance, arrogance and self-importance. He hated their collective lust for money and power, and their intoxication with themselves.

They had degraded the entire coal industry; these conceited pencil pushers disguised as high and mighty corporate executives. Pinheads who knew less about the business than the lowliest bone-picker in the smallest dog mine of Appalachia. Their daddies had built their companies with pride and resourcefulness and knowledge and trial and error, but in the end by quirks of nature these brats had fallen into line to take over their fathers' enterprises.

It sickened Howard Mills to think what this one egotistical loser had done to the company, especially its people. He still remembered all the good things Henry Hutson, and for that matter old man Carter, had done: his way with people, his wise embracing of the local union and how he had taken great pride in the workers. His *family*, as he called them, were to be treated and paid fairly, given decent housing and recreation, and their children encouraged to become company men—homegrown mechanical and mining engineers from the best regional universities, their costs paid by Champion.

And now this slick-haired perfumed narcissist had taken the company to the brink of ruination. He had managed to infuriate Local 6026 with his edicts and mandates. The worst one was his decree that a miner's death in the company mine meant the forced removal of his family from company housing, all within two weeks of their loss—no compassion and no money for the widow, just the boot from Coalwood and Caretta. He reasoned that a widow and her children hanging on would just demoralize the other families, making them worry about the risks of continuing to work the mine.

Mills remembered that day. The day this snake shocked them all. Marianne was enraged—she kept asking J. Frank, "Are you serious? Are you serious?" Then, realizing that he was, she begged that a company truck and workers be supplied to help move the family, and that the widow be given a two-hundred dollar death benefit, so she could pay a few month's rent and provide for the needs of her family. She pointed out that *his* father had treated families who had lost fathers with respect and had kept them in the community and made sure their sons and daughters were given a good education, and that the widows wanted for nothing.

J. Frank shot back that he wasn't his father and that he would run the business the way he saw fit, that nobody deserved special treatment or rewards just for dying. But he did agree reluctantly to move the grieving family within a twenty-mile radius, but not to the death benefit, saying, "If we give them that they'll soon want more and it'll become an issue with the union. What I will do, though, is give them fifteen dollars worth of merchandise and food from the Big Store. That should keep them going for a week or two."

Mills looked across the room at J. Frank. "Yes," he spit out the thought, "There he is, the devil of Youngstown, lean, suntanned, healthy-looking, French cuffs, gold links, finest Italian shoes, white silk shirt and all. He's all icing and no cake; a painted shell of a man with no soul. Pitiful. He's a true testament to the deterioration of our universities and degeneration of American society. What would his father think?

"I must be just plain too old for this. Can't fight much longer—fifty years is too long to be in this business, and now to have to put up with this nincompoop. I remember, though. I remember when Henry and I first left Carroll County and headed for The Clear Fork. Young men, we were, full of fire and determination, and we found it. We found the coal and we built an empire based on honesty and trust, and now this—"

An apologetic Hubert broke Howard's daydreaming, "Mr. ...Mr. Hutson, Judge Lucas is here."

"Send him in," J. Frank shouted, not lowering the mouthpiece of the telephone.

A visibly perturbed Howard Mills strode hastily up the steps of the red colonial brick governor's mansion overlooking the Kanawha River at Charleston, West Virginia. Stepping under the white columned portico, he sharply greeted the lone security guard, "Mills, Sheet and Tube. Here to see Singleton. Tell him I'm waiting."

The guard hunched away from Mills and whispered something into his walkie-talkie, then answered, "Yes, sir, right away."

"Follow me, please, Mr. Mills."

Mills lingered momentarily to take in the gleam of the 293-foot high state capitol dome. He had always found it fascinating knowing that coal company money had carved out a place in the mountain wilderness to build the largest capitol dome in the nation. "Yes," he grimaced, "King Coal will be alive for many more decades in this god-forsaken state. The politicians have always owed big coal and they have always known where their power lies. But it's different than it used to be. At one time, there was some compassion and honor to it, but today, they just can't resist lining their pockets, I guess. These young punkish execs and politicos have replaced honor and consideration with greed and disrespect."

He had no sooner stepped across the threshold when he saw a bushy-haired, slightly graying, rather portly Governor Singleton enter the huge foyer, left hand adjusting his bifocals, right hand outstretched, smiling broadly.

"Howard, it's good to see you. How's the wife and family?"

Mills hated the obligatory greetings that always went with a politician's handshake. "They're fine, thank you. And Elizabeth?"

"Same, she's down at the Greenbrier. Some kind of women's get-together, she said. Let's go into the study." Singleton swung his arm, beckoning Mills into a room on the left side of the reception area.

"Have a seat, Howard." Singleton pointed to a comfortable-looking camel-color side chair that faced a huge colonial fireplace. Drink?"

"Walker Red on the rocks."

"Sounds good. Think I'll have one myself."

As Singleton mixed the drinks, Mills watched him contemptuously, all the while thinking what a weak person they had put into office. "J. Frank spent hundreds of thousands getting this creep elected," he thought. "Now, it's time for him to start the payback. J. Frank will demand complete loyalty."

"Here ya go! People say I'm the best whiskey mixer in the state. Had plenty of practice, that's for sure." Singleton laughed expecting a chuckle from Mills but all he got was a sour look between two gulps of scotch.

"Singleton, I'm here for J. Frank, for some reciprocity."

"What's that mean?"

"You know what it means. You owe him he says. Now, it's your turn to step up to the plate. The company needs some help."

"He wants me to help out with what Champion is trying to do in McDowell County, doesn't he?"

"That's right. You know the problem."

"We've followed them for days. The entire country is watching them gather. I've heard reports they represent every economic level, every occupation and every category of education and nearly every state. I hear they are well armed, well led and determined. 'Frightening,' I've heard some say."

"Yes, they've got company property surrounded and now I hear they've sealed off the county courthouse."

"I heard that. Got a report this morning that the locals are giving them food and drink, and they seem to be quite popular. There's been no violence, no problems that we have discerned."

"No problems?" Mills exploded in disbelief. "What's *your* problem? Think man! Of course, there's a problem. The problem is that if you don't do something to break this up, *you*, my friend, will be replaced—no more coal money for you. That's from J. Frank's own mouth."

"You threatening me? Don't!"

"No, not me, J. Frank. He says 'you're bought and sold.' You know the game. What've you done to help the company?"

Singleton gazed through squinted eyes, cleared his throat and replied, "I've called out the Guard, just in case there's violence. They've already massed along the border now."

"The Guard? That's fine, that's fine, but that's not going to help. Get a judge in there who understands the company position; a judge who'll work for the betterment of this pitiful state. Get a judge who will ensure that you have a second term. You understand what I'm saying?"

"I understand, but it's not that easy."

"Just do it. J. Frank expects you to do the right thing."

"Right thing?"

"Yeah, the right thing! You know, he wants Lucas on the case."

"Lucas, huh?" Singleton eked that out through a tight mouth. "I'll see what I can do."

Mills stood, took Singleton's limp hand, winked and coolly stuffed an envelope into the governor's side pocket, "J. Frank said to give this to you."

Singleton frowned releasing a long breath.

"Good, good, now that's the right attitude. J. Frank will like that."

"I'll bet he will."

"Of course, if you can't get Lucas, I'll bet ole Judge Ballard would love to have the job. Do the right thing, Governor. Do the right thing." Mills paused momentarily, just long enough to catch Singleton's puzzled eyes. "Do the right thing," he whispered with a grin, slightly nodded and strode from the room, not waiting for a reply.

Governor Singleton peered through the huge side window watching Mills step into a long black limousine and thinking that Mills had sounded unusually sarcastic throughout their whole conversation. He stared, perplexed, as the limo disappeared into Charleston's rush hour traffic.

Singleton sat down at a small desk, pulled the envelope from his coat pocket and counted out fifty one hundred dollar bills. An obviously hastily scribbled note read, "More after the ruling. J. Frank" He sighed, ashamed that he had let things go this far. Ashamed that he had been so ambitious, that he had gladly taken their campaign money, and now Hutson figured he was bought and sold. "Yes, bought and sold," he thought, "and weak, no better than a prostitute. He doesn't even take the time to write a decent note or hide his identity. He just *expects,* and he's *so confident* in his ability to corrupt."

He pushed his spectacles up on his forehead, chugged his drink, slammed the glass down and fell back into the chair. Head bowed, chin resting on tense thumbs, fingertips touching covering his nose, he rocked back and forth for several minutes.

"Do the right thing, huh? Bought and sold, huh?" He exhaled loudly, and then mumbled, "Well, I guess I can do one of two things."

Picking up the phone, he dialed a number and touched the receiver to his ear just in time to hear, "Ballard."

"Wendell, this is Singleton, I have something I'd like you to handle. Can you meet me...?"

20

The Discovery

Near the Head of Mankins Hollow

Bat Cave was situated slightly over the ridgeline from the old log collection point once used by Top Notch Timbering Company. A clump of dense laurel that stood at the back of a small mountain bench hid the cave. The bench had been formed from thousands of years of erosion, and it lay inconspicuously above a small ravine.

Once the dark green leaves of laurel were negotiated, one could see a gigantic black hole spreading between horizontal layers of rock. The cave was at the base of a primordial cliff that jutted like an odd nose from the face of the mountain wall.

Jack and Norm exhaled loudly, shuddering at the sight of the black abyss that filled the space inside the circular rim of Bat Cave. It was the first time they had been allowed to see the cave. It took their breaths, frightening them at first. Burrhead forged ahead, flashlight blazing, not scared at all by the mammoth hole of darkness before him.

It was a hard decision for the boys to make, remembering how Jack and Norm had wanted little to do with the misfits. Burrhead was easier to get along with, but he was not noted for any close association with the misfits. As a matter of fact, just the opposite was true. He was more closely allied with Jack, Norm and their elite friends. But Hub insisted that the three were needed, more eyes and more hands to search. "Besides," he said, "Jack has the car. If he's on our side, we'll be able to move about faster. Anyway, he's already involved, watchin' Brownlow and Marty."

They all agreed, and so did Hobe. But he insisted that Jack, Norm and Burrhead take the oath. They did, and after seeing the serious looks on their faces everyone was satisfied that the secret of the cave would be kept.

Once inside the cave, Hobe paused in the large cave-room to give instructions. "Okay, youngins, the rest of ye turn on ye lights. Now, I'm goina lead ye down this passageway over hyeh," he pointed his light to a small narrow opening that led away from the main room, "and we'll all spread out in a big long line. Look fer little openin's in the walls or anythang unusual, and iffin ye see somethin' whistle reel hawk-like."

The boys searched up and down the tenebrous passageway, crouching, kneeling, tiptoeing, and looking for any spot that might be a hiding place, or anything that might hide one. For hours they hunted with no luck, and then suddenly they heard it— the roaring *W-h-o-o-s-h* of returning bats. They had heard them many times before but were still unaccustomed to the strange, ear-piercing, high-pitched, hell-like echoes.

As the sounds grew louder, Norm, Jack and Burrhead stumbled into each other, fighting for positions against the cave wall, fingernails digging into its surface, their contorted bodies cringing from the ghastly, shadowy images careening past them. The endless river of bats flowed past them, assaulting their senses and their courage. Then just as it had begun, it ended in an eerie silence.

In the spray of flashlights, the three newcomers were a comical sight. Burrhead lay on his side plastered against the wall, head between two bent elbows, hands locked behind his head. Norm and Jack had each plunked down on their knees, and had burrowed against the wall. The other boys laughed and pointed at them, remembering how they had reacted when they had first experienced the torrent of bats. Embarrassed, the three quickly tried to regain their footing.

Burrhead, a stout boy of considerable flesh, finding support by which to drag himself up, clawed the side of a boulder that protruded from the cave wall. As he rose, his weight pulled against the rock and it suddenly rolled free.

"Look at that! Hobe, Hobe, you better come fast!" Norm yelled.

"I see it, too! Hobe can't hear us. I'll whistle," Jack answered excitedly, "Pssssst, psssst, psssst, pss—"

"—Oh, I'll do it," Burrhead, now standing, interrupted sarcastically, and immediately his shrill tone shattered the heavy cave air.

Down the passageway, lights could be seen skipping toward them. Obviously, every boy who had been searching places farther down the tunnel was now running at breakneck speed toward them. Hub was the first to arrive. He slid to a dusty stop, just as Hobe careened past him, lurching to see what the threesome had found.

"Whut, whut is hit?" Hobe asked.

"I found somethin' in the wall. Look at that!" Burrhead pointed to a narrow opening that the shoulder-high boulder had hidden.

"My, my, I thank ye dun found somethin' reel impor'nt. I thank ye dun found Micager's secret hidin' spot. I bin all over this cave and I ain't nev'r seed this b'fore. Lut me crawl in thar." Hobe bent his knees, turned sideways, placed one leg knee-first straight into the hole, dragging the other as he squeezed through. It was a ferret-looking maneuver, one that likely had been passed down from his cave-dwelling ancestors. He disappeared quickly into the slit, and just as suddenly darkness covered his dim light. Minutes passed, but no sounds from Hobe, no signals, no nothing.

Fidgeting about and becoming more frightened with every moment without hearing from Hobe, the boys' imaginations offered up explanations. "He's been attacked by a hibernating bear." "He's fallen into a hole and it's so deep we can't hear his screams." "As soon as he squeezed through, a big rock fell on his head." "Starving bats ate him in seconds, only his bones and spent flashlight are left."

Sheer panic had begun to grip and consume them all, when suddenly they heard Hobe's animated voice. "Youngins, we dun found out a secret. Yes, sirree, I think we dun found somethin', and that ain't all. We dun found the big secret of Bat Cave. We dun found hit fer shore. Pappy's goina be so happy, 'cuz we dun found hit. Poor Pappy, before his own pappy cud tell 'em the secret he wuz kilt. Now, poor Pappy'll know fer shore. Lut's go, boys! We gotta git to Welch courthouse, fast-like!"

The boys turned quickly, jabbering about "not much time," and stampeded toward the cave opening at Mankins Hollow.

"Hey, youngins! Wait up, turn your feet around, right now! We gotta skedaddle this-a-way. We gotta go out the other entrance.

"Whaaat? We can't—"

"—Y'all disremember? Hit's on the other end of this hyeh tunnel. Hit's on the Roderfield side and lots more closer to Welch. 'Member?"

"You told us not to go back—"

"—I told..." Hobe trailed off, then remembered that he had once told them there was grave danger in the dark tunnels of the cave. "I know, I know, I gotta tell y'all lots more 'bout hit, though. Lut's go now, right now, youngins!"

21

Judge Ballard's Court

Welch, West Virginia—1963

Most **public hearings at the** McDowell County Courthouse attracted little attention but for this one. Litigants for the plaintiff and friends of the defendant pushed their way into the courtroom. Within minutes, not one empty seat could be found, and stragglers from all over the county elbowed one another in animated attempts to find standing room along the walls.

Folks from every corner of Appalachia had come to see for themselves the strange little man who had brought thousands of men of kindred tribes from across the nation to McDowell County. Several beefy contingents of those men positioned themselves along the inner perimeter of the courthouse as if they had been assigned by some unknown commander to reconnoiter and report on the activities of the day.

Inside the courtroom Marianne Bretz, Jonathan Turley, Horace Maynard Whitaker and Gail Jacobucci huddled with Pappy around a small conference table on the defendant's side of the room.

A smiling, freshly groomed, impeccably dressed J. Frank Hutson joked with Champion's lead counsel on the other side. From time to time he gazed across the aisle at Marianne Bretz and mouthed something that obviously was not complimentary.

When Judge Ballard entered the room, there was a loud rattle of wooden chairs as everybody stood. Pappy removed his slouchy black hat and placed it over his bosom as he took to his feet quickly, stiffly standing before the man who embodied the spirit of the great people of McDowell. His defense team followed his lead.

Still sitting and talking loudly to his hired guns, J. Frank Hutson ignored the call "All rise."

Ballard's eye caught the scene, and he heard J. Frank's piercing, harsh voice. He sat down smoothly as the bailiff shouted, "Court is now in session. The honorable Wendell C. Ballard is presiding. Take your seats, please."

The courtroom grew unnaturally quiet as spectators settled into their chairs, and folks standing along the walls waited anxiously for the judge's first words.

The plaintiffs were still babbling on like hens before a feeding. J. Frank asked, "Where is Judge Lucas? Who is this Ballard fellow? Do we have him—?"

"—Plaintiffs approach the bench, please," Ballard commanded without a response.

"No, no, we don't know who he is. The defense must have requested a new judge, and they brought this one in."

"I said, 'Plaintiffs approach the bench.'" The judge bellowed behind a heavy gavel.

J. Frank's head cocked and he grew silent, now keenly aware of the judge's dissatisfaction. His team approached the bench.

"Gentlemen, don't you like being in my courtroom?"

"I'm sorry, Your Honor, but I'm not quite sure what you mean," answered J. Frank, preempting his counsel.

"I'll tell you what I mean. If I see you disrespecting this court again, I'll have you thrown into jail for contempt of court. From now on if the bailiff tells you to do something, even stand on your head, you'd better do it. You understand me, Mr. Hutson?"

"Yes, sir, I do."

"And how about this army of lawyers you brought with you?"

"Yes, they understand."

"Good! Now get back to your seats, and shut up."

Judge Ballard appeared to wait patiently until the plaintiffs took their seats, but his steel-gray eyes belied his outward composure. They told a different story; he obviously was upset with the whole bunch of them.

He began, his voice oily and smooth, "This hearing was called at the behest of the defendant. Case # 2034-21; Champion Sheet and Tube on behalf of the county of McDowell versus Ezekiel Whitaker, also known as Pappy; first heard 24 August 1963; Judge Lanceford Paul Lucas presided. Mr. Whitaker's legal representative, Marianne Bretz, wishes to present new evidence to the court."

"New evidence? No one told us of any new evidence. We object to these proceedings, Your Honor. We thought this hearing was set only to work out the particulars of Mr. Whitaker's removal. We request a continuance, so we can study the new evidence."

"Overruled."

"Then we request a recess, a postponement."

"Request denied. I have studied the new evidence and find it quite convincing, although I have not seen the actual document. We will not delay its presentation any longer. The defense may now proceed."

"Thank you, Your Honor." Marianne Bretz rose and moved to the center of the floor, "The defense offers this document to the court, but first, at your pleasure, I will relate some of its contents to the court."

"You may."

"This document was presented to Micager Whitaker, great-great-great grandfather of the defendant. Thomas Jefferson, President of the United States of America, signed it on December 4, 1803. The document was discovered at the Montgomery County Historical Society, at the Old Courthouse in Fonda, New York. It was found after many hours of searching by Gail Jacobucci, who is the county historian. If the court pleases, I would like her to relate the circumstances by which this document was found."

"I will allow it, although it is unusual."

"Do you swear to tell the whole truth, and nothing but the truth so help you God?"

"I do."

"Mrs. Jacobucci, please proceed."

"Your Honor, the court, many circumstances affected our search. First, in 1772 Tryon County, New York, was formed from Albany County. It was given its name in honor of William Tryon, former royal governor of North Carolina. While still governor of North Carolina, he led his troops into Orange County in 1771, and near the village of Alamance brutally defeated a ragtag group of poorly armed colonists styling themselves 'Regulators.'

"When the frightened and badly beaten settlers retreated into the woods, it is said that Tryon ordered his troops to set fires in the dense pine forest, sparking a terrible firestorm in which many young men and teenage boys perished. Many believe the battle at Alamance was the spark for the Revolutionary War, and not Lexington and Concord.

"As a result of Tryon's actions at Alamance, backcountry settlers and mountain people felt a revulsion and boiling hatred for him. He quickly arranged for his sister in London to finance his bid for another governorship. She did, and he left the colony quickly to become governor of New York."

"Your Honor! This has nothing to do with this case. Who cares about what happened in North Carolina and New York two hundred years ago, and—"

"—Mr. Hutson, sit down! I'll determine what's germane to this case. Please continue, Mrs. Jacobucci."

"Thank you. In 1784, at the end of the Revolution and due to anti-British sentiment, Tryon County was renamed Montgomery. Therefore, not knowing whether the paper had been filed by date of issue or date of presentation, we were not sure in which county it reposed. There was even the possibility that it had been transferred to the State repository at Albany. There was much confusion for several decades after the Revolution.

"The only information we had was that given by Horace Maynard Whitaker. He had only an oral history of the family, so we had to piece together why the document would have ended up in New York in the first place. After interviewing him, we learned about Garfield Whitaker's accident, his removal to New York and his subsequent death at Hootmocker Hospital, which was in another county—that being Yates. If Your Honor pleases, I will not get into great detail, as it is all explained in written documents already presented to the court?"

"That will be fine. Please proceed."

"Well, when we checked our log for *Whitaker*, we found nothing, although we searched for hours. It looked hopeless until Horace Maynard casually remarked that his mother married a Johnson. We guessed that her new husband might well be a descendant of William Johnson. Historians in our part of the country know very well the history of Sir William Johnson. He served as superintendent of Indian affairs for all of North America, and was knighted in 1755 by the king of England. He married a Mohawk Indian and his son, John Johnson, and brother-in-law, Joseph Brant, led the Iroquois League against the Americans during the Revolution."

"I object, Your Honor. What has this got to do with this case? Furthermore, I don't believe—"

"—Your Honor, Mrs. Jacobucci is simply laying the historical basis for her testimony." Marianne interrupted.

"Overruled. Proceed."

"Well, this was the same family that Garfield's widow married into, so evidently when she found the thin bear-greased tin and went to the courthouse to file it, the clerk, not looking inside the greasy tin, simply logged it in under her new name, *Johnson*. That's where it was, under *Johnson*, in the log. It read, 'one tin' and was dated 'July 8, 1927.' The tin had never been opened, and it was perfectly preserved. After inspecting it, we determined that it was the original tin—the tin that the document was first placed into, probably sometime during the very early 1800s. It is undeniably the original, authentic without question."

"Thank you, Mrs. Jacobucci."

"You may step down now."

"But, judge don't we get to ask any questions?"

"Not necessary. The court believes the document *is* the original. Continue the reading, Mrs. Bretz."

"Yes, Your Honor. First, though, may I ask your patience? We have set up an overhead projector, so the court and spectators, and also plaintiffs, may follow along. We will go line by line. Would you please allow us a short recess, say five minutes?

"You may, but neither you nor the plaintiffs may leave the courtroom. All spectators are to remain in place. No talking, whatsoever."

After a short delay Marianne began her presentation by reading the full contents of the document. Jonathan Turley pointed to each line, following her on the projector as she progressed through the document:

THOMAS JEFFERSON, President of the United States of America
To all to whom these presents shall come—**GREETINGS:**

KNOW YE, That in pursuance of the Act of Congress passed on the first day of June 1795 entitled "An act regulating the grants of Land appropriated for Military services and several acts supplementary thereto passed on the second day of March 1799, and on the eleventh day of February and first of March 1800, there is granted unto
Micager Whitaker, a Private in the late army of the United States; in special consideration of his exemplary Military Service at the Battle of Eutaw Springs along the Congaree in South Carolina, September 1781,
a certain tract of Land located in *Tazwell County in the State of Virginia that lies between the head of Peerycamp Branch, including Wolfpen Branch, and the junction of Clear Fork Creek and to the band of Tug River, encompassing all the Land from the first rise of the slopes on each side of the main mountain runs beyond Big Branch on the West and the head of Little Indian Geek on the East, contiguous to the mouths of several hollows or branches from Premiere Mountain to Shabbyroom herein above designated;* **surveyed and located in pursuance to the acts above recited: To HAVE and to HOLD the said described tract of land, with the appurtenances thereof unto the said** *Micager Whitaker and to his heirs and assigns forever subject to the restrictions, condi-*

tions and provisions contained in the said recited acts, except in the case of taxes: A waiver of All taxes has been granted by George Washington, first President and Father of the United States of America, to the said Micager Whitaker and his heirs and assigns FOREVER, including but not limited to taxes on land, whiskey, gunpowder, furs, timber, animals and all else that the said Micager Whitaker, his heirs and assigns might ever own, produce, make, barter, buy or sell in the United States of America and its territories, if any.

In WITNESS whereof, the said **Thomas Jefferson**, President of the United States of America, hath caused the seal of the United States to be hereunto affixed, and signed the same with his hand, at the City of Washington, the *fourth* day of December in the year of our LORD 1803; and of the Independence of the **United States of America**, the twenty *eighth*.
BY THE PRESIDENT   *Thos. Jefferson*
James Madison, Secretary of State

    Marianne read the document line by line, speaking clearly and pausing for the importance of each line to sink in. When she finished, the stone silence that had pervaded the courtroom continued. Only shallow breathing could be heard. Not a word was uttered for several seconds until J. Frank jumped to his feet. "Your Honor, if I may?"

    "You may speak, Mr. Hutson."

    "First of all, even if the document is authentic, and it will never be proven to me, the Whitakers have nothing. Their land is completely surrounded by Champion land. Their egress and ingress is over and through Champion property. They can't mine, timber, go to stores, to the Post Office, to the county seat, and, of course, to this Court House without crossing our land."

    J. Frank paused as the huge courtroom door screeched opened. He continued as he watched a man he knew to be Hobe Whitaker enter the courtroom. A group of grinning young teenage boys filed through the door behind him.

    "We will not allow the Whitakers or their friends any access whatsoever to places outside their property, nor will we allow their friends to cross our land. We will not sell them anything from our company stores, and we will ask our fellow coal companies to do the same. The Whitakers have nothing..... I say they have nothing. They are backward half-breeds that deserve what will surely come their way. We are not scared of them or their half-breed kin—we have our own security force that will deal with these Out-clans and In-bloods, or whatever they call them.

"In fact, they are on our land at this very moment. We will take all measures necessary to protect and defend company property. Let them just try to cross our land. We will levy huge tolls on their movements and even charge fees for their water if we choose. Ha! We are on perfectly legal grounds.

"Judge Ballard, we now ask you to issue a writ to prohibit any further encroachment on Champion land, and an order for the removal of all these half-breeds from our land. We also call for a writ to restrain them from violence against our property and our persons. You and the State are charged with the responsibility of ensuring our safety."

Judge Ballard hung his head, knowing that legally he could do nothing. "It is with deep regret that I lawfully must allow it. The writ will be—"

"—*Ye honor, ye honor!* We got somthin' to show the court, right hyeh! We got hit right hyeh," yelled a breathless Hobe from the back of the courtroom.

"You've got what *right here*?"

"We dun found somethin' in Bat Cave, right hyeh, ye honor. Can I give hit to me pappy?"

"*Bat Cave?* Judge Ballard repeated, pausing, looking perplexed, and then continued, "Yes, give it to him. Mrs. Bretz, see what he has."

Marianne Bretz took a greased buckskin pouch from a puzzled Pappy. She carefully loosened its ancient string to reveal a small scroll cushioned and protected by what appeared to be dry leaves from a papaw tree. She gingerly peeled away the leaves, and began reading the paper they had protected. Her expression turned from curiosity to bafflement, then a smile spread across her face. Jonathan Turley looked over her shoulder. He touched her arm and whispered excitedly, "It's real! It's real!"

She turned for more assurance, and he nodded, "It's real. It's okay. Do it."

Marianne beamed across the aisle at J. Frank, and then addressed Judge Ballard. "Your Honor we have new and profound evidence to enter. Evidence that has been verified as authentic by Doctor Turley, the nation's foremost expert on such things. May I approach the bench with the evidence."

"You may approach."

Marianne gingerly handed the old paper to Judge Ballard. He took a minute or two to read the document. Then he looked up; his face radiated pure simple delight. He began to read the document out loud:

Andrew Jackson
President of the United States of America

TO All TO WHOM THESE PRESENTS SHALL COME, GREETING:

KNOW YE, That in pursuance of the Acts of Congress appropriating and granting Land to the late Army of the United States, passed on and since the sixth day of May 1812, *Oxendine Whitaker*

having deposited in the General Land Office a Warrant in his favor number 26.2054 there is granted unto the said Oxendine Whitaker, son of Micager, and late a Private in Blackstone's Company in the Seventh Regiment of Infantry, a variance to the above-stated Acts. Granted is a certain tract of land outside the appropriated Tracts granted for Military Bounties. Said land lies in the State of Virginia and County of Tazwell and contains an unknown amount of land beginning on the south at a Blackjack at the mouth of John's Branch running Northwest along Dry Fork to Threefork Branch continuing to Buck's Fork thence to a double sycamore at the mouth of Johnnycake Hollow. Thence North in a straight line to a rock beside a white oak at the head of High Fork Branch, thence East passing the heads of the Twin Branches, Left Fork, Davy Branch, and thence South Southeast to Upper Shannon Branch, thence directly South to Sugarcamp and continuing to Split Fork, and thence in a straight line to the Beginning. Within this larger tract lies a Bounty Land Grant previously made to Micager Whitaker for his late Service in the War of Independence; this land being now part and parcel of this most recent larger grant. All waivers made by the original grant are to remain operative forever.

TO HAVE AND TO HOLD the above described land with the appurtenances thereof, unto the said Oxendine Whitaker and to his heirs and assigns forever.

IN TESTIMONY WHEREOF, I have caused these Letters to be made patent, and the Seal of the General Land-Office to be hereunto affixed. Given under my hand at the City of Washington this *twenty-seventh* day of *February* in the year of our Lord one thousand eight hundred and *thirty* and of the Independence of the United States of America the *fifty fourth*.

By the President
Andrew Jackson

Pappy stood quickly, proudly, face flushed, hat against his breast, body rigid. "Jedge, I knowed of me great grandpappy Oxendine—they called him Ox—he was at that big Battle of Nu Orleens. He wuz the youngin of all Micager's chillun. Yes, sirree, me pappy, Erasmus, and grandpappy, Nimrod, both told me he wuz thar wit Old Hick're. Fact wuz, he loved Old Hick're so much he swore he'd name his first-born youngin' *Andrew Jackson Whitaker*—and he did. Yes sirree, he did, and he called that youngin' *Jack*. She didn't like hit none neither. Poor girl grew up reel sour-like. Me pappy told me that she wuz shore 'nough a mean one—didn't like nobidy at all and..." Pappy trailed off to a low mumble.

Dropping his eyes and shaking his head, he sighed loudly, then continued, "Well, anyhow, me great forebear, Ox, wuz a big hero, but I jest didn't know how big. Ye know, Jedge, air fam'le hepped win that war fer Old Hick're, and now me and me kin are goina hep out the good people of Coalwood and all of Mack Dal Coun'e. We goina keep the men a-workin' in them coal mines, and all the women-folk 'll be at home a-cookin', a-cleanin' and a-raisin' 'em youngins. We goina make life reel good fer all the people. And...and iffin they wont, we goina send 'em misfit boys to college fer a-heppin' and a-believin' in Whitaker werd. And we goina move this hyeh coun'e cap'tol from this hyeh Welch back to Peeryville, back to whar hit was stole from me cuzins' town. Yes, sirree, we goina make that poor town right agin and—"

"—Yes, yes, Mr. Whitaker, but we aren't finished yet," the Judge, exasperated, motioned with his hand for Pappy to sit down.

"Okay, Jedge, I'll hold me horses, but I know all that land ye're talkin' 'bout. I know hit reel good."

"Mr. Hutson...bailiff, hand me a county map and a pencil."

"This one, Your Honor?"

"Yes, yes, that's it, right there."

The bailiff reached the map to the judge, and quietly returned to his corner of the courtroom.

"Thank you. Let's see now, from John's Branch to Dry Fork, over to Johnnycake, and then to..." The judge's voice trailed off leaving only a name here and there to be heard as he scratched the points on the map, "Davy... Shannon Branch... and then back to the beginning. Yes, that's it.

"Sheriff Christian, would you check this to make sure I'm right. I hear you're known as the Walking Man, and that you know this country better than any man alive."

Greenwalt Christian took the document and map, and inspected them thoroughly. "Yes sir, Judge Ballard," the sheriff offered, handing the map back. He turned toward the spectators, opened his arms, and began, "I've walked every foot of that land. I know every dog, cat, bull, mule, wild animal, man and woman, and I've kissed every sorghumlipped child in these ancient mountains. I know every family personally and I know what the people of this county need. I was born and raised a mountain man and I understand mountain people, and I know about what kind of man you need in off—"

"—*Pleeeease*, Sheriff, we're not running for office here. Just tell me if my conclusions are correct, *pleeeease*."

"You're right, Judge Ballard, exactly right."

"Now, hand this paper to Doctor Turley, and sit down."

The judge's eyes smiled above gold-rimmed bifocals at Marianne and Pappy, and then he turned his gaze to the plaintiffs. "Mr. Hutson, if I am not mistaken," he sneered, "this document, which appears authentic in all respects, states clearly that most of

McDowell County by way of a Bounty Land Grant from Old Hickory, himself, is owned by the Whitakers. Is that how you see the paper and the map, Doctor Turley?" The judge turned for a nod from a glowing Jonathan.

"So, It appears that you and your company and all your cronies are on Whitaker land. I hope you understand the gravity of what I am saying. You are trespassing on the property of Pappy Whitaker. If your company desires to continue to operate its businesses you must come to terms with Mr. Whitaker."

"I object," J. Frank squealed.

"There's nothing to object to. Overruled."

"Exception," yelled the chief counsel.

"Noted, but irrelevant."

"But judge, please..." J. Frank pleaded, voice trailing off, suddenly coming to terms with his new circumstance.

"Case is dismissed. Any motions entered by the plaintiffs, past, present or future, are hereby denied. Justice has now been served."

The courtroom erupted in laughter, as J. Frank and his team of slick northern lawyers scooted from the courtroom, jumped into their limousines and sped off toward U. S. Route 52.

213

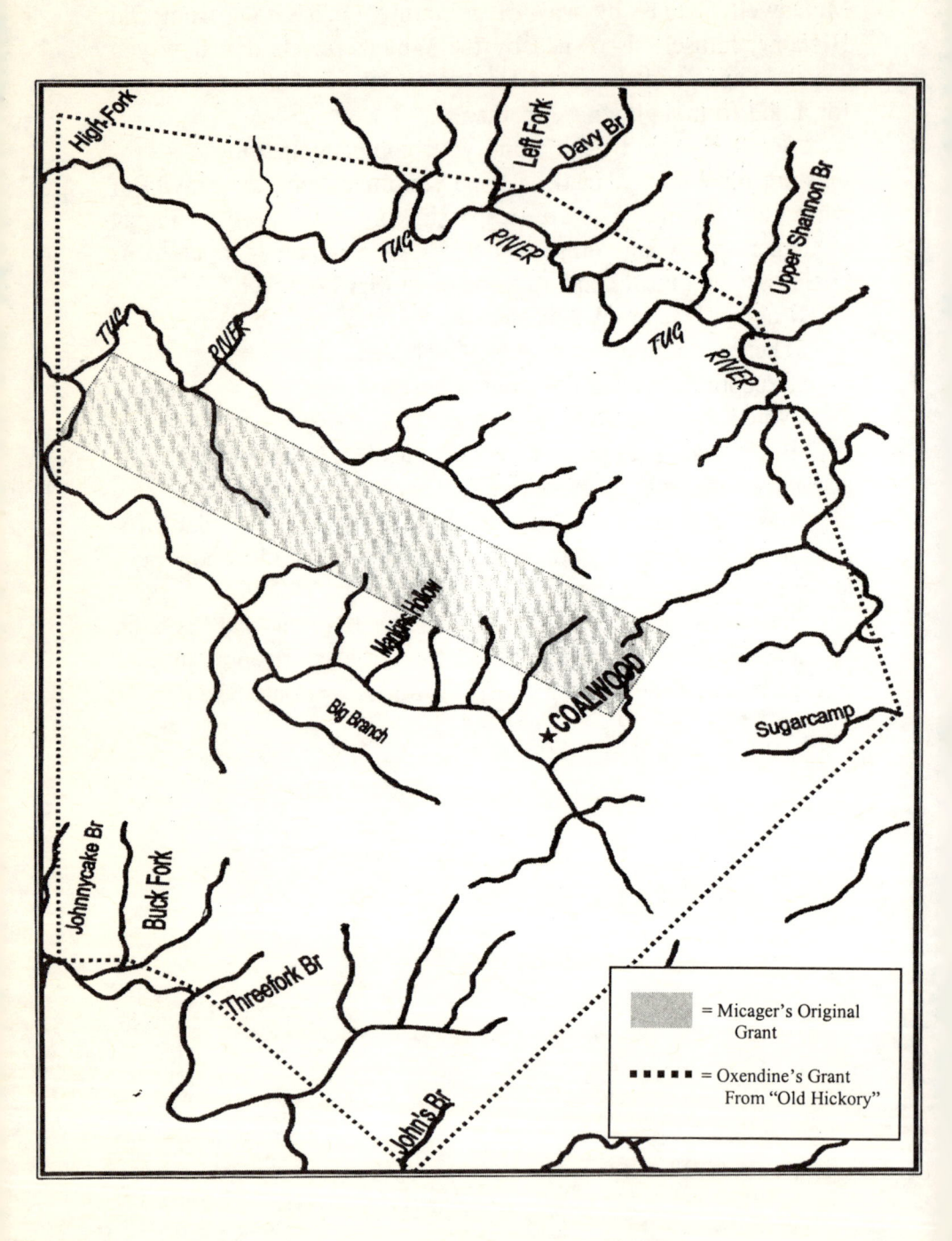

22

The Reckoning

Youngstown, Ohio—Late 1964

The man in black prepared to address his board of directors. He signaled to one of his cronies to close the lone mahogany raised-paneled door and dim the lights in the windowless room. He flipped a switch to a backlit map that abruptly illuminated the entire forward wall of the room. He could hear huffs and gasps of surprise from the eight men and one woman who comprised the board.

"Hit's shore funny," he thought, "a two-mule-high map that covers almost the entahr wall, ever detail crisp and clher agin the backlight!" He grinned openly in the darkness of the room's corner. "Jest wait 'til they hear whut me goina say," he mumbled to himself. He drew the metal pointer from the side of his boot, extended it to its full six-foot length, and clomped to the edge of the map. He began smoothly and confidently rolling every word in heavy mountain brogue that some would say sounded much like broken Elizabethan English:

"Mornin', boys." He chuckled to himself, knowing that line would catch the attention of the one female board member—to make her a little more perky. "We ain't got no time to waste, so I'll git right to the point. The land sets along this hyeh nair ridgeline," he tapped the pointer's end twice against one end of the ridge, and moved it slowly along the run of the mountain, "Startin' on the bank of Wolfpen Branch...hyeh...hit passes by Snakeroot and Mudhole hollers, Vint Carroll, and Mankins hollers, and runs on down to Daycamp, Meathouse, Abbcamp and

Copperhead Junction; din hit follers this ridgeline in the same gen'ral dierection all the way...to hyeh...right hyeh to the junction of Clher Fork and Tug River.

"Now, youngins, we dun found the richest coal seam ever found in North America. Hit's on the edge of the Pokeyhuntis....and thar's more me boys.

"Ye see, best we can figger, thar wuz a bunch of reel hot rock that hid two or three miles under that mountain. Well, hit made that boiling', scorchin' watery stuff go up through a fault. Yes, sir, a big long crack in 'em mountains. 'em highfalutin educated men figger hit starts and stops right hyeh at The Clher Fork."

The man in black paused and smiled widely, head tilted, big bright eyes beaming over flared nostrils and a wide smile. "But *sumbidy* sed hit *might* foller that ol' map that Micager and Vardy done drawed up yers ago—ye know, that'un Hobe and 'em misfit boys found in the cave.

"Yes sirree, that big crack *might* go on down through the Cumberlands an' hit *might* take a turn up to whar 'em Mullens boys live down on Straight Crick...an' hit *might* go along that big Pine Mountain...an'...an' din hit *might* run on over to Cleghorn an' Meadow cricks in ol' Carolina."

"Hit...hit's a *mighty* long fault line fer shore." Somebody blurted out between chuckles.

"Fer shore hit is, youngin. But, me gots lots more to say. Ye see, after a spell that hot watery stuff an' hit's pressure set down a whole bunch of minerals, includin' gold and silver. Yes, sirree, gold and silver, hit did! An' as hit did, that same pressure pushed this hyeh big, big, rich coal seam right up close-like to the top of the ridge."

"But, iffin the seam's that big and rich, why ain't operations done happened?" Asked a board member, face shrouded in darkness.

"And thar's the rub, me good boy. Ye see, Olgey Coal and Chaimpyun don't own the property!"

"Whut'll ye mean, we 'don't own the property'?" 'Course, we own hit. We bought off ever politician and jedge in Mack Dal Coun'e! I know that fer a fact. I paid a couple off meself!" Someone howled, stammering as he giggled.

"Yes, sirree, we did git all the s'port we could. An' boys, everbidy cooperated, 'cept fer one. 'Member, that feller who wouldn't talk to us? No, sirree, that man jest didn't wont to talk, not even a lit'l bitty bit.

"We never found hiz or hizzin, 'member? We never got after that land, 'cuz we never thought to look fer coal on a mountain-top. After all, hit ain't like the Pokeyhuntis Fields; thar warn't no outcroppin's to be seed. No way fer us to know of 'em big, big, *big* deposits.

"Well, boys, that same man owns the whole dadblame mountain range from Wolfpen Holler all the way down to the Tug." Mocking frustration, the man in black banged the pointer several times on the map. *"He owns hit all!"*

"That's right! Now, I recollects. Hit was that Whitaker feller. They call him *Pappy*. His reel name is Ezekiel," someone offered from the dark.

"Yep, that's right, Pappy Whitaker. I doubt witout a litt'l hep he'll ever sell to us. He's one of 'em backwoods inbred hill-billies—he'll be hard to deal wit, fer shore."

The room exploded in laughter, and its cacophonous sounds reverberated through the windowless walls. Outside, pedestrians stopped on the downtown streets of Youngstown listening to the laughter that continued for several minutes. They grinned and elbowed one another, and some chuckled loudly as they walked past the dozens of big black mules tied at the newly installed hitching posts outside the corporate headquarters.

Inside, the man in black turned to his crony. "Ye can hit 'em lights now. We dun had air lit'l fun. And after ye do, ye brang me and Howard and the boys sum big ol' ham samiches an' a jug or two of that thar brew. Hit's summers over yonder. Hurry now, hurry now, J. Frank! We got lots more corpret werk to do!"

Ten Years Later

McDowell County Seat, English, West Virginia

They stood arm-in-arm, her hand in his, staring proudly across the narrow valley at the new running-light sign on the gigantic skyscraper's marquee. It flashed, "Whitaker Worldwide Enterprises," "Home of Whitaker Sheet and Tube," "Whitaker Coal and Coke Companies," "Whitaker Pure Sparkling Spring Water," "Whitaker Adult Beverage Companies," "Whitaker Precious Metals," "Whitaker China" and "Whitaker Aeronautics." A trailer flashed by announcing, "Coming soon, a car called *Pappy*."

His eyes caught hers. Smiling, pride showing, he whispered, "Whut ye thank, Mayrianne? Ain't air litt'l biznus purty?"

She squeezed his arm and kissed his cheek lightly and giggled, "Yes, Pappy, air biznus is the purtiest thang I ever saw!"

Afterword

After Pappy Whitaker gained control of Champion Sheet and Tube, he made many changes in the way Olga Coal Company operated its businesses at the sister communities of Coalwood and Caretta, West Virginia.

The first change he made was that Brownlow Bean was no longer required to answer to corporate executives at the Youngstown headquarters. As Pappy said, "Cuzin, Brownlow, ye run this hyeh comp'ne the way ye see fit. Nobidy from haidquarters is goina bother ye, me boy, and iffin ye need to set and talk a spell, jest brang a jug and ye own bidy to see ol' Pappy."

At the same time, Pappy created a permanent position at Olga for an elected representative of Local 6026 of the United Mine Workers. He told newly selected Sam Wilson, "Now, youngin, ye got oodles of union work to do, makin' these hyeh mines safe, makin' shore 'em families are taken care of and makin' shore ye work reel close-like wit Brownlow. Make this ol' cuzin proud of ye, me boy."

The second change, and by far the most profound for the miners, was that the Big Store lowered its prices and Pappy changed the value of scrip. Miners and their families could still exchange one-dollar American for one-dollar scrip, but once changed into scrip their money increased its dollar value by three. The company stores did a huge business, and as a result of lower margins, higher sales and greater turnover, profits had never been better.

The miners and their families had never had it so good, and when Pappy offered each of them a small piece of the company, things got even better. Coal production reached new highs and company profits broke all records. People were happy in Coalwood and Caretta, and on rare occasions when adults and children alike glimpsed Pappy silently riding above his big black mule up and down the streets, they began to call him simply *Pappy*, thinking of him as a great benefactor. Nowhere was a man more revered. Not even Pappy's good friend, the wildly popular Governor Singleton, commanded as much respect.

To show their admiration, the miners insisted that the name of company money be changed from Olga Scrip to Pappy Scrip. A greatly embarrassed Pappy reluctantly approved the change; and a very becoming image of his proud Whitaker face was stamped into each new coin. Eventually, the miners were paid in nothing but Pappy Scrip. Funny thing about that new scrip, though, it was made of a shiny yellowish substance that the Whitakers provided. Supposedly, it came from a mysterious cave; and when merchants all over the region heard about Pappy Scrip, they began to run ads in the Whitaker Daily News attempting to lure the miners into bringing their new money to Tazwell, Grundy, Charleston, Beckley and Bluefield.

The boys, who some called "Coalwood's Misfits," were given the opportunity to attend college with a full scholarship from Whitaker Enterprises. Pappy was quite surprised when he found that the Misfits were a much larger group than he had thought, "Whut?" Rubbing his hands together and smiling, Pappy exclaimed, "Ever boy in Coalwood is a misfit? And, and Caretta, too! Now, I see why 'em boys know everthang. Dadgummit, we goina have us some big graduation parties. Ain't we, Mayrianne?"

Well, after the new procedures were established at Coalwood and Caretta, Pappy began to expand them to cover the rest of his operations in McDowell County. Thousands of workers from outside the county came in hopes of joining Pappy's company. Not wanting to turn them away, he cut a deal with the Gibson, Mullens and Collins clans to open up their land for development. Many were hired in McDowell County and transferred to Wise, Dungannon, Coeburn, Sneedville, Jacksboro, Pineville and Cumberland in southwest Virginia,

East Tennessee and eastern Kentucky to help work coal, saltpeter, gold and silver mines. Some were hired to run support institutions, such as stores, medical centers, schools, libraries and hotels.

But Pappy took his greatest pride in The Whitaker School of Commerce, Industry and Aerospace at Mankins Hollow. He was proud that people from all over the country had contributed to its construction, and particularly pleased that J. Frank Hutson himself had been kind enough to contribute $5,000 dollars through Governor Singleton's office.

Construction took three years and required an expenditure of over twenty-five million dollars. And when it was completed, the nation's top names in business law, economics, management, aerospace, engineering and history were recruited. Jonathan Turley was appointed Chancellor. His first official act was to employ Howard Mills to teach a class in business ethics.

At its dedication Pappy said, "Hit's a purty thang fer shore. Too many winders fer me, though. But, I got to admit my heart flutters when I see hit. Mammy Whitaker would've liked hit a lot, too, 'em rockets and that big statue of Micager out front. I betcha ol' Cager's summers out yonder grinnin' and proudin'."

Well, you can see that Pappy made a huge difference in how the people of Appalachia lived their everyday lives. The adults were healthy and happy, and their children sound and well educated. But the biggest improvement was in the way folks thought about Melungeons.

You see, once word filtered out that Brownlow Bean, Marty Messer, the Hootmockers, Mullenses, Collinses, Gibsons and a great number of other families were kin to the Whitakers, it seemed that everybody from Knoxville to Charleston and Lexington to Roanoke claimed to be Melungeon—just to be in vogue. Pappy thought it was funny, saying, "Why, youngins, thar never wuz nothin' wrong wit bein' Melungeon."

New and Old Place-names

Bristol, VA/TN once known as **Sapling Grove**
Castlewood, VA once know as **Castle's Camp**
Coalwood, WV once known as **Snake Root**
Coeburn, VA once known as **Gist's** or **Guest Station**
Cumberland, KY once known as **Poor Fork**
English, WV once known as **Peeryville**
Galax, VA once known as **Bonaparte**
Kingsport, TN once known as **Long Island**
Norton, VA once known as **Big Glades**
Paintsville, KY once known as **Paint Lick Station** and **Paint Creek**
Pineville, KY once known as **Cumberland Ford**
Roanoke, VA once known as **New Antwerp,** then **Gainesborough** and then **Old Lick**
Six, WV once known as **Peery Camp**
Tazwell, VA once known as **Jeffersonville**
War, WV once known as **War Creek**

THE CLEAR FORK SERIES

The Clear Fork Series was first introduced in 2001. Each book is loosely connected with the others in the series.

The following is an up-to-date list of the books that are part of this series.

The Coalwood Misfits, first published in 2001
The Kindred Gathering, published in 2003
Shoddy and Ox, published in 2003

The Coalwood Misfits, published as a revised and longer book in late 2003 or early 2004.

Books of

The Clear Fork Series

may be ordered by title at

www.amazon.com

or by writing:

BV Wespat
Box 197
1641 North Memorial Drive
Lancaster, OH 43130